THE DAUGHTER'S PREDICAMENT

THE QUILTING CIRCLE SERIES

The Widow's Plight
Book One

The Daughter's Predicament
Book Two

What people are saying about *The Daughter's Predicament*

"Once again, Mary Davis has charmed me with a sweet story of love and forgiveness. Tackling delicate issues, Davis helps us to examine our own hearts as we live the story through her memorable characters."

~Kimberley Woodhouse - Best-Selling and Award-Winning author of The Heart of Alaska Series

"The heroine caught my fancy from the start and kept me intrigued until the last page. I actually returned to several scenes, just to enjoy her attitude once more."

~Donita K. Paul, author of romantic fiction and fantasy

THE DAUGHTER'S PREDICAMENT

The Quilting Circle Series

By Mary Davis

The Daughter's Predicament
Published by Mountain Brook Ink
White Salmon, WA U.S.A.

The website addresses shown in this book are not intended in any way to be or imply an endorsement on the part of Mountain Brook Ink, nor do we vouch for their content.

This story is a work of fiction. All characters and events are the product of the author's imagination other than those stated in the author notes as based on historical characters. Any other resemblance to any person, living or dead, is coincidental.

The author is represented by and this book is published in association with the literary agency of WordServe Literary Group, Ltd., www.wordserveliterary.com

Scripture quotations are taken from the King James Version of the Bible. Public domain.

The Team: Miralee Ferrell, Nikki Wright, Cindy Jackson
Cover Design: Indie Cover Design, Lynnette Bonner Designer

Mountain Brook Ink is an inspirational publisher offering fiction you can believe in.

Printed in the United States of America

Dedication

To my daughter, Jessica. I'm so very proud of you!

Acknowledgments

A special thanks to Miralee Ferrell for believing in my stories and editing my manuscript, to Nikki Wright for marketing help, to Lynnette Bonner for another beautiful cover, and to Sarah Joy Freese and WordServe Literary Agency. I'm so thankful to work with all of you!

One

Central Washington State, 1893

ISABELLE ATWOOD RODE HER BICYCLE ALONG the main street of Kamola, pumping with one foot then the other. The tepid fall air fanned her face. The bicycle had emancipated women like nothing else. She no longer had to wait for a man to hitch up a buggy or saddle a horse. Her Bloomer bicycle dress, with the blousy trousers under the mid-calf length skirt, made riding so much easier. No more bunching up her skirt and petticoats to keep the hems from getting caught in the greasy chain. She steered around a chuckhole in the road and wobbled but kept her conveyance and herself upright.

Ahead, the White Hotel came into view, and not to disappoint, Grant Dawson sat on the bench out front. He worked as a desk clerk there. A smile broke across his face, and her insides fluttered.

She squeezed the brake lever with her right hand and slowed to almost a stop before putting her feet out as the bicycle tilted to one side.

Shaking his head, her best friend stood. "Izzy, you're twenty-two. Why do you ride that thing?" He was the only one who called her Izzy.

"Because it gives me freedom, and it's fun." She leaned it against the boardwalk railing.

"You're going to get hurt."

Like her father and stepmother, Grant worried too much. He lived in a small room at the back of the hotel. He had the early shift at the desk and sometimes got called to help during the night if a problem arose. Though he could afford to rent something bigger, he was saving every penny to buy a house someday. Such a practical man.

Isabelle unstrapped the food basket from the back of her bicycle. "I brought lunch."

He relieved her of the basket and offered his assistance.

She clasped his steady hand, stepped up onto the boardwalk, and sat on the bench, then unpacked the food and held out the bowl of cold fried chicken.

Grant chose a drumstick and took a bite. "Mmm."

She bit into a piece of her own.

After polishing off the drumstick, he wiped his hands and mouth on a cloth napkin. "I've been invigorated. I'm ready now."

"For what?"

"Bringing me lunch usually means you're trying to soften me up for the next young lady you plan to set me up with."

Isabelle had nearly exhausted the supply of suitable ladies in town. "No one this time." No one was quite right for her childhood friend, but she hadn't given up. The right lady worthy of her best friend was out there, and she would find her.

She dropped her half-eaten chicken into the bowl and licked her fingers while she pulled a folded piece of paper out of her Bloomer skirt pocket. "Yesterday, I found this wound between the spokes of my bicycle."

"What is it?" He picked up the bowl of chicken, gazing into it lovingly, and licked his lips.

Men. More interested in food than anything.

She unfolded the paper. "This is a love poem."

"A what? What are you going to do with that?"

"Don't look so scared. I'm going to read it."

"You are?" Grant's voice cracked. "Why would you do that?"

"I want to share this with you, my friend. Maybe you'll get a little inspiration."

He held up one hand. "Oh, no. I'm not sending a *cloying love poem* to a lady I've never met."

"No, silly. It was left for me by a secret admirer." So exciting and romantic. "Let me know what you think."

He groaned. "I'll need more nourishment to endure oversentimental musings written by some confused, lovelorn sap." Grant took another piece of chicken.

"It wouldn't hurt you to write a few sweet lines to a lady. Maybe then you would find one who doesn't think you completely emotionless."

"I'm not going to be someone I'm not. A lady's gotta take me as I am, or what's the point?" To punctuate his earnest words, he ripped off a big bite, and motioned for her to proceed.

He made her job of finding him a suitable wife more challenging than it need be. Isabelle cleared her throat.

"The rose is red,
The violet's blue,
The honey's sweet,
And so are you."

He stared at her sideways, frowning. "Is that it?"

She nodded. A few well-chosen words could say so much.

Grant made a retching sound.

She slapped his arm with the paper. "Don't be like that."

"Ow." He clutched his arm, pretending to be injured. "That isn't even original." He put his chicken-free hand over his heart. "*The man is boring, not a brain in his head, you'd be better off, filling him with lead.* See I can do it too." He tore off another bite of chicken.

"Stop it. That's not nice."

He laughed.

She shook her head. "You're impossible."

He stopped laughing and made an effort to not smile. "Do you seriously like this kind of mushy sentimentality? It's not even a very good poem."

"Shows what you know. It's not about the poem or even if it's any good, but the thoughtfulness of it. Someone I don't know thought enough to secret this onto my bicycle. There's something romantic and enticing about that. And I'm going to find out who he is. Your problem is you're too practical. You could learn a thing or two from him." She held the poem a little higher.

"Let me guess. You're hoping he leaves you another one of these."

"Most definitely. Why are you so disparaging?"

"Not disparaging, realistic. I don't want to see you get hurt." He lowered his head. "What about that cowboy you've been talking about?"

"*Rancher*. He's a cattle *rancher*. Shane Keegan." Just saying his name made her a little giddy. "I hear he has quite a place outside of town."

"He's still a cowboy. I can't see you with a *cowboy* stuck out on a ranch all winter. You would be bored inside of a month. Tedious before the honeymoon was over. He'll be gone for weeks at a time, and you'll have nothing to do. And when he is at home, what will you talk about? You have nothing in common with his type."

"I could find many things to occupy my time. I can sew and bake and read and crochet doilies."

He sputtered out a laugh. "I don't think ranchers have doilies."

"A rancher with a wife does."

"If you say so." He chucked his second chicken bone into the trash bin outside the hotel and licked his fingers. "So, in all the ladies you've tried to set me up with, why never Adelaide?"

"My half-sister? Oh, no. She is *all* wrong for you."

"How so? She's mighty pretty with her blond hair and alluring round face."

"I love my sister, but she's a bit selfish and about as deep as a saucer." Adelaide was one of those people who remained immature and naïve longer than others. "You would literally have nothing to talk about with her. *You* would die of boredom."

"Being pretty has to count for something."

Her sister *was* the picture of beauty with ringlets around her face and rosy lips. Isabelle couldn't blame Grant and other men for falling for her, but Isabelle wouldn't subject her good friend to life with Adelaide. "Is how a lady looks all men care about?"

Grant held up a cookie he'd fished out of the food basket. "And cooking."

"Impossible." She threw her hands up. "Well, maybe I *will* arrange something between you and my sister. You're both shallow and self-centered. You deserve each other."

"Because 'the rose is red' has so much depth and is so profound."

"If you bothered to think about the poem for even a minute, you would know it's not about the color of the rose. It's about the truth of the statement. Not one. Not two. But three true statements to validate and give extra weight to the fourth. The important one."

He squinted at her. "You got all that out of those four little lines?"

"I did. And, it's not the words themselves, but the fact some gallant man thought to pen them and deliver them is what makes them special."

"Gallant?" He glanced away then pointed down the street. "Speaking of boredom, isn't that your cowboy coming out of the telegraph office?"

She cast her gaze that direction. "That's him." She sighed. Shane Keegan, a rancher who stood well over six feet tall, with a saunter that said he was comfortable with who he was, and a smile that crooked up on one side that could fairly make a lady swoon. And when he tipped his hat and said *good-day, ma'am...* all sense and reason left her.

"Maybe he's your secret admirer."

A rush of anticipation swooped through her at the thought. She'd run into him a few times, saw him at church once or twice, but not regularly. She'd never had a lengthy conversation with him though she'd like to. "Do you think so?" She would very much like it if he were the one.

Grant shrugged. "As good a guess as any. You should go talk to him."

"Talk to him? You think that's a good idea? Not too forward?" A surge of excitement warmed her cheeks.

"Sure. Ask him what he thinks of dull, sappy poetry. Unless you're scared."

She knew a playful taunt when she heard one. "Maybe I will."

Grant folded his arms. "Bet you don't."

"Why do you say that?"

"I've known you a *long* time. I've never known you to be daring, except to ride that fool bicycle. You talk about doing exciting things, but you seem content to read about others doing them."

He was right. Her head told her to be careful, but her heart told her to be bold. If she took a risk, she might get hurt, either physically or emotionally.

She squared her shoulders. "I'll do it. What should I say?"

He spoke in a voice a few octaves higher than his normal one. "Tell him what a big strong man he is, then bat your eyelashes at him." He clasped his hands together under his chin and batted his own lashes. "The rose is red, the violet's blue, the honey's sweet, and so are you.'"

She swatted his arm. "*You* are no help."

"You could drop your handkerchief and wait for him to pick it up."

"Seriously? Would you fall for that? Because I don't think a man like him would. Why do I even bother asking you anything?"

"Because you know you'll get an honest answer." He pointed down the street. "He's getting away. You lost your chance."

Maybe she would get an opportunity another day.

Shane Keegan stopped near the livery and talked to the sheriff.

"He's been waylaid. Now or never." Grant elbowed her.

Dare she go? *No, don't think about it, just take action.* Stuffing the paper back into her pocket, she gulped in a deep breath, grabbed her bicycle, and peddled down the street, wobbling at first until she got going. She would head over and say hello to the sheriff and pretend not to see Mr. Keegan. At first.

Right as she drew near and was about to squeeze the brake lever, a horse spooked, neighed, and stepped backward into her path.

She swerved to avoid running into the horse's hindquarter but put herself on a collision course for Shane Keegan.

Oh, dear!

Shane Keegan stood outside the livery, talking to Sheriff Rix when a shriek cut through the air.

"Oh, no! Look out!"

Shane jerked around at the panicky words.

A woman on a bicycle careened straight toward him.

He jumped back, and as she swooshed past, Shane reacted without thinking and plucked the frantic woman off her bicycle. Though she rested safely in his arms, her vehicle went on alone and crashed into the side of a wagon.

Uh oh. Had he ruined this lady's transportation by plucking its driver off? He had neither meant to grab her nor wreck her bicycle. "Are you all right?"

She turned toward him, her pretty face inches from his. He held her in his arms. He'd just had the misfortune of harassing the affluent Miss Isabelle Atwood. She lived in the upper tier of Kamola society, a different class from a saddle tramp like Shane altogether. A polite *how do you do?* was the most he ever expected from someone like her toward someone like him, and she smelled of flowers.

"Are you all right, Isabelle?" Sheriff Rix asked from somewhere beside him.

Miss Atwood stared up at Shane. Probably in shock from him grabbing her. "Um, I think so."

His heart pounded. All he could do was stare. Wisps of brown hair framed her heart-shaped face. Clear blue eyes. Lips the color of ripe strawberries. And a fetching blush to her cheeks. Of course, a lady was more than her appearance.

He shouldn't be holding her, so he set her down but kept her in his arms. "I want to make sure you're steady on your feet before I turn you loose." She was likely fine. He was the unsteady one, using her shakiness as an excuse to be close to her.

Strangely, she didn't pull away from him in disgust. "I'm quite well. Fit as a fiddle, in fact." She almost seemed pleased to be near him.

Couldn't be.

The sheriff cleared his throat. "Good thing Mr. Keegan caught you."

Oh, right. Shane wasn't alone with this alluring, young filly.

She looked from the sheriff to Shane. "Did you snatch me off my bicycle?"

He offered her a lopsided grin. "I guess I did." He had not so much caught her as acted out of self-preservation. When someone was heading straight for him, he either needed to duck out of the way, stop them, or punch them. Well, he had known enough not to punch the lady, and he had been too caught off guard to duck. So, he'd done the only thing he could. Wrapped his arms around her. She did fit nicely there.

She gifted him with a smile that could make a man do almost anything for her. "Thank you for rescuing me."

Rescue? Is that what she thought he'd done? "I didn't want to see you get hurt. I can't rightly stand the sight of blood." Now she was going to think he needed mollycoddling.

"Not a scratch on me thanks to you."

Was she flirting with him?

Sheriff Rix tapped him on the shoulder. "You can let go of her now."

Shane released Miss Atwood and glanced toward her bicycle. "Let me get that for you." He walked over to the corpse of her contraption and wheeled it back, the front tire wobbling. "It appears to be damaged." *Great going, Shane. You sure know how to impress a lady, destroy her property and tell her you're a milksop.* "I'm afraid that's my fault. I can't help but feel if I hadn't been so hasty, you probably had everything well in hand."

"I can assure you, I did not have it well in hand. The horse spooked, and I swerved. If not for you, I would've been in a heap right along with my bicycle."

Nice of her to spare his feelings by being polite.

"If you say so. These things can be dangerous. You should be more careful." He should not have criticized her. He wasn't handling this situation well at all. He found her riding a bicycle endearing. It showed an adventurous side to the fair Miss Atwood.

She gripped the handlebars. "I will. Thank you very much for retrieving my bicycle and for rescuing me."

"Mighty welcome, ma'am—I mean miss." He touched the brim of his hat. "I'm fairly new in town. I recently acquired the old Bristol ranch. I don't believe we've been properly introduced." Though he'd asked around and knew much about Miss Isabelle Atwood. "I'm Shane Keegan."

"I know—I mean I've heard your name mentioned before. Townsfolk talk."

The sheriff suppressed a soft chuckle. "Shane, this is Miss Atwood."

Shane tipped his hat. "Pleased to meet you, Miss Atwood." So very pleased.

"Do call me Isabelle."

Bold move to offer him the use of her first name. But he preferred ladies who didn't put on pretentious airs. He felt the right side of his mouth automatically hitch up. "A beautiful name for a beautiful lady. *Very* pleased to make your acquaintance, Miss Isabelle." But his delight was short lived when he glanced up the street. He motioned. "Your fella's waiting for you." He had seen her with the hotel clerk often.

Isabelle turned toward where he'd indicated. "Grant? He's not my... fella. He's only a friend. We've been palling around since we were children."

Not her beau? Strange, he could have sworn the pair were sweet on each other. But good news he wasn't. "Very pleased to hear that." Her smile emboldened him. "Would the lady think it too brazen of me to inquire if she has a beau?"

Her widening smile encouraged him even more. She wasn't as unapproachable as he'd imagined.

"The lady *would* think it quite brazen."

He'd stepped in it now.

"*And* no, she does not have a beau." Though she'd made a point to let him know she was unattached, she glanced away shyly.

"Would the lady consider eating with a brazen

rancher? Say Monday, noon, White Hotel dining room?" He should have waited for her to answer the question before giving a time and place.

"Lunch Monday?" She paused as though thinking. "I'll have to consult my social calendar and let you know Sunday after church."

Was that a delayed no? Or the game ladies played where they feigned disinterest or pretended to be neutral to string a fella along? Make him wait in anticipation of her answer. Drive him mad with wonder. He folded his arms. How could he get out of the rendezvous and save face for both of them? "I'm not going to be able to make it into town on Sunday."

Her expression shifted from playful to disappointment.

He hurried on. "I usually do some sort of Bible reading and such for my men—who would never cross the threshold of a church. So, I'll tell you what. I'll be at the White Hotel's dining room at noon on Monday. If you show up to eat with me, I'll consider it as the good Lord smiling down on me." A graceful way for her to back out.

"And if I don't show up?"

What he expected would happen but still disappointing. "I'll be eating alone. A man's still gotta eat." He was not up for her inevitable rejection in person and so turned to the sheriff. "I'll talk to you later." He tipped his hat to Miss At—Miss Isabelle and strode away, resisting the urge to run. Why was talking to ladies so nerve wracking? She was just a person, just like him. No, she was nothing like him. She was refined. He was a dusty cowboy.

Come Monday, he'd be eating alone.

Isabelle watched Shane Keegan saunter away. She'd received several smiles, two cowboy saunters, two hat tips, and a lunch invitation. As well as being rescued and held in his arms. Strong arms. She sighed. Quite a productive interaction. She'd wanted to accept his invitation right away, but it would be considered poor etiquette for a lady to answer too quickly. Could make a man think she was desperate. Didn't a lady need to seem elusive to keep a man's interest? Yet, he'd been the elusive one and had piqued *her* interest.

She nodded at the sheriff. "Good day, Sheriff Rix." She walked her wobbly bicycle back up the street to the hotel, her insides as unsteady as the wheel.

Grant frowned. "You made quite an impression on that scoundrel."

"Scoundrel? He was very chivalrous." Like a perfectly set romance novel.

"Chivalrous? I saw the way he grabbed you. Opportunist, if you ask me. You have to watch out for his kind."

"Well, I *didn't* ask you." She didn't want to talk about Mr. Keegan anymore and rocked her bicycle forward. "The front tire is bent. Will you help me fix it?"

"You mean will *I* fix it?"

"Please?"

He shook his head. "If you are going to insist on riding this thing, then you need to learn to repair it. We can work on it together."

She smiled. "Thank you."

He smiled back. "When have I ever been able to say no to you? Park it around back by Hurley's workshop. Meet me here in the lobby Saturday morning."

That's what she liked about Grant. He didn't treat her like a helpless female. He'd taught her how to do many things, like fish, balance the hotel ledgers, ride a horse—*astride* no less—and even shoot a gun. She'd only done that once. The sound had hurt her ears, but she'd hit the target he'd set before her.

After parking her bicycle, Isabelle walked home then headed into the two-story house by way of the kitchen entrance. She snatched a small handful of raisins from a ceramic canister on the worktable.

Molly, the cook, tsked at her. "You'll spoil your supper."

Isabelle chewed and swallowed. "No, I won't. Nothing

could spoil today." She had a social engagement with Shane Keegan.

Marguerite stalked in from the front hall. "Finally, you're home. Where have you been?"

Even her stepmother couldn't spoil her buoyant mood. "My bicycle got banged up. I had to take it to be repaired."

"That thing is a menace. You're a young lady, not a hooligan. Not to worry. You won't be riding that anymore."

"Why not? It's mine." Isabelle's bicycle gave her freedom. That it irritated Marguerite was a bonus.

"Because it's unladylike. Come into the parlor." Her stepmother strode back the way she'd come. "Your father and I need to talk to you."

Isabelle tagged along in her wake. She didn't like the superior tone in Marguerite's voice. It always meant trouble for Isabelle. "About what?" She stopped short over the parlor's threshold.

Her father stood by the fireplace with a worried expression. Her eighteen-year-old half-sister sat on the settee, picking at a thread on her sleeve cuff.

Something menacing hung in the air. "What's this all about?"

Her stepmother eased herself onto a wingback chair. "Your life is about to change. *All* our lives are about to change."

"Change? How?"

"We've arranged a marriage for you."

Isabelle sucked in a breath and choked on the air. She coughed several times before she could speak. "What? To whom? I don't want to marry someone I'm not in love with." Right now, she wasn't in love with anyone.

"Mr. Oliver Mallory."

"The banker? He's so old."

"Watch your tone," Marguerite snapped. "He's only thirty-six. That's not so old."

Isabelle shook her head. "Why would I agree to marry *him*?"

Her stepmother, sitting on the edge of her seat, didn't blink. "It's for the good of the family."

Marry a banker? For the good of the family? Isabelle

shifted her gaze to Father. "Are we in financial trouble?"

He gave a snort of dismissive laughter. "Don't be silly."

"Then why would you want me to marry a banker I don't love *'for the good of the family'*?" When her father remained silent, Isabelle turned to Marguerite. This had to be her doing. "Why?"

"It seems our precious Adelaide has gotten herself into a little bit of trouble." Her stepmother's voice wavered slightly on the last word, and she fidgeted with her handkerchief, tugging at the corner. A sure sign something had unnerved her. She rarely ever got rattled.

"What kind of trouble?"

Marguerite's jaw worked back and forth, and her lips parted as if to speak.

Isabelle shifted her gaze to her sister. "What kind of trouble are you in?"

Adelaide chewed furiously on her bottom lip as she spoke. "I... sort of... I'm kind of..."

Her father finally blurted out the words. "Your sister has gotten herself in the family way."

"What?" Isabelle sat on the settee next to her sister. "How did this happen?"

Adelaide didn't have a beau. Did she? She was barely eighteen, old enough to get married, but still young. "He said he loved me."

"Who?"

An odd animal-like sound came from her sister.

Marguerite narrowed her eyes. "She won't tell us, but that really doesn't matter. The boy would never be suitable for her. You will marry Oliver Mallory and pretend to be expecting right away. When we can no longer conceal Adelaide's condition, she will remain in seclusion for the duration of her time. After the child is born, you'll say it's yours, and my dear sweet Adelaide will be free of this burden."

While saddling Isabelle with it. Unbelievable. "Has Mr. Mallory agreed to this?"

"He owes your father a favor."

Probably not one this big that will last the rest of his life. "Why me? Why doesn't Adelaide marry him?"

"You're the oldest. You must marry first. Adelaide is too young."

Obviously not.

Isabelle turned an imploring gaze on her father. "Say I don't have to do this."

"I think your mother knows what's best." He looked resigned.

Isabelle wasn't. This couldn't be her fate.

First of all, Marguerite wasn't Isabelle's mother, but Isabelle wasn't allowed to voice that fact. Hers had died when she was very young, and Marguerite never truly treated Isabelle as a daughter.

Second, her stepmother *didn't* know what was best for Isabelle, and third, her father didn't argue with his wife. Marguerite wouldn't let him. He always gave in to her because it was easier.

"I won't do it. You can't make me."

Marguerite raised one pale eyebrow. "Can't we?"

That look sent a cold shiver down Isabelle's back. "Why must I pay for Adelaide's mistake?"

"Because she has a bright future. I've been in correspondence with Lord Blaine in Boston. He's interested in meeting your sister and will make a wonderful match for her. You wouldn't deny your sister the opportunity to marry a titled man, would you? Don't be selfish. Think of her future."

Her stepmother was attempting to arrange a marriage for Adelaide with a lord, so Isabelle was to be the sacrificial lamb to sweep Adelaide's transgression under the rug?

Adelaide sat next to her on the settee with her shoulders hunched and arms crossed over her stomach.

"All things work together for the good. And this marriage is for the good of the whole family. Don't be selfish by thinking only of yourself."

Isabelle hated it when Marguerite spouted Scripture for her own benefit. She understood her stepmother's need to protect her daughter, but to sacrifice Isabelle to do it wasn't fair. She didn't have much choice when Father sided with his wife. Was there any way for her to get out of this?

Two

Isabelle waited until Marguerite turned in for the night. She approached her father's study and knocked softly on the door. She needed to talk to him alone so her stepmother couldn't overtly influence him.

"Come in."

Taking a deep breath, she turned the knob and eased the door open.

Father didn't offer her his usual smile. "Come all the way in. We were expecting you."

"We?" Isabelle darted a glance around the room. No one else was there.

"Your mother and I. We have spoken at length and are in agreement. She said you'd come to me alone. To try to persuade me to change my mind. She's a smart woman."

Indeed. Cunning was more like it. She'd likely coached Father on how to best rebuff Isabelle's attempt.

No worries. Isabelle was every bit as smart as Marguerite. "May I try anyway?"

Father rose from behind his desk and motioned toward the wingback chairs flanking the fireplace. "I'm always open to hear what you have to say."

Meaning he would listen, but he'd already made up his mind. Placating her. Even so, she wouldn't waste this opportunity to plea for her freedom. She sat and smoothed her hand across her skirt. Dying embers glowed in the hearth.

After crossing to the chairs, Father lifted a teal and gold patterned teapot. "All I have to offer you is cold tea left over from earlier."

"No, thank you. I'm fine." Or at least she would be once she'd convinced him that there had to be another way.

He set the teapot down and took the adjacent chair. "Go ahead. Speak your piece."

She appreciated her father's willingness to let her express her objections to this plan, but his tone said her efforts wouldn't do any good. She would simply have to change his mind. "I beg you to reconsider this marriage. We can come up with another solution." One that didn't involve her being married off.

"Your mother and I have gone over every scenario. This is the best option. Trust me."

"I know this is all Marguerite's idea."

Father didn't mind her using Marguerite's given name instead of Mother when it was only the two of them.

He leaned forward with his forearms on his thighs and clasped his hands together. "Though she did propose the initial plan, I came to see her reasoning."

Reasoning? "Why does it have to be me? It should be Adelaide. It's her mistake. Her baby. She should be the one to marry."

"Don't get me wrong, I love Adelaide. I love you both. But you and I both know she's not as responsible as you. I'm sorry to say she gets that from me. People like Adelaide and myself need loved ones like you, Marguerite, *and* your mother to keep us from turning into complete disasters."

Adelaide had proven how irresponsible she was to begin with. Would her sister ever grow up? Perpetually a child. She often acted without considering the consequences.

"*You* were always the nurturing type, caring for animals and then your baby sister when she came along. You are the most sensible one of us all. Can you imagine Adelaide looking after an infant at her age? She's still a child herself."

"She was *old enough* to get herself into this mess. Lots of women are mothers at her age. Some even younger."

"You're right. She's not my little girl in pigtails anymore. But you must agree she will do better in a house with a staff to take care of her and whatever children who come along. It will be best if they come later, giving her the opportunity to grow into the idea."

Her sister did seem to need someone to look after her.

"But I don't want to be forced to marry. This isn't fair."

"Few things in life are. We must do the best we can with the situations we find ourselves in. Trust me, this will all turn out for the best."

"Best for who? Adelaide? Marguerite? You? Certainly not for me. I want to marry for love."

"Romantic love is admirable in daydreams, but it's not what holds a marriage together. Commitment is. Oliver Mallory is a man you can grow to love. Give him a chance."

She didn't want to. "But it's happening so fast." She liked her freedom and making her own choices.

"I know. I also know you are strong enough to handle this." He took her hand. "I'll tell you what I'll do. I can delay the wedding a week, not much longer."

"A week?" She couldn't imagine it happening so quickly. "Oh, please give me at least a month."

"I can't. For the baby's sake it needs to be as soon as possible. You need to be married long enough for it to be plausible for the baby to be yours."

She hadn't made any headway. "I don't even know the man."

"I've known Oliver since before he arrived in town. We had corresponded. I vouched for him. He's a good, Christian man. I would never suggest a husband who I didn't think could take care of you and be good to you. He will provide well. I can try to push this out to two weeks, but I won't tell your mother. I'll let her think things are going according to her schedule."

Isabelle appreciated that. Two weeks wasn't much but better than a few days or a week. It would give her a little time to come up with another solution which would benefit everyone.

During the night, Isabelle woke with the sensation of her

bed jiggling. Rolling over, she found Adelaide climbing into her bed. Her sister hadn't come into her room since she was young. Then, it had been a common enough occurrence. Any little thing—a noise, a bad dream, being lonely—would send her scurrying in. Isabelle wrapped her arm around her sister.

Adelaide snuggled close and cried against Isabelle's shoulder. "I'm scared."

"Shh. I know. We're going to figure this out."

Why did Adelaide have to be so naïve and gullible? She'd always been one to believe most anything anyone told her. It had become a game with some of the older school children, and Isabelle had needed to watch over her. If Isabelle ever discovered who the man was who'd taken advantage of her sister, she would have words with him.

Isabelle stroked her sister's hair and once again pressed. "Who's the father? You can tell me."

Adelaide shook her head against Isabelle. "No. I can't. I won't."

"Why not?"

"It wouldn't do any good."

"Father could make him marry you." That would solve this whole problem.

"He doesn't want it. He would just say it wasn't his."

True. With no way to prove the identity of the father, Adelaide had few options. To openly accuse this man would shine a light on her sister's transgression.

Isabelle didn't want that. "Sweetie, I need you to tell me something."

"I won't tell you his name."

"I wish you would, but that's not my question this time. Are you sure this man didn't force himself on you?"

Adelaide shook her head.

Isabelle was glad of that.

"He said he loved me. And I loved him. But now, I don't think I love him. I've made a mess of my life."

Her sister certainly had. Maybe after this, she would think twice before believing everything people said.

"If you tell me who he is, we can at least get Father to make him leave town, so you wouldn't have to see him all the time."

Adelaide shook her head again. "I want to forget all about him. And about being..." She put her hands on her lower abdomen. "But I can't, can I?"

"I'm afraid not."

"Will Mother truly make you marry Mr. Mallory?"

Yes. "I'm sure we all will figure out another solution." And by "we all," Isabelle meant herself, because no one else cared more about her future than she did. Marguerite wanted to rescue her own daughter from her mistake and her fate. Father would go along with whatever Marguerite decided in matters concerning her daughters. And Adelaide was too young to think beyond herself.

Which left Isabelle to figure a way out of this situation everyone else had created for her and accepted.

Mr. Mallory wasn't a detestable sort. He attended church and spoke cordially to people, but Isabelle didn't really know him, and he was so much older than her. Women married gentlemen twice their age and more all the time and were perfectly happy, but Isabelle always imagined marrying someone close to her own age. Someone she could grow old with and spend many happy years together. Someone she was in love with. Not someone so advanced in years and who would die long before her, leaving her alone later in life. But even then, there were no guarantees. People died young all the time.

Her sister's breathing slowed and deepened.

Oh, silly Adelaide.

Would it be wrong of Isabelle to pray for the Lord to touch her sister with a miscarriage? It would save everyone a lot of heartache.

Lord? A miscarriage would solve so many problems for Adelaide and myself, but... I won't pray for such a dreadful thing. That is up to You. But I do ask for me to not have to marry someone I don't want to. So if I'm going to have to marry Mr. Mallory, make me want to. But I'd much prefer a different solution. Show me a different way.

The words from her secret admirer's note drifted through her head. Was he the different way? She huffed out a breath. Isabelle didn't know him any better than

Mr. Mallory. Even less.

She longed to fall in love with someone and have her own happily ever after. Was that even passible? Did that kind of romantic love exist only in fairy tales and romance novels?

Though she longed for love, a part of her needed to protect her sister. Adelaide never intended to get herself into difficult situations. It was just so easy for her to do so, and this time her mistake was bigger than usual. If Isabelle had been paying more attention, maybe she could have seen this trouble lurking before it happened. Had this been Isabelle's fault for not looking after her sister better? Paying the price for her own self-centeredness. Amusing herself with the whim of her bicycle.

Too late for regrets now. The only thing to do was to figure out a way forward.

If she went away with Adelaide until after the baby was born and gave it to a deserving Christian couple to raise, that could work. Marguerite might even be agreeable. Adelaide's reputation wouldn't be marred, and she could still marry a titled man.

Leaving Isabelle free to fall in love. A handsome rancher's smile flashed in her mind. Maybe even fall in love with Shane Keegan.

Three

IN THE MORNING, THEIR DRIVER, EDWARD, steered the carriage through town. Isabelle rode in the back with her sister and Marguerite.

The rocking conveyance lulled Isabelle, and she yawned for the third time in as many minutes. After Adelaide had climbed into bed with her last night, Isabelle's thoughts had raced like a stampede, hindering her sleep most of the night.

Marguerite preened over Adelaide and spoke in a whisper. "Don't worry about a thing. You aren't showing yet and won't for a while. No one will know." She leaned closer to Isabelle. "You're not to say a word about your sister's condition."

Did Marguerite think she would? "I would never betray her."

By using a low voice, her stepmother likely hoped to prevent the servants from finding out about Adelaide's condition. How long could that last? One of them would overhear at a doorway or walking into a room. And what about when Adelaide started showing? Hopefully, the staff would be discreet. If they wanted to keep their positions, they would be blind to Adelaide's changing body.

"Mother?" Adelaide's voice squeaked. "I don't feel well. I think I'm going to lose my breakfast." She had been ill a lot lately.

Isabelle groaned to herself. Not ill. Morning sickness. Since Isabelle had never imagined her sister could be in the family way, she hadn't thought much about her stomach troubles lately. "Do you need to go back home?"

Adelaide's voice came out weak. "I think I should." It would be difficult to conceal Adelaide's condition if she threw up everywhere she went.

"No." Marguerite shook her head. "Take deep breaths. Tell yourself you feel fine. When I was carrying you, I resolved not to... you know. It's very unladylike. It's a matter of strength of character."

Isabelle couldn't believe Marguerite's callousness. "It has nothing to do with character. Some women have morning sickness, and some don't."

"She's far enough along, she shouldn't be nauseous any longer."

"Some women have it for the whole nine months." Turning in the seat, Isabelle scrutinized her pale sister. "Adelaide, what do you want to do?" She hoped her sister chose reason.

Marguerite squinted at Isabelle then patted her daughter's hand. "If you shirk too many commitments, people will wonder. When Isabelle has a baby too soon after getting married and she's not been ill and you have, people will figure it out. You don't want that, do you? You'll be fine. I know you can manage."

Adelaide nodded and parroted her mother's words. "I'll be fine. Thank you for your concern, Isabelle. I'll go to quilting circle. It'll be nice to visit with all the ladies."

Marguerite beamed. "That's my girl."

Though her stepmother thought she meant well and was doing the right thing, Isabelle didn't think the advice was best. Adelaide should be resting. Isabelle would keep an eye on her sister.

Marguerite's comment about Isabelle not being ill niggled at her. Would her stepmother insist upon Isabelle feigning morning sickness to throw suspicions off of Adelaide? Probably not until after the wedding, which would be far too soon for Isabelle's liking.

For now, she would voice her plan. "I was thinking, if Adelaide and I went away for several months to a year, and return when she's no longer expecting, then no one would know, and she could still marry the lord."

"That's exactly the plan. A day or two after you're married, we'll get an urgent telegram from your sick aunt back East and send the two of you away. You'll write your new husband to tell him he's going to be a father and how happy you are. Then the two of you will return with Mr. Mallory's child in hand. A man of his age will be thrilled to have a child."

"You haven't told him about Adelaide?"

"Why should we?"

"It wouldn't be fair not to tell him. He may not want to raise another man's child."

"Are you suggesting we abandon our own flesh and blood? What would you do with the little one if not bring it back?"

Isabelle hadn't thought about that. The trouble was Adelaide's condition, not the baby itself. "Maybe we could find someone who can't have children to adopt it."

Adelaide's face brightened, and she nodded.

"You would deny your father and I the pleasure of seeing our grandchild grow up? I never thought you so selfish." Tears welled in Marguerite's eyes. Real tears? "This child is our own flesh and blood. You expect us to just give it away. We have to keep this little one in the family." Her stepmother obviously wouldn't agree no matter how much arguing Isabelle attempted.

The baby *was* family, Isabelle's niece or nephew, and she, too, wanted it to remain with them. Then the perfect plan flashed in her mind. "Marguerite, you—"

"I told you not to refer to me by my first name. I'm Mother."

Isabelle bristled and pressed her lips together. "Anyway, *you* could pretend to be expecting and say the baby is yours." This would solve everyone's problem.

"I'm too old. It was a miracle we had Adelaide. No one would believe this baby is mine." Marguerite had wanted to have a big family but had to settle for a daughter and a half. And so, she had poured all of her hopes, dreams, and aspirations into her one child.

"It could be another miracle."

"I'm sorry, Isabelle. It would never work. Don't you think we already considered that option? I'll hear no more of this nonsense." Her stepmother wouldn't be swayed. She likely didn't want to be saddled with the day to day raising of a baby.

Isabelle would have to think of another solution.

After arriving at Aunt Henny's, Marguerite took

Adelaide's arm. "Isabelle, would you be a dear and bring in the food?"

Every week, the quilting circle met at Aunt Henny's boarding house. She wasn't actually Isabelle's aunt, and as far as Isabelle knew, the older woman, around fifty, wasn't aunt to anyone in town, but everyone called her Aunt Henny. Come to think of it, Isabelle didn't even know the woman's last name.

Isabelle looped her sewing basket over one arm and balanced a pan of rolls on that hand while holding a pie in the other. Did her stepmother think no one would find it odd she alone carried everything except Marguerite's and Adelaide's sewing baskets?

The driver stretched out his arms. "Do you want me to help you with those?"

"Thank you, Edward, but I have them." At least, he noticed the disparity of the situation.

"If you're sure, then I'll return this afternoon for you ladies."

"We'll see you then." Isabelle caught up to Adelaide and Marguerite on the porch.

Leaning on her cane, Aunt Henny opened the screen door. "Come in." She still limped from her recent broken leg, though out of the cast now.

Marguerite entered first, then Adelaide, and lastly Isabelle.

"Oh, my. Let me help you." Aunt Henny took the pie and gave Isabelle a questioning glance.

Another person to notice the inequality. If Marguerite wasn't careful, she would give away their secret.

Isabelle pretended not to notice the silent inquiry. "Thank you."

Aunt Henny closed the door behind her and followed her into the parlor. "We're all here now."

Marguerite waved a gloved hand in the air. "Sorry we're late. You know how it is getting young ladies ready."

Isabelle bit back a retort.

Marguerite hadn't assisted with either of them getting ready for many years. Once Father had inherited money, she'd been more concerned with her own appearance and standing in the community.

Seven ladies sat around in the circle in their usual places with the double-wedding-ring quilt to be auctioned off at the Founders Day Festival in the middle on a quilting frame. Aunt Henny and the Atwood women made eleven all together. Three chairs in a row waited for Isabelle, Adelaide, and Marguerite. Isabelle wished her stepmother could sit away from her and her sister. But if anyone got displaced, it would send a ruckus through the group like a bunch of disrupted hens, all squawking and flapping.

Trudy MacVay tilted her head. "Adelaide, you don't look well."

"Trudy." Agnes Martin's eyebrows shot up. "No woman likes to hear such unfavorable things."

"I'm concerned about her." Although nearly thirty, Trudy had never married. She had held out for love and had been left alone. But she was happy, wasn't she?

Isabelle would rather be like Trudy than stuck in a loveless marriage for the rest of her life, but Marguerite had different plans. Was being a spinster so bad? Could a woman only be fulfilled if she had a husband and children? Isabelle longed for both of those things, but she didn't want to give up on the prospect of love to have them.

Marguerite waved her hand in the air. "She's fine. The ride was a little bumpy."

"All right, but maybe she should sit down." Trudy indicated Adelaide's usual chair.

Franny Waldon scooted the chairs apart a little for Adelaide. Franny worked at her father's mercantile and dry goods store. Like Isabelle, she was waiting for the right man to come along and sweep her off her feet.

Agnes Martin, who was almost as old as Aunt Henny and generally wore a sour expression, nodded. "She does appear peaked."

The other four women around the circle, Dorthea Albert, Betsy Jones, Neva Whittier, and Lily Hammond, nodded their agreement.

If these nice ladies knew what troubles had befallen the Atwood household, what would they think of Marguerite's solution? Each would undoubtedly have an opinion, some stronger than others. Would they come up with a better solution? Marguerite would never agree and have Isabelle married off by the end of the day.

If the focus didn't get off of Adelaide, someone might figure out what was wrong. "Neva, you appear to be well. When is your baby due?" Neva Whittier had married a couple of years ago and was expecting her first child. For the fifth time.

Marguerite narrowed her eyes at Isabelle.

Right. Putting the focus on someone else who had a child on the way probably wasn't wise.

Neva didn't seem to notice and put a hand on her protruding belly. "Three months. I can't wait." This was the longest Neva had carried a child. The baby was active and seemed to be doing well. And with that, everyone focused on Neva.

Aunt Henny settled in her chair. "I think we can finish the quilting on our donation before lunch."

Agreements murmured around the circle.

The group had worked together to make the quilt, as well as other items, to be auctioned off at the Founders Day celebration. The money raised would go a long way to build a gymnasium for the school so the children would have someplace to run around during the cold winter months.

Each lady said what else she was donating to the auction, from canned and baked goods to embroidered linens and hankies.

Would there be any baby clothes or items? Even if there were, it wouldn't be wise for Isabelle or her family to bid on them. She mentally shook herself. Less than twenty-four hours and she was already thinking about how to take care of the little one.

Henny watched the three Atwood women across the circle while she wove her needle in and out of the fabric before her. Something was up with them. A different conflicting emotion peeked out from behind each of their feigned smiles. Isabelle's pinched eyebrows indicated her angst, Adelaide's paler than usual light complexion made Henny wonder if she were on the verge of being sick, and hints of worry snuck out around Marguerite's false cheeriness.

Something was going on in their household. Henny wouldn't bring it up in front of the whole group, but maybe the Lord would see fit for her to be alone with one of them before the day was through. If not, hopefully, they would be the last to leave, and she could speak to them then.

Henny tied off her thread and cut it. "My section is complete. It looks as though everyone else is almost done as well."

Chatter rippled around the auction quilt about how much each woman had left to stitch.

Isabelle snipped her thread. "I have this section done as well. Is there another place that still needs quilting?"

Henny stood and spoke before anyone could direct Isabelle to more quilting. "I could use your help in the kitchen, setting out lunch while the others finish up."

"I would be happy to." Isabelle scooted her chair back from the quilting frame and stood.

This must be God's hand at work.

In the kitchen, Henny leaned on her cane to relieve some of the ache in her injured leg. She didn't heal like she used to and looked forward to getting rid of her cane, but not today. She missed having Lily around with her sweet little boy. They had been a big help while she'd been laid up and had brought so much life into the boardinghouse and to Henny. She was happy the troubled mother had found love for the first time with their sheriff. The two made a delightful couple and wonderful parents to their three children.

Isabelle took the yeast rolls from the pan they'd arrived in and placed them into a bowl. Then she proceeded to rearrange them, turning each one ever so slightly, making them fit more tidily in the dish. Fastidiously so.

Henny touched the girl's arm. "Is everything all

right? You've been more quiet than usual."

Isabelle glanced at Henny, opened her mouth, then closed it again and shifted her gaze away. "I... I can't say."

That made Henny's insides crimp. "Your father's well I presume."

"Oh, yes."

"Then the trouble's with Marguerite?"

"Partly." Isabelle sighed. "This time it's my whole family. Please don't let her know I spoke about it. I shouldn't have said anything."

"I won't." Not that she knew anything to tell. "I'm here for you. If you need someone to talk to, I'll listen. No judgments, just a compassionate ear." Something Henny had wished she'd had all those years ago.

"Thank you, but I really can't."

Henny patted the girl's hand. "Try not to worry. I'll be praying for you and your family."

"I appreciate your concern." Isabelle carried the bowl of rolls out into the dining room off the parlor.

Henny watched from the doorway.

The Atwoods had troubles. Bigger troubles than any of them were letting on with their fabricated demeanors.

Henny could feel it.

Four

THE FOLLOWING MORNING, ISABELLE TROTTED DOWNSTAIRS and into the dining room for breakfast in her bicycle Bloomer dress.

Marguerite stared at her. "What are you wearing?"

Maybe Isabelle would skip breakfast to avoid Marguerite, but it might be more fun to irritate her with her outfit. "Good morning." She grabbed a plate from the credenza and scooped the various food offerings onto it.

Father, in his usual place at the head of the table, read the newspaper with Marguerite next to him.

"Where's Adelaide?" Isabelle sat across from her stepmother.

"She's resting. You haven't answered my question. What are you wearing?"

Isabelle took a big bite of hash browns and chewed ever so slowly.

Marguerite glared at her the whole time while Father ignored them both, preferring the news.

Isabelle swallowed, stood, and turned in a circle. "My bicycle Bloomer dress. Practical and fashionable."

"It is entirely unsuited for today."

She knew that tone. Marguerite had made plans for her without bothering to inform Isabelle. "This is very much suited for today's activities. Grant is helping me repair my bicycle, and I'll be riding it home." She returned to her seat.

"No, you won't. Your father has spoken to Mr. Mallory. He's coming for lunch today. You want to make a good impression. Wear something light and airy to offset your dark hair and complexion. The pink organza with the ruffles, I'd say. It will enhance all your good features."

Whether Isabelle liked it or not, their plans for her

future crept forward, rendering her helpless to stop them. She had hoped if she ignored it, they would as well and not progress with their plans. She wasn't ready. She hadn't come up with an alternative Marguerite might agree to. And now, every time she wore her favorite pink dress, she would think of Marguerite's manipulation. But disregarding this problem was like Adelaide wanting to wish her condition away. Only God could do such a thing for her sister.

Isabelle stood again. "I haven't agreed to this marriage. Papa, please can we think of another solution?"

"Don't use *Papa*." Marguerite again. "Honestly, Isabelle, we don't live on the farm anymore. Dignified people say Mother and Father."

Isabelle hadn't called her father Papa in years. Not since he'd inherited money and they'd moved into town and Marguerite had groomed them all in the ways of polite society. She missed *Papa,* and those simpler days. "Father?"

He lowered his newspaper. "Your mother knows best when it comes to these matters." Though he sided with his wife, he offered his first daughter a conciliatory smile, and one eye twitched in an almost wink.

Even with Father's moderate understanding, Isabelle gritted her teeth. She had different ideas of what was best. Letting Isabelle choose her own future was best, not having it dictated to her.

Father took a drink of his coffee. "I know you think this unfair and too difficult to bear, but it's high time you married. You're twenty-two. You should be married with a child or two by now. Where are the grandchildren I should be bouncing on my knee?"

Adelaide was taking care of that.

"I need to know you're settled and have someone to take care of you."

"I can take care of myself."

He folded the paper, set it aside, and pinned Isabelle with a hard gaze. "But you're not. I'm the one who sees to all your needs, your clothes, food, a roof over your head. Without a husband, how would you manage these things for yourself?"

She didn't know.

Father studied her, no doubt waiting for an answer.

An answer she didn't have. She would suggest he give her a small monthly stipend, but he would just say he would still be supporting her. "Perhaps, I could get a job until I fell in love with the right man."

Father shook his head at her paltry attempt. "Right man? Fall in love? Do you have someone specific in mind?"

She heaved a sigh. "No, but—"

Father cut her off with the raise of his hand. "Mr. Mallory is a good man. I considered several men before agreeing to him. He has the means to provide well for you, and he's a God-fearing man."

Marguerite's expression, though neutral, had a hint of triumph twinkling in her eyes.

Isabelle hadn't conceded defeat yet. "But I don't love him."

"Give him a chance and you might. It won't hurt to get to know him."

She'd hoped Father would relent but wasn't surprised he didn't. It had been worth a try. With an unladylike flare, she grabbed a piece of buttered toast and two strips of bacon off her plate—with her hands.

Marguerite gasped, more for effect than real shock.

Isabelle nibbled a bite of toast and marched out of the room.

Marguerite's voice followed her. "Jackson, I've tried with that girl. She doesn't want to better herself."

Isabelle picked up the cloth bundle of cookies she'd prepared for the maintenance man at the hotel. A small compensation for use of his workshop and tools. She tucked the bundle into a cloth bag and hung it from her arm.

Once outside and having lost her appetite, she prepared to pitch her breakfast into the bushes when Tramp scampered up. She crouched to pet the scruffy stray. His brown and tan fur held mats, dirt, and debris. "You hungry?" She held out a strip of bacon.

Tramp sniffed it once then gobbled it down in two bites. The second one as well as the toast disappeared equally as fast. He put his paws on her bent legs and sniffed the cloth bag with the cookies.

"These aren't for you." She petted him and stood. "That's all I have today." She headed off toward the White Hotel at an inappropriate pace for a well-bred lady. But then she hadn't been born into money, Father had come into it after the farm girl in her had been well established. And that precocious farm girl, who had climbed trees and gone fishing, needed to find another solution to her grown-up problem. There had to be one.

By the time she entered the lobby, she still hadn't thought of a way out. Marguerite had shot down her only two ideas. When she reached for the door handle, a male voice spoke beside her. "Let me get that for you."

She hesitated, and a man Isabelle's height with shocking red hair opened the door.

"Thank you." She stepped inside.

"My pleasure." He smiled, closed the door, and headed down the boardwalk backward, watching her. The man was as bold as his hair.

She shook off the encounter and approached the desk. No Grant. He'd said to meet him in the lobby. "I'm looking for Mr. Dawson."

The older man behind the counter turned from placing a key in one of the slots. "Since he was hanging around, I sent him to the telegraph office to pick up any messages for the hotel or our guests. He should be back soon."

"Thank you." Isabelle sat in a lobby chair. Her knees bounced uncontrollably. She pressed her palms on her thighs to still them, but that succeeded for only a few moments. She stood and crossed to the window. Where was he? With her feet planted firmly on the ground, the jittering from her knees traveled up to her arms, and her hands twitched now.

Oh, this was ridiculous. She marched out the door and up the street.

She hadn't gone more than a block before Trudy MacVay and Franny Waldon from the quilting circle strolled down the boardwalk in her direction. Trudy spoke. "Isabelle. We're headed over to the mercantile.

Franny says they received a shipment of yard goods. Come with us."

Would Trudy marry a man she wasn't in love with if she had the opportunity? Then she would no longer be an old maid in her thirties. What about Franny? A year younger than Isabelle. Would she accept a solid proposal to make certain she didn't end up a spinster? Would either of them understand Isabelle's dilemma? Or would they think her silly for worrying over it? Foolish for not snatching up a catch like Mr. Mallory post haste? Many women were happy to have any husband at all.

Isabelle forced a smile that felt more like a grimace. "I wish I could, but I'm in an awful hurry. Tell me all about them at quilting circle next week." She scuttled around the pair and pressed on.

Grant exited the building a half of a block before she reached the telegraph office. He smiled when he saw her, but his cheery disposition fell away the closer he came to her. "What's wrong? I know that look."

Isabelle fisted her hands and gritted her teeth. "Oh, you don't know *this* look. *This* is a whole new look."

"All right." He took a step back. "First, are you angry with me for something I know nothing about?"

"No." She touched his shirtsleeve. "You are the one person I can count on not to betray me."

He blew out a breath. "That's good to know. Now, tell me what happened. Who betrayed you?"

She pulled her hand back and picked at her fingernail. "I don't even know where to start."

He held up a stack of telegrams and envelopes. "I need to get these back to the hotel. Tell me on the way. Just spill it. I'm sure we can sort it out."

She could always count on Grant and fell into step beside him. "Adelaide is a foolish girl, my stepmother is intolerable, and my father is no help whatsoever."

"I might be able to help if you gave me some frame of reference."

Her thoughts and emotions had jumbled into a flying mess, knocking her this way and that. How could she sort it out to make any sense to him? "Well... I mean..."

Any words she could think to say, didn't make any sense. This whole situation didn't even make much sense to her.

"You're really upset. Start at the beginning."

She opened her mouth and closed it again. The beginning was weeks ago before her sister got herself into this difficulty. "I can't. I sort of got dumped into the middle of this myself. It started with Adelaide— Oh, you *really* don't want me to set up something between the two of you now." Not that she could tell him about her sister's condition. "Besides, my stepmother is trying to arrange a marriage for her with a lord back East anyway. And you don't have nearly enough money nor a title for Marguerite's liking. I've gotten off track, haven't I?"

He rubbed a hand across the back of his neck. "I have no way of knowing. You haven't made one lick of sense so far."

She supposed she hadn't. None of it made sense to her. "The beginning?" She took a deep breath to order her thoughts. "For me, this started Thursday afternoon— after I left you. But my father is in on it too. They are all conspiring against me." Life had been simpler when they lived out on the farm. Oh, if she could go back, she would. To have nothing more important to do than gather eggs, milk the cow, or lie in the meadow and watch the clouds drift by.

"Izzy, please tell me the worst of it first."

She stopped short. The worst of it? Which part was that? It was all awful.

He faced her. "What is it? It can't be all that bad."

"Not all that bad?" Tears blurred her vision, and she stomped her foot. "I'm getting married."

His mouth dropped open. "You can't be serious? Who?" He stretched his neck forward. "Not the cowboy? I thought you only talked to him for the first time on Thursday."

"Of course, I'm serious. I wouldn't make light about such a thing. It's not Mr. Keegan. And he's a rancher. I wouldn't be one bit upset if it were him, but Marguerite would never agree to him. It's... it's... it's Mr. Mallory." She bit her bottom lip, and her insides wrenched up into a tight ball having spoken his name.

Grant pulled his head back into his shoulders, and his eyebrows flinched together. "The banker?"

"Yes."

"He's so much older than you. I didn't know you were interested in him. Why would you marry him? This doesn't make sense."

Why indeed. "I'm *not* interested in him. It's Marguerite's idea. She's convinced my father to make me marry him."

"I should have guessed *she* was behind something like this. So, you don't want to marry the banker?"

She shook her head and continued walking.

His shoulders relaxed, and he matched her pace. "Well then, don't marry him."

"But they'll make me."

"You're the one who has to open your mouth to say 'I do'."

If it were only that simple. She could easily refuse to marry Mr. Mallory, but what about Adelaide? "You'll pray for me, won't you?"

"Of course. I always do. And especially now. What if there was someone else to marry?"

"My stepmother has her sights set on the socially acceptable banker. There's no swaying her. I've tried. He meets all her criteria."

Grant shook his head, seeming as troubled as she was. It was nice to finally have someone on her side, even if he couldn't do anything about her problem.

In the lobby, he dropped the telegrams and mail at the front desk and walked Isabelle through the back passageways of the hotel. "Let's fix your bicycle while we contemplate a solution." Once behind the building, he stopped at the workshop. "Howdy, Hurley."

The older man stood at a bench outside his shop. He had a wiry white beard and a fringe of matching hair circling his head. It was as though the hair that had once inhabited the top of his head had slipped down onto his face. His brown bib-overalls attested to the dirtiness of his job. His arms were beefy, and his stomach protruded, stretching the waist of his overalls tight over his midsection. With a hammer in one hand, he turned. "Don't you 'Howdy, Hurley' me. This here's my workshop."

Grant chuckled at the burly man's false bravado. "Miss Atwood has a bent rim on her bicycle. We only want to fix it."

Hurley waved his hammer above his workbench. "You come in here, mess my tools all up, and I cain't find nothin' fer a week."

Isabelle stepped forward, her offering in hand. "For me? I brought you cookies."

Hurley's expression softened. He took the cloth wrapped bundle and beamed. "Miss Atwood, you know I cain't say no to you. Iff'n I was thirty years younger, I'd be a courtin' you." He turned to Grant. "You should take heed. Use whatever you like but put things back where you find them this time." He scuttled off with his treat.

Hurley was nothing but a big kitten who got grumpy when someone played with his toys.

Grant flipped the bicycle upside-down and grabbed a wrench.

"Do you really not put his tools back where you get them from?"

"I'm very careful to return everything to its proper place."

That sounded more like Grant.

"So why does Hurley say you don't?"

"He likes to fuss." Grant twisted one of the bolts holding the front tire on. "What does your father have to say about you marrying Mr. Mallory?"

"He's all for it. Thinks it's time I settle down. He wants grandchildren."

He gave her a sideways, wide-eyed look. "Why does your stepmother want you to marry the banker in particular?"

What could she tell him? She didn't feel right divulging Adelaide's transgression. "There's a lord back East Marguerite wants my sister to marry. She says Adelaide can't marry until I'm married. You know, the oldest daughter marrying first and all." Without the whole story, he would never truly understand. Even then, he might not. Isabelle barely understood all the nuances of the situation.

"That hardly seems fair. I still think you should refuse." He removed the front tire.

If she did, what would become of Adelaide? "I tried to refuse, but no one listened to me. They've invited him for lunch."

"If it's a matter of you simply marrying, why don't you pick someone? Someone you already know." He gazed at her steadily as though trying to tell her more.

Because not just any man would have the right qualifications. Blond hair, money, and a high standing in the community. "I wish I could, but Marguerite and Father are very particular."

"So, if someone came up to you and proposed right now—?"

"Who would do that?"

"I don't know." He shrugged. "Someone. The cowboy. If you married him—or someone else—right now, today, then they would be free to marry Adelaide off to the lord, right?"

"He's a rancher, and Marguerite would never agree to him, and he wouldn't likely propose soon enough."

"So, money and a title mean a lot to your stepmother." His shoulders slumped as though disappointed. "What about you?"

"I don't care one whit about titles. I prefer a man without a title. A simple man who loves me. I'm still that farm girl at heart."

"Then decline their offer."

If not for Adelaide's condition, she would.

"Where's your independent spirit I admire?"

"You admire me?" Marguerite would say Isabelle's independent streak was her downfall. Not something to be commended.

"Of course, I do. It's what gives you spunk."

Spunk? She liked that.

In the two hours Grant patiently tried to teach her how to repair her bicycle, he came up with no viable solutions but not for lack of trying. She hated to have to shoot down all his suggestions. Most he shot down himself before finishing them. She loved that he tried so hard. A little too hard. His friendship meant more to her than most things.

If, in the end, she did marry Mr. Mallory, her new husband would need to understand that her friendship with Grant was a permanent fixture in her life.

Five

OLIVER MALLORY SAT IN THE ATWOOD'S parlor with Jackson Atwood and his wife. Being a man of means made him desirable as a husband to a lot of women and to the parents of young ladies, but he didn't have near the money Jackson had inherited.

This favor Jackson had called in wasn't really a favor. Not in the true sense of the word. If this wedding did happen, he would feel even more indebted to the man.

Oliver didn't know how he'd been so fortunate to catch his first wife. But it had become apparent shortly after the wedding that his sweet Francine had manipulated events and meetings to catch him, and he'd fallen helplessly in love with her. Thankfully, she'd been a devoted wife. Her passing seven years ago had crushed him. He figured he'd never marry again. Too much trouble to court a woman in hopes she might say yes in the end but never knowing if she truly cared for him or his bank account.

Then this. He knew where he stood in an arranged marriage. No emotions to muddy the waters. Like a business transaction beneficial to both parties. Nothing more.

"I don't know what could be keeping her," Mrs. Atwood said for the third time as she folded and refolded her handkerchief.

"She'll be here. I've sent the stable hand out to find her," Jackson replied for the third time.

If Oliver wasn't indebted to this man, he would have graciously left by now, but he paid his debts. If not for Jackson vouching for his character a year ago when he'd been mistaken for an outlaw on a wanted poster, he could have lost his position at the bank. Everything had gotten resolved quickly because of Jackson, or else the whole town would have thought him an outlaw and would mistrust him from then on. Not a good position for a banker.

A woman like Isabelle Atwood wouldn't be interested in his money since she had more—or rather her family did. Hopefully, she wouldn't think he was after *her* money. He would make it clear he was only doing this as a favor to her father. That didn't sound good. He didn't want her to feel like a charity case. He'd seen Miss Atwood around town and at church. He never thought much about her. She could likely have any gentleman in town she set her cap for. Why he was the fortunate one chosen, he didn't know.

The front door opened and closed.

Oliver stood to greet his intended. If it was, in fact, her.

Mrs. Atwood rose to her feet. "You stay here. I'll get her." She rushed out of the room.

Female voices drifted in from the entry.

"Already? He's early. I'm not presentable."

That must be Miss Atwood, because it didn't have the grating sound of Mrs. Atwood.

"You're a mess." Mrs. Atwood's voice scraped along his spine. "Look at your filthy hands and shirtwaist sleeves. And your hair. Let's get you cleaned up." She changed her tone to cheery and spoke louder. "We'll be right back."

Oliver glanced at Jackson.

He shrugged. "I'm not even going to pretend. I'm sure she won't be long."

From his vantage point, he could see the ladies from the knees down as they climbed the stairs. Miss Atwood wore a Bloomer bicycle dress outfit. A smile pulled at his mouth. Good. He wouldn't be able to stomach a mousy kind of wife. He wanted one with strength of character and a presence about her. One who could speak her mind—without being belligerent—would keep him on his toes and make life interesting. He sensed his betrothed was just such a person.

Ten minutes later, the ladies descended the stairs. The bicycling outfit had been replaced with a pink gown that subtly shimmered when Miss Atwood moved, hinting at more than met the eye. Like the woman who wore it?

He took her hand and bowed over it. "Miss Atwood." Some of the aforementioned stains remained in the corners of her nails. A socialite who wasn't afraid of a little dirt. Endearing.

"Please call her Isabelle," Mrs. Atwood said. "You're practically family. We'll leave the two of you to get acquainted until lunch is ready." The pocket doors slid closed behind her parents.

Oliver had hoped he would get to visit with Miss Isabelle alone. One could hardly get to know a lady with others around. He indicated the furnishings. "Shall we sit, Miss Atwood?" Regardless of what her mother had said, he would wait for the young lady to grant him permission to use her first name.

"Thank you, Mr. Mallory." She sat in a wingback chair and not on the settee where he might sit next to her. She also didn't offer him the use of her given name.

He took the settee. "Please call me Oliver. Formalities can get tiresome."

"Oh. All right." She paused. "Oliver."

She seemed surprised by his request but still didn't return the friendly gesture.

He smelled coercion and shook his head. "This wasn't your idea, was it?"

She lowered her shoulders but didn't answer. She didn't have to.

"It's all right. You won't hurt my feelings. I had convinced myself you wanted your father to arrange this match between us. I ignored our age difference and hoped you cared for me, but it's clear that's not the case. So, why arrange a marriage?"

She took several breaths before answering. "They want to marry my sister to a lord back East."

He waited, but she offered no further explanation. "What does one have to do with the other?"

She worked her lips back and forth, and her blue eyes studied him. "They're old fashioned. Need to marry off the oldest daughter first."

He stared. She was serious. "That's a poor reason to marry. I can call this off."

"But what about the favor my father has called in?"

"I'll make him understand." Jackson likely wouldn't be happy.

An array of emotions he couldn't identify flickered across her sweet face. Some positive and others not so, with several iterations of confusion.

This had been a nice dream. Even as short lived as it was. He stood. "I'll let your father know. I'll take full responsibility."

He crossed to the sliding doors.

"Wait." Her voice came out a little strangled.

He turned.

She stood, twisting one hand in the other. "My parents are set on me marrying. And soon."

"Then pick someone you actually might want to marry. I'm sure there are dozens of men in town who would fight for a chance to marry you."

"But not you?"

"If I thought you cared and would want me to win, then of course, I would fight for you. Who do you fancy fighting to win your hand?"

Her shoulders sagged. "It wouldn't matter. My parents won't allow me to marry just anyone. They're... particular."

He should leave and tell Jackson he would owe him double next time. Trifling with someone's life—the rest of their life—made him uncomfortable. This wasn't some quick solution which would blow over in a day or two. This was the rest of her life and the rest of his. But something inside of him didn't want to let her go so easily. If he thought she could come to care for him even a little, he would fight for her. He would never know if she could if he didn't fight at least a little.

He motioned toward her chair. "Shall we sit again, Miss Atwood? Perhaps talk?"

She sat and smiled at him. "Thank you. And do call me Isabelle. I agree that formalities can get tiresome."

"You're welcome, Isabelle." He returned to the settee. "I'm not a man who likes secrets and subterfuge. So tell me honestly, would you really agree to marry me so your sister can marry a lord? Why don't you marry the lord? You are the eldest."

"Me? I have no interest in having a title, and I'd hate to move from Kamola. This is my home. And yes, I would marry to help my sister."

Devotion and passion. A nice combination.

He put his hand on his chest. "Please don't think I've agreed to this arrangement because of your father's money. I simply owe him a favor."

"This is quite a commitment in repayment."

"It surprised me as well, but I've seen you around town and in church, and people speak highly of you."

"They do?" Her head tilted like a bird's.

"You doubt that?"

She smoothed her hands over her skirt as though uncomfortable with praise. "I guess I never considered what people said about me."

"It's all been good."

She narrowed her eyes. "I thought you didn't like subterfuge. I know quite a few people who have definite opinions about my choice in transportation. None of them good. What do you think of a potential wife who rides a bicycle?"

"I shall purchase one for myself and go riding with you."

Her smile turned genuine, and he knew he wanted to make this work. He wanted to take care of her. Protect her from her mother who he suspected had orchestrated this whole matter.

A maid slid open the parlor doors. "Luncheon is ready."

Oliver rose to his feet and proffered his hand to Miss Isabelle.

She took it and stood.

He tucked hers around his arm and escorted her to the dining room.

Jackson sat at the head of table with his wife and youngest daughter near him along one side. On his other side, two place settings waited for Oliver and Isabelle. The younger man held out her chair until she was situated then seated himself.

The meal was far more elaborate than he was used to for his noon meal. The conversation jerked from one awkward topic to another that had nothing to do with anything. Something to talk about to avoid the subject on everyone's mind—the question of his impending marriage to their eldest daughter.

The younger Miss Atwood dabbed her napkin to her lips. "Mr. Mallory, where did you live before you came to Kamola?"

"Philadelphia, then California, then here."

"Were you a banker in those places as well?"

"I was."

"Do your parents live in Philadelphia?"

"They do."

"Adelaide," Mrs. Atwood scolded. "Let the poor man eat in peace."

"I simply want to get to know the man who will be... who is going to marry my favorite sister."

Mrs. Atwood thinned her lips. "She's your only sister."

"Even if she wasn't, she would still be my favorite. She's always doing nice things for me and helping me when I have a problem. So, my favorite."

What a charming girl.

A noise came from Isabelle beside him that sounded like a stifled laugh.

He looked her way.

Her mouth worked back and forth as though suppressing a smile. She raised her napkin to her face, likely to hide her mirth. When she lowered it, she had regained her composure. "You are my favorite sister as well."

Mrs. Atwood narrowed her eyes at her eldest daughter, then slid a sideways glance at her youngest. "We'll all have plenty of time to get to know Mr. Mallory, *later.*"

He didn't mind the younger Miss Atwood's questions. He found her captivating. If his intended was too shy to inquire, he was glad her sister wasn't. Refreshing. He glanced at Isabelle who kept her gaze on her plate. Or perhaps, she had asked her sister to make the inquiries on her behalf. "I'm happy to answer any questions she might have."

Adelaide gave a bashful smile. How endearing. "Do you have any brothers or sisters?"

"Four sisters, no brothers." The reason his parents wanted him to marry again so his offspring could carry on the family name.

"Are they older or younger? Any of them married?"

"One older, three younger, all married with children. They and their families live in Philadelphia as well."

"You must miss them all terribly."

"I do." But he also didn't. He didn't miss their badgering him to take a wife again. It had been easier to remain aloof some distance away. But if this arrangement with Isabelle worked out, his mother would be exceedingly happy. He could get her to cancel the Christmas soiree to parade the eligible debutantes in front of him. An event he'd been loathing. If he could return home with a fiancée or wife, everyone would be happy. That the decision whom to marry had basically been taken out of his hands and he didn't have to court a woman in the traditional manner, made the whole thing less unpleasant.

"Do you plan to move back there as well?"

"Honestly, Adelaide. Take a breath. One would think you were betrothed to the man." Mrs. Atwood picked up her goblet and took a drink of water.

"I'd like to know if he plans to take my *favorite* sister far away."

He chuckled inside. She would keep him on his toes as well. "At present, I have no plans to move from Kamola."

The younger Miss Atwood shifted her gaze back to him. "Marrying someone is no trifling thing. You must have owed my father a huge favor."

"That's quite enough, Adelaide." Jackson set his fork firmly on the table. "That's a private matter. Apologize for your impertinence."

Miss Atwood looked duly admonished. "Pardon my forwardness, Mr. Mallory."

"Of course. No harm." Oliver felt bad for Adelaide.

With Mrs. Atwood's protest earlier, he hadn't noticed if Jackson had been irritated by the conversation.

Jackson and his wife both appeared upset with their youngest daughter.

Oliver turned to Isabelle.

Her expression held compassion for her sister. Good to know.

He didn't want a wife who would be harsh with their children.

Six

The following morning, Isabelle debated whether or not to feign illness. If Shane Keegan decided this would be a good Sunday to make an appearance at church after all, she would need to keep him away from Mr. Mall— Oliver. He'd sounded as though he wouldn't attend, but she *had* said she would let him know today after the service if she would meet him tomorrow or not. He might have changed his mind and decided to come after all to get her answer to save himself a trip into town tomorrow. Why had she said that? Her parents would be cross if they saw her talking with him. And she couldn't exactly avoid him. If Mr. Keegan did show up and if the two men spoke to her at the same time and found out about the other or if her parents caught her...

She pushed the unpleasant thoughts away. No sense dwelling on something that might not happen. She would deal with the situation if it arose.

Upon entering the church, she stayed at the back, considering each man in turn to determine if the handsome rancher had come. Most of the men had removed their hats indoors, which made the process easier. Mr. Keegan didn't appear to be in attendance.

A male voice came from behind her. "Looking for me?"

Sucking in a breath, she spun around to face Oliver. "Oh. Good morning." She pretended not to hear his question, not wanting to lie nor tell the truth. Let him believe he had been the one on her mind.

He'd been so sweet yesterday, offering to call off the arrangement. She'd wanted to dislike him, to give her father a reason to revoke the tentative betrothal, but he'd been nothing but respectful and considerate. The kind of man a woman ought to marry.

"May I sit with you and your family?"

Yes and no warred to cross her lips. Yes because, if her parents had their way, she would end up marrying him, and he was quite likeable. No because, if Shane decided to make an appearance, he would see them together and presume she wasn't interested in him—which she definitely was. He had also been kind *and* rescued her.

Father approached. "Oliver, you must join us in our pew."

Oliver looked to her for approval.

She smiled. "Yes, I would like that very much." The answer expected from her and surprisingly not distasteful.

He held out his arm, and she tucked her hand into the crook of his elbow.

Tomorrow, she should tell Shane she couldn't see him anymore. Or she could simply not go, and he would figure it out. That would be discourteous when he'd made a point to let her know he would eat alone if she didn't meet him. Besides, she wanted to have one rendezvous with him. For a short time, forget about her family's troubles and possibly find an alternate solution. Marguerite wouldn't be mollified for very long. If Isabelle could avoid agreeing to any definite plans for her future—marrying Oliver—she might find a way out of this. Possibly find the baby's father and make him do right by Adelaide.

Oliver sat next to her in the pew. Tongues would waggle now. Rumors and suppositions about his presence with their family. Exactly what Marguerite would want. Isabelle hoped none of them got back to Shane Keegan before tomorrow. Not likely since he mostly stayed out at his ranch. There had to be a lot to do on a place like his.

After the service, Oliver stood outside with Isabelle and her family. "It's a beautiful day. I've had my cook prepare a picnic. Won't you all join me?"

Adelaide beamed. "I love picnics."

Marguerite looped her arm with her daughter's. "How very thoughtful of you, Mr. Mallory, but we'll leave you and Isabelle to enjoy the feast."

Adelaide faced Father. "Please may I stay?"

Oliver kept his attention on her father. "I would like to get to know Isabelle's family, and a chaperone is always prudent for a young lady's reputation."

Marguerite's pinched face bespoke her displeasure with the idea of Adelaide staying behind, but Father nodded his consent.

Oliver smiled. "Very good. I'll see to it your daughters arrive home safely."

"I appreciate that." Father took Marguerite's arm and walked off.

Adelaide lunching with them pleased Isabelle, but not for any of the obvious reasons. Not as a chaperone. Not because she didn't want to be alone with Oliver. But so Adelaide could get to know the man who might be raising her child. For that had likely been the reason for her slew of questions yesterday.

Oliver pointed. "If you ladies will find a patch under the tree over there, I'll fetch the picnic lunch I had made for us."

"I can help." Adelaide popped up on her toes and back down.

Isabelle should have been the one to offer. "That leaves me to claim our spot in the shade." She headed off for the tree.

Grant strolled up beside her. "Are you seriously considering marrying him?"

She didn't want to. "I have to, at least, consider it for my family's sake. He's not so bad. He's congenial."

"Congenial? That doesn't sound promising."

"I could do a lot worse."

"You could do a lot better."

"Could I?" Other than his age and not being in love with him, there was nothing wrong with Oliver.

"He's old."

If she didn't know better, she might mistake his concern for jealousy. "He's mature. Much more preferable to someone who is a ruffian or one without a lick of sense in his head."

"Speaking of ruffians, what about Cowboy Keegan?"

"*Rancher.*" She stopped in the shade and turned on

him. "Why are you so reluctant to refer to him as such?"

He shrugged. "Nothing more than a fancy word for cowboy. So, you've given up on him?"

"Not entirely, but I can't afford to wait for him to propose."

"Propose? You're that certain about him? If you're so sure, why don't you propose to him?"

"No, I'm not sure. I wish I had time to find out. And I will not propose to him nor any other man."

"Why not?"

"And look desperate?"

"Aren't you? Why are you in such a rush to marry?"

She couldn't tell him about the baby. "Why are you so worried about whom I marry?"

"We've been friends a long time. I've always looked out for you. I don't want to see you get hurt. This is the rest of your life you're playing with."

"I appreciate your concern. You're like the brother I never had." From whom she'd once hoped for more, but that was a long time ago. "Like I said, Marguerite's eager to arrange things with the lord back East for Adelaide." When he didn't say anything, she parroted her father's words, "It's time I married. I don't want to turn into an old maid."

He shook his head. "Since when have you been worried about that?"

Since she was being forced to marry and avoiding spinsterhood was a socially acceptable reason for a woman to marry when she wasn't in love. "I think about such things a lot." Think about, but not worry about. "Even if I haven't been *worried* about becoming an old maid, that doesn't mean I don't want to marry."

"Promise me you won't rush into this for the sake of your family."

Exactly what she was being forced to do. Or at least considering it until she could figure a different way. She couldn't say she wouldn't rush into anything, because she had no other choice without an alternative. "I'll be fine."

He stared at her hard before speaking. "May I show you something this afternoon?"

"This picnic aside, Marguerite had the day planned with Oliver. I think she is quite pleased he took the initiative to organize something."

"You're using his first name already?"

"Why not?"

"It makes you sound settled on this as your fate. What about tomorrow? Go with me then." His eagerness to show her something meant it must be important to him.

"I can't. I'm having lunch with Mr. Keegan."

"You're still going through with that even though you are practically engaged to *Oliver*?" Now, he really did sound jealous, but she knew it wasn't so.

She nodded. "Of course. How about Tuesday?"

He nodded this time. "Noon, for my meal break? In the lobby?"

"Sounds good."

Adelaide sauntered up with Oliver. She held a quilt draped over her arm.

Oliver set a basket of food on the ground and held out his hand to Grant. "Mr. Dawson, good to see you." Grant shook his hand. "Would you like to join us? I have plenty of food with Isabelle's parents turning me down. It will even up the numbers." He tilted his head toward Adelaide.

Isabelle touched Grant's arm. "Oh, yes, do join us." Since it was Oliver's idea, she didn't feel bad about encouraging him to stay.

Grant shrugged. "All right."

Adelaide held out the quilt. "If we each take a corner, we can get this spread out in a jiff."

With the quilt laid on the ground, all four sat, one at each corner, Isabelle across from her sister and the men opposite each other.

Oliver removed small china plates with silver filigree edge work, slim crystal goblets, and silver utensils.

Isabelle fingered the rim of the plate. Had the fineries been to impress her parents? Or her? Didn't he realize there was no need? Her parents were already set on him for a son-in-law, and such things didn't impress her.

Oliver handed two loosely corked bottles to Grant.

"Would you pour the lemonade?"

Grant took the bottles and did.

Oliver unpacked the food. "Nothing elaborate. Bread and the makings for sandwiches. I thought everyone would prefer to select what they like on theirs."

How thoughtful. She hated it when simple decisions like this were made for her. Maybe she and Oliver would be a good match.

"Ladies, you go first."

"Hmm," arose from her sister.

Oh dear. Food and Adelaide weren't exactly the best of friends most days. "Adelaide?"

Her sister lifted her gaze and could evidently sense Isabelle's apprehension. "This looks delicious. I'm starved."

A relief, but the tide could turn quickly. Isabelle would keep an eye on her sister just in case.

Halfway through the meal, Oliver turned to Adelaide. "I hear you'll be engaged to a lord soon. Are congratulations premature?"

Adelaide beamed her captivating smile at him. "A little. Nothing is set yet. It may not even happen."

Oliver returned her smile and held her gaze a moment longer. "Then I'll wait on the good wishes."

Everyone ate in awkward silence. Isabelle certainly didn't know what to say. Since she had the strongest connection to each of the other three people here, she supposed the duty fell to her to facilitate the conversation. But who to engage first? Dare she ask Adelaide something, which might trip her up to say something she oughtn't? She should try to get to know Oliver better, but honestly didn't have the desire to. Lastly, Grant. She already knew everything about him. Think of something. This silence couldn't go on. But it did with a few strained comments now and then from one person or another.

After lunch when all the dishes and food were packed and stowed in the back of the buggy, Oliver turned to Grant. "Can I give you a ride? I promised Mr. Atwood to see his daughters home."

"No, thank you. It's not a bad walk. Thank you for

lunch." Grant headed off.

Was he upset? Isabelle couldn't imagine why.

Oliver drove them home and parked in front of her house. "Stay right there, both of you. Let me help you down." He set the break, climbed out, and rounded the vehicle. His buggy had a step, so the only assistance he needed to offer was a hand to steady oneself with. Adelaide went first, then Isabelle.

Though he worked behind a desk most of the time, his hand seemed strong. His warmth comforted her. "Isabelle, may I speak with you a moment longer? Alone?"

Adelaide curtsied. "Thank you for lunch, Mr. Mallory."

"You're welcome, Miss Atwood." He watched her sister dash inside.

"What did you want to speak with me about?"

He turned his attention from her sister to Isabelle. "Since your mother seems to be in a hurry, are we supposed to announce our engagement and set a date? I wasn't sure how much I could say in front of Mr. Dawson."

Marguerite would like nothing better than a fast wedding. The faster the better. Not to mention Adelaide needed her to marry quickly. She would start showing soon, and if Isabelle appeared to have a baby who was too premature, no one would believe she'd conceived after the wedding. Most importantly, Oliver needed to believe. But it was probably already too late for anyone to be fooled anyway. "Do you mind if we wait a bit? I'd like to get used to the idea." Time she could use to find the father or figure out an alternate solution. She almost felt bad for Oliver. Given time, she might actually fall in love with him, but time was not something she had right now. Not if Marguerite got her way.

"Since we are soon to be engaged, may I ask another question?"

"Of course."

"Feel free to refrain from answering if you wish. Who is Mr. Dawson to you?"

"Grant? We've been friends for years. You have nothing to worry about from him." Once, many years ago, she'd fancied the idea of her and Grant as a couple, but she'd gotten over that a long time ago. A ridiculous notion that had caused strife between them.

He studied her a moment then nodded and walked her inside.

Marguerite and her father met them in the foyer. Her father spoke. "Do come in."

"Only for a few minutes."

Once they all sat down, Marguerite got straight to the point. "Do the two of you have anything to announce?" She was not going to relent, determined to push Oliver into this. Like a hunter with her prey in her sights.

Oliver shifted forward. "I couldn't be more pleased with this match, but I'd prefer to spend some time getting to know Isabelle before announcing anything."

So kind of him to take responsibility. Marguerite would accept that.

"We understand," Father said.

Oliver stood. "I need to be going."

After he left, Isabelle climbed the stairs to her room. She had no sooner shut the door when Adelaide burst in, as giddy as a schoolgirl. "You were right. Mr. Mallory is a nice man. I like him, Isabelle. I think he'll make a good father for my baby," she put a hand on her abdomen, "and a fine husband for you."

Isabelle thought so too. She wished she didn't. She wished she could dislike him. She wished he would do something unacceptable to make Father change his mind. But at every turn, he was a charming gentleman.

If she spent the rest of her life with him, her future wouldn't be so bad. Though she hadn't settled her fate yet, she could picture herself with him.

Mrs. Oliver Mallory.

She shook that thought free immediately.

Oliver sat in Andrew MacVay's parlor across the chessboard from the older man as he did most Sunday afternoons. Today he'd arrived later than usual because of his picnic lunch with the charming Atwood ladies. He moved his knight.

Andrew scrubbed his hand across his chin. "Hmm. Are you sure you want to make that move?"

That could mean his host felt he was getting backed into a corner. Or Andrew could have realized that Oliver had picked up on his pattern of saying the same thing when he was in trouble in a game and using it against Oliver. It didn't matter. He still enjoyed the game and the challenge. "I've taken my hand off the piece. I can't change my mind now."

Andrew took Oliver's knight with his bishop. "Check. You're distracted today. What's on your mind?"

Too soon to talk about his arrangement with the Atwoods. Jackson might want to make the announcement himself. "I'm not at liberty to say at this time."

Andrew's mother sat across the room, working on a needle project. "I saw you sitting in church with the Atwoods—right next to Isabelle—and after church you lingered with their girls."

People would figure out something was up if he kept company with the Atwoods and Isabelle in particular. "Yes, I have some business dealings with Jackson." Oliver moved his king.

The elderly Mrs. MacVay harrumphed from the settee. "You know, if you're looking for a wife, our Trudy is closer to your age."

Oliver hadn't been looking. Miss Atwood had been offered up, but she didn't seem keen on the marriage.

"Our Trudy is a fine cook and can keep a neat house."

Mr. MacVay lifted a pawn and set it back down on its same square. "Mother, Mr. Mallory doesn't need you meddling in his personal life. I've found someone who can challenge me at chess, so don't go scaring him off."

The topic of the current discussion, Trudy, strolled into the parlor. "Grandmother, have you seen my crochet hook. I was working on a doily yesterday, but my hook has disappeared."

Mrs. MacVay's voice took on a cheerful tone. "I haven't, but there's a young man here looking for a wife."

Oliver coughed.

Trudy stared wide-eyed.

Andrew stood. "Mother, Oliver isn't interested, and neither is Trudy. Now leave this be."

Oliver gave Trudy a sympathetic smile.

"Well, the girl needs to find a suitable husband."

Some women never married for one reason or another. It was none of Oliver's business why this pretty woman hadn't married. She must have had offers.

Mrs. MacVay continued. "And we have an eligible bachelor right here looking for a wife."

"He said nothing about looking for a wife."

"He implied it."

"He did no such thing." Andrew waved his hand. "Trudy, you're excused and take your grandmother with you."

The old woman stood. "I don't need any help. I know when I'm not wanted." She glided to the doorway.

"You are most definitely wanted. However, your meddling isn't." Andrew met his mother at the doorway and kissed her on the cheek. "I love you, Mother."

"I know you do." She patted him on the cheek.

The two women left.

Andrew returned to his seat. "I'm sorry about that."

Though it was none of his business, Oliver asked anyway. "You don't feel as your mother does, that your daughter should be married?"

"I tried years ago but finally gave up. Whose turn is it?"

"Yours. Your daughter's determined to remain single?"

"Not necessarily. When she lost her heart to a man and then lost him to another woman, she never recovered from it. Whenever I'd bring up a potential suitor, she knew just how much lip quivering and tear blinking to do to get me to back off. I never could handle a woman crying. I prefer the good old fashion tongue lashing of my mother—all in good humor." Andrew moved his queen. "Check. Checkmate in three moves."

Oliver studied the board. Indeed. Checkmate in three. He toppled his king.

"You've been off all through the game." The older man reset his pieces. "I could have been playing my mother for the amount of challenge you provided today."

Oliver followed suit with his pieces. "I am distracted."

"Your *business* with Jackson Atwood?"

"You could say that. I've agreed to... a transaction that I'm unsure about." Oliver pointed to the board. "Another game?"

Andrew moved a pawn. "Is there anything inherently wrong or illegal in the *transaction*?"

"No." Oliver moved a pawn.

"Then what's holding you back?" Andrew moved another pawn.

"One of the parties seems reluctant." Oliver moved another pawn.

His host moved a piece. "Has this party requested to back out?"

"No." Oliver moved.

"Have you let this party know they can back out if they wish to?" Andrew moved.

Oliver moved. "Yes."

Andrew moved. "Is this party an adult who can make their own decisions?"

"Yes." Oliver moved.

"Then you have done your part, it's up to the other party to make her—or his—decision. If this party hasn't taken your offer to back out, then they have made their own choice."

Oliver supposed that was true. Maybe he just wished Isabelle wanted this more.

Andrew moved. "Checkmate in eight."

Oliver huffed a sigh and toppled his king. He hoped he didn't topple as easily.

Seven

IN THE FULL MOONLIGHT, HE GLANCED over the page. Would the beautiful Miss Isabelle Atwood like his words? Not his own creation, but they conveyed how much he cared about her. Time would tell. Why was it so hard to approach a lady and tell her how he felt? Because if she rejected him in person, his hope and his heart would be crushed. For now, this would have to do.

He stood outside her house and gazed up at the second-floor windows. She likely sat behind one of them in her room, reading or doing needlepoint. He moved around the outside of the house to the barn where she kept her bicycle and waited until the stable hand exited the building.

To conceal himself, he pulled back into the shadows and held his breath. When the man moved out of sight, he released the air in his lungs and crept up to the barn, as he had done with the first poem. He eased the door open just enough to slip through, minimizing the creak. Though black inside, he knew where to go, but there could be unknown obstacles.

He retrieved the candle from his pocket and struck a match. It ignited with a hiss, and he lit the candle. Isabelle's bicycle leaned against a post near the far wall. In between him and his destination lay a rather large barn cat. He stepped around the stretched-out orange fur to the bicycle.

Isabelle Atwood looked adorable when she rode it. Now, to attach his missive. How long would it be before she noticed this one? More prepared than last time, he wrapped the folded piece of paper around one side of the handlebars and secured it with a blue ribbon the color of her eyes. He hadn't planned to give her this one so soon, but he needed to accelerate his timetable. He'd wanted to tuck a flower in with the note, but it would be wilted by morning or whenever she rode her bicycle next.

A noise startled him. The crunch of dirt under the sole of a shoe. The stable hand must have forgotten something. He blew out his candle as the door hinge creaked, long and loud.

He stepped around the bicycle, behind a dividing wall, and into the shadows.

The cat rubbed against his leg.

He waved his hand at the furry pest.

Isabelle glided in, carrying a lantern.

What was she doing out here?

"Marmalade. Here, kitty-kitty-kitty."

He shooed with his hand and mouthed, "Go."

"Marmalade? I brought you some milk."

The cat trotted away.

From his vantage point, though in the shadows, he could see Isabelle. He wanted to reach out to her. Tell her how he felt. But the fear she would laugh at him held him back, silenced his tongue.

She crouched, setting a saucer of milk on the floor.

With the speed of the wind rushing down the canyon, the cat lapped at it.

After petting the feline, Isabelle moved closer to where he hid. Her light invaded the edge of his hiding spot.

Would she see him?

He halted his breathing.

She stopped at her bicycle only a few feet away. "What's this?" She set the lantern on the dirt floor less than a foot from his boot. The light touched and illuminated the tip. Dare he drag it backward and risk making a sound?

She pulled the ribbon free. The paper crinkled as she unwound it from around the handlebar and unfolded it.

He took advantage of that opportunity to withdraw his foot from the light disguised by the paper noise. He could have left a flower after all.

She picked up the lantern and held it close to his missive. "Another poem! When was this left?" She read aloud. "But soft! What light through yonder window breaks? It is the east, and Juliet is the sun.'"

She sighed. "Romeo's soliloquy to Juliet on her balcony."

He released his breath. He'd chosen well. As she continued to read the entirety of Romeo's monologue, he closed his eyes and let her lilting voice caress him.

"'It is my lady. Oh, it is my love. Oh, that she knew she were!'"

The way she read with such emotion, such passion, made him believe she might feel the same. Dare he reveal himself? He pictured the scenario in his mind. He would step out from the shadows and say, *I love you.*

She would startle. Drop her lantern, and the barn would catch fire.

No, this was not the time. For now, he would listen. And dream.

"'*See how she leans her cheek upon her hand.*
Oh, that I were a glove upon that hand,
That I might touch that cheek!'"

She clutched the paper to her chest. "So romantic." She picked up the cat who had finished its milk. "Did you see who left this?"

Yes, he had. Good thing the cat couldn't talk.

Maybe one day, he would win the hand of the fair Isabelle Atwood. But for now, it was better to love her in secret than to have his hopes crushed.

Eight

On Monday, Isabelle smoothed her hands down the sides of her lavender silk-chiffon dress with a taffeta underlay. She studied her appearance in her standing mirror. Shane Keegan couldn't help but be impressed.

"You look beautiful." Her sister's small voice came from the doorway.

She twirled to face Adelaide. "Thank you."

"Are you going to meet Mr. Mallory?"

Heat rose to her face. "I'm not planning on it, but one never knows who one will chance to meet." She crossed to her sister. "How are you feeling today?"

"Well."

Isabelle studied her sister's pale complexion. "You don't look well."

"I wish I wasn't expecting. I'm causing so much trouble for everyone. Mostly for you."

She took Adelaide's hand and patted it. "There's nothing we can do about your condition now. We simply have to figure out the best way forward."

"I wish I could do like you said and go away, have the baby, then come back and pretend none of this ever happened, but Mother won't let me."

Not if she knew about it. But what would become of the baby if Isabelle swept Adelaide away to have it in secret? No, they had to keep the little one in the family. They had to. So, she must come up with an alternative, like finding the father. "Let's go down to breakfast."

In the dining room, Marguerite gave Isabelle an approving nod. "You look like a proper lady fit to marry a banker. After you eat, we'll go over the wedding plans."

"Plans? We haven't even— Nothing has been— It's too soon."

"Nonsense. If anything, we're late in making

preparations. Today is Monday... hmm... See if you can get Mr. Mallory to agree to Wednesday."

"Wednesday for what? Another lunch?"

"The wedding of course. Haven't you been listening? The sooner the better. Your sister can't wait."

Wednesday was only two days away! Isabelle exchanged looks with her father.

He cleared his throat. "Certainly it can wait until after Founders Day. Everyone in town is so busy. It will be difficult for people to squeeze one more thing into their already full schedules."

Marguerite sat silent for a moment. No doubt trying to figure out how to get her way. In the end, she yielded. "Your father's right. Waiting until after the Founders Day Festival will have to do, but it will give us much needed time. We have a lot to do before then."

Isabelle gave her father an appreciative glance, but she had lost her appetite.

A half an hour later, she sat in the parlor with her stepmother and Adelaide.

Marguerite had a folder with a stack of papers in it. Each one had something written or drawn on it, lists and diagrams. It appeared as though *someone* had already done quite a bit of preparations.

Her stepmother folded her hands on her lap. "When you speak to Mr. Mallory about choosing a date, push for early next week, Monday or Tuesday. We don't want to put this off any longer than absolutely necessary."

One week? Was that all the time she had? Better than this week. "What if that doesn't work for him? He does work. The bank needs him."

"I'm sure they can do without him for a couple of hours. Insist upon immediacy. I'm sure you can persuade him. He'll want to please his young bride. And a few tears wouldn't hurt if need be."

"I'm not going to shed false tears to manipulate him." Any more than her parents already were orchestrating everything to their advantage. "Next, you'll have me dropping my handkerchief in front of him."

"Now you're thinking. Men like to feel useful. Our cook will make all the food except the cake. I'll order that from the bakery." She handed Isabelle a sheet of paper. "Choose which hors d'oeuvres and other foods you would like to have served."

Isabelle stared at the list. "I don't want any."

"You have to make these decisions. It is your wedding after all."

Anger flashed inside Isabelle. "Is it? I'm not the one who wants this. You do. You decide." She tossed the paper back. Whatever cuisine Marguerite wanted to serve would be fine. She obviously already had in mind what she wanted. So why invite Isabelle to have an opinion which ultimately wouldn't matter?

"Now, don't make a fuss. We're going to keep the whole affair quite small. We'll have the ceremony in the back garden, unless it turns cold or the weather is bad. If that happens, we'll clear out all the furniture from in here." Marguerite stood and waved her hand toward one end of the space. "We'll have the minister stand there, near the piano. Oh dear. Having it outside will never do. Too much trouble to move the piano and everything else outside in so short a time. This room will have to suffice. Adelaide, you'll play the Wedding March. Isabelle, you'll come down the stairs and meet your father at the bottom and enter through there." She pointed. "The guests will be seated in chairs on that side of the parlor."

"Guests? Chairs? I thought this was going to be small." The fewer people who witnessed this farce, the better. "How many people are you planning on?"

"I think we can squeeze in forty."

"Forty? No. Why can't we simply stand in the preacher's living room with you and Father and Adelaide? We don't need anyone else." Isabelle wished *she* didn't have to be there.

"That would never do for an Atwood wedding. What would people think? Honestly, Isabelle. We have to give the appearance that this isn't a rushed wedding."

"But it is rushed."

"No one needs to know that. It will deflect suspicion off your early spring arrival."

"Won't a big spectacle draw attention to it?"

"It's all in how you look at it."

Adelaide had sat silently on the settee but spoke up now. "I agree with Isabelle. It would be better with fewer people."

How sweet of her sister to side with her, because Adelaide never disagreed with her mother.

Marguerite gave her a wide-eyed look of astonishment.

Her sister's shoulders slumped, and she turned to Isabelle. "Forty's not so many."

Her poor sister. One small moment of bravery squashed with a look.

Pleased to have won the battle, Marguerite returned to her seat. "Now, tomorrow afternoon we have an appointment with Mademoiselle Celeste Dumont."

"For what?"

"Your wedding gown, of course, as well as several other outfits for your new wardrobe."

"I have plenty of clothes. I can wear one of the dresses I already have to get married." She didn't want anything new or special for her very un-special day.

"Absolutely not. You need a proper gown, and you can't wear last year's fashions after you're married. We don't have time for a whole new wardrobe to start with, but we can get you the basics and order the rest. It's all settled."

Maybe for her stepmother, but not within Isabelle. She stood and crossed to the doorway.

"Where are you going?"

To get away from this madness. "You seem to have everything figured out, so I'm not needed. I have an appointment in town."

Marguerite grinned and raised an eyebrow. "With a certain banker?"

Isabelle didn't want to lie by saying no, so she simply shrugged one shoulder and glided out of the room. Evasiveness was acceptable for a lady. Let her stepmother think what she wanted to. Isabelle gathered her reticule and shawl and hurried out the back door before anyone else could waylay her.

In the barn, she gathered the hem of the full skirt on her fancy dress around each of her calves and tied them with strips of fabric, sort of makeshift bloomers. It would keep her hem from getting caught in the greasy chain. She swung on her shawl and pinned it in place with a pink cameo brooch to match her shawl.

Isabelle arrived at the White Hotel well before noon but not as ahead of schedule as she would have liked. Although she'd planned her escape from the house with plenty of time to spare, she'd been waylaid too long by her family. Mostly by Marguerite and her wedding plans. Plans that Isabelle was determined not to need.

After leaning her bicycle against the boardwalk railing, she untied the strips of fabric she'd used to keep her silk dress out of harm's way. She hadn't wanted to wear her bicycle dress for her rendezvous with Shane Keegan, choosing pretty over practical.

She shook out her chiffon skirt and its taffeta underlay, then brushed her hands over the rumpled fabric. "Oh, bother." She'd hoped to avoid wrinkles by carefully tying her skirt out of the way. At least her hem and mudguard had been successfully spared a battle with the chain. A small consolation. Hopefully, Mr. Keegan wouldn't notice.

She unpinned the cameo and removed her shawl before entering. She approached the front desk where Grant stood on duty but stopped short and twirled in a circle. "What do you think?"

He stared but didn't say anything.

"What is it? Is this outfit terrible? I should have chosen something different. It's too wrinkly at the bottom." She shook her skirt again in hopes of straightening more of the creases then twisted to look at the back. "Did I get mud on it or something?"

He gave his head a little shake and cleared his throat as though uncomfortable. "No. No, you look fine. More than fine. Quite fetching, in fact. Beautiful." He cleared his throat again. "Where are you having lunch with him?"

Since when did Grant stammer. Men. Ask them to assess a dress and they act like a squirrel searching for its lost stash. "Right here in the dining room."

"Lunch at the hotel? Not very original." He scrunched up his face. "Are you sure about this fellow?"

"Of course not. That's why we're sharing a meal, to get to know each other." She pulled open the top of her beaded drawstring reticule and retrieved a piece of paper, waving it in the air. "I received another one."

"Another what?"

"Poem. From my secret admirer."

"More drivel about flowers and honey?"

"No." She wished Grant could appreciate poetry and things of the heart. "This one is from Romeo and Juliet. The most romantic play ever." She sighed then read aloud Romeo's entire soliloquy to Juliet on the balcony.

Grant remained silent for the duration.

When finished, she sighed and let the paper rest on the counter. "Doesn't it make everything seem right?"

"Can't say that it does. It's overly sentimental. Romeo doesn't even know Juliet."

She straightened. "You haven't a romantic drop of blood in your entire body."

"Oh, I think I'm capable of still surprising you."

She couldn't imagine how. She'd known him too long for that. "When you fall in love with someone, you'll wish for a hundred poems to express your feelings."

"If you say so. Who can even understand that twaddle?"

"Obviously, not you."

"Don't they both die at the end?"

"That's beside the point."

He reached across the counter and took her hand. "I don't want you to put too much of your hopes in these notes."

His touch comforted her. "I'm not. It's nice to think someone has these feelings for me when I'm faced with an impending marriage I don't want."

"So, you've decided to marry Mr. Mallory?"

She shrugged, not wanting to set her fate yet even if Marguerite had. "What did you think of Oliver?"

He hesitated. "He seems like a pleasant enough fellow."

She stared at him, waiting for more. None came. "No cutting remarks? No 'you'll be bored within a month'?"

"Would they do any good? I wish you'd put this off

for a while."

"I wish I could."

"You can."

She shook her head. "I don't have much of a choice. My parents are determined I marry immediately." But not for the-eldest-daughter-must-marry-first reason he knew about. Her stomach roiled as she longed to confide in Grant the real reason for the haste, but she wouldn't betray her sister.

"You have choices. Everyone has choices."

"You're a man. You don't understand what it's like for women. Contrary to your beliefs, women can't simply choose what to do. Unless we have money of our own— which men are reluctant to give us—" Her father was proof of that. "We are at the mercy of men. I could refuse, but what if my parents turn me out for disobeying them."

"You could get a job."

"I thought of that, but what job? The handful of opportunities *men* would actually give a woman don't pay well. Generally, only a half or a third what they pay a man for the same work. Could you live and support yourself on that?"

He shook his head. "Doesn't seem fair."

"It's not, but it's the way the world is. So, until things change, I have little recourse but to capitulate to their wishes."

He silently studied her. No doubt trying to devise a solution to her predicament. If his mind were a clock, she'd be able to hear the gears whirling as fast as a speeding locomotive.

She didn't want to talk about nor think about her future beyond lunch with a handsome rancher and folded the letter. "I think you might have been right that Mr. Keegan is my secret admirer. I imagine him riding into town under the cover of darkness and secreting this onto my bicycle. Then waiting in the shadows for me to find it."

"You can romanticize anything, can't you?"

"You sound surprised. You've known me long enough to know that."

"That I have."

She held the letter up. "It can't be a coincidence I received this the night before I'm to have lunch with him. What do you think?"

"Coincidences are rarely truly coincidences."

"Precisely."

A few minutes later, Shane Keegan opened the door, then stepped aside for a lady to exit and tipped his hat to her before he strode in. The woman smiled at him and blushed. A lady standing by the dining room entrance with her gentleman turned and, with a soft smile, studied him.

Isabelle leaned a little over the front desk and sighed. "Now that's the way to enter a room."

Grant fisted one hand and pressed it into his other palm. "I'd like to be a glove upon his face."

So, he had been listening when she'd read Romeo's words.

"Stop it. You could never best him in a fight."

"If he hurts you in any way, I will fight him."

She touched his sleeve. "Don't be silly." After stuffing the poem into her reticule, she lifted her hand and wiggled her fingers. Her heartbeat quickened, and her cheeks warmed.

Nine

SHANE STRODE INTO THE WHITE HOTEL. Fifteen minutes early. He adjusted his bolo tie and stopped short over the threshold. Miss Isabelle Atwood stood at the front desk counter, talking to that fellow who she insisted was *not* her beau.

But she was here. She had come. Though he had planned for her to be here—just in case—he had not truly expected her to be. He had intended to secure a table and be ready for her. Now what should he do? The muscle under his left eye twitched once, twice, then took up a regular rhythm like a prancing horse as it often did. He would ignore it, and it would go away.

His mouth hitched up on one side, and he crossed the lobby. "Miss Atwood. I had hoped to arrive ahead of you and have a table waiting." Please let her not turn him away. Not now that his hopes had been raised. And in front of an audience.

"That's all right. We can wait for the table together. Shane, this is my good friend Grant Dawson. Grant, Shane Keegan."

Shane shook Grant's hand. "Good to meet you."

"And you," Grant replied. "I recommend the pork chops. They seem to be particularly good today."

"Thank you." Shane cocked his elbow toward Miss Atwood. "Shall we find a table?"

She hooked her delicate hand around his arm, sending a tingle all the way up to his shoulder. "We shall." She fit nicely on his arm.

At the entrance to the dining room, the matronly hostess greeted them with a static smile.

"I'm Shane Keegan. On Thursday, I requested to have a table saved for me today."

"Right this way." The hostess wound her way

through the bustling room to a table in the corner by the front window. "Your menus are on the table. Noreen will be with you in a few minutes to take your order." She walked away.

He held out a chair for Miss Atwood then sat across from her. The menu had five items. Roast beef, ribs—both from his cattle—baked chicken, chicken pot pie, and pork chops. Each came with potatoes, green beans, and sliced bread, with cake or pie for dessert.

His dining companion looked particularly beautiful today. A mite too good for a wretch like him.

She glanced up. "Everything smells wonderful."

"Are you going to have the pork chop as Mr. Dawson suggested?"

"It does sound good. You?"

"Haven't decided." He would prefer to have one of the beef options but wondered if that would leave a poor impression if he ordered beef, which had come from his own ranch.

A minute later, Noreen, a younger version of the hostess, waltzed up to the table with a welcoming smile and set two glasses of water on the table. "Have you decided?"

Shane inclined his head for Miss Atwood to order first.

"I would like the roast beef."

"Good choice. It comes from one of the local ranches." Noreen turned to him. "And you?"

Since Miss Atwood had unknowingly ordered his beef, so could he. "I'll also have the roast beef."

"I'll have those out to you straight away." Noreen strolled off.

As they waited, Shane leaned forward. "Can I confess something to you, Miss Atwood?"

"I told you to call me Isabelle. And you may, provided it's nothing illegal."

The muscle twitch under his eye picked up its pace. *Ignore it.* "You think me a scoundrel?"

"I have no way of knowing, but I wouldn't want to have to call the sheriff on you if you confess something dastardly." She tilted her head.

She had been teasing him. He liked that.

She leaned forward, presumably to match his posture. "What deep, dark secret do you wish to divulge?"

"Well, Miss Isabelle, it's not so deep nor dark." She had the most remarkable blue eyes. *Shane, focus.* "I didn't think you would show up today."

A worry line formed between her eyebrows. "Why not?"

"I'm not exactly the type of fellow who a person like you socializes with."

"A person like me?" She straightened. "And what kind of person is that?"

"Wealthy. Socialite." Unapproachable.

She chortled. "All misnomers. Can I tell you a secret?"

He raised his eyebrows. "Provided it's nothing illegal."

She gifted him with a smile. "*Touché.* Five years ago, we lived on a small farm at the edge of town, scraping by enough to eat and pay on the mortgage. My father inherited money from a relative back East. Suddenly, we were viewed as better people. As though money could make the person on the inside somehow better, more valuable. Money can be taken away, character can't."

"A farm girl?"

"Are you disappointed?"

"Quite the opposite. I find that endearing." Not as unapproachable as he had imagined. She was definitely the kind of girl he could see out on his ranch. She wouldn't likely wilt under adverse conditions.

"Tell me all about being a rancher."

"It's hard work, but I enjoy it." At least for the time being.

"What exactly about it do you enjoy?"

Everything. "I get to be out of doors." Cooped up inside made his muscles restless. "Riding across the countryside. Tending to livestock."

"How big is your place?"

"You mean spread. That's what we call the whole of a cattle ranch." He shouldn't have corrected her. That hadn't been very cordial.

He liked her curiosity. It wouldn't do to have a wife with no interest in what held tremendous joy for him. "A thousand acres of decent grazing land and a little over three hundred head of cattle. Two-thirds of them I'll be driving to market soon before winter sets in."

"A cattle drive? That sounds exciting."

He liked her enthusiasm. "They can be. But I prefer a drive without excitement."

"I thought cows were taken by train nowadays."

"Most are, but there are still places the rail lines don't go."

"Do you have a bunch of ranch hands and a bunkhouse?" She took a sip of water.

"I do. I get along well with five hands. On a drive, I'll hire others if I need to."

"Do you have a house? Or do you stay with the other men?"

"The house is the best part. The ranch came with an amazing five-bedroom homestead. Has an indoor pump in the kitchen and a water closet upstairs."

"Quite civilized, you are. What do you like to do when you aren't out in the countryside with your cattle?"

"I work around the ranch, break in new horses, and make sure everything's in good repair."

"Other than work, what do you like to do? When all your work is done?"

She was fishing, and he knew what for. To find out what kind of companion he would be. The very same reason he'd invited her to lunch, to learn about her.

He picked up her hand and held it in both of his. "On long winter nights, I like to read."

An attractive blush tinted her cheeks. "You do? Poetry? Perhaps Shakespeare?"

He wasn't fooled. She wanted to know if he was a sentimental type. Ladies like her thought cattle drives were romantic, as well as the cowpunchers on them. They were plain hard work. "Shakespeare's a bit hard to understand, but I've read some poetry. I like Emerson and Longfellow. What I mostly read are..." Time to put a little reality into her starry-eyed notions. Would do no good to raise her expectation unrealistically. "...cattlemen's journals. I need to keep up on the latest trends to maintain healthy livestock. There's more to ranching than having a herd, turning them loose to graze, and then selling them when the time is right." No need to mislead her into thinking he would be a romantic sap with nothing but dreams in his head. He wasn't opposed to romance, but he wouldn't let his livelihood suffer because of it.

"Emerson and Longfellow. I like their works. Have you read Emily Dickinson?"

Oh, no. She didn't want to get into a discussion about poets, did she? He'd about reached his limit on the subject. He knew a couple of names and read a few poems in his school days, because he had been forced to. "Haven't read Dickinson, but maybe I'll have to get one of her collections." His eye twitch became most annoying. He resisted the urge to rub it. He'd probably only end up punching himself in the face.

Noreen returned with their meals in time to spare him from exposing his lack of knowledge. Miss Isabelle may have grown up on a farm, but if she was like most girls, she'd read, lived, and breathed poetry, and saw romance potential in every mundane daily task.

After a most delightful meal with a charming companion, Isabelle took Shane's offered arm. So sad this had to end.

"Thank you for a wonderful time." He walked her outside.

"I enjoyed it as well. Thank you for lunch." Enjoyed was an understatement. It had been everything she'd imagined.

"So." He cleared his throat. "If I were to ask you to go to supper with me, might you say yes?"

Yes! "I might. But you'll never know if you don't ask."

He flashed her his crooked grin. "Would you do me the honor of having supper with me on Wednesday night?"

"I would like that very much." She would need to figure out how to get out of the house for the evening.

"Shall I meet you here again?"

"I'll pick you up at your house."

That would never do. Her parents would have a fit, and it would be impossible to explain his presence at the house. "Um. It might be better if I meet you."

He narrowed his eyes. "You don't want your parents to know you're going to supper with me, do you?"

Perceptive. "Not quite yet. They have plans for my future that I'm not set on."

"Is this a discreet way of saying the farm girl turned socialite is embarrassed by a scruffy cowboy?"

"Rancher." Oops. He wasn't Grant. She didn't need to correct him. "What I mean is, you aren't part of *their* plans for my future. I need time to change their minds." Time she didn't have. "You'll give me that, won't you?"

A frown flickered on his face, then he gave a slow nod. The muscle under his left eye twitched. He shifted his gaze beyond her and pointed at her bicycle. "You got it fixed, I see."

"I did. I even took part in repairing it myself."

"You did? I'm impressed. I like a woman who can handle herself. On a ranch, everyone needs to be capable. Can't have someone who faints at every inclination."

Oh, dear. He was speaking of a woman on his ranch and speaking of it to her. What did that mean? Was he hoping she would be that woman? Time would tell. "I don't recall ever fainting." She almost had once when her corset had been laced too tightly.

"Good to know." He leaned forward and kissed her on the cheek. "Until Wednesday." He strode away.

She resisted the urge to sigh out loud or put her hand to her cheek still warm from his kiss. A very pleasant lunch. But now, what should she do? She was more confused than ever. She'd thought she could break it off with Shane; instead, she'd convinced him she wasn't embarrassed by him and for him to give her time to bring her parents around. He'd been so sweet, and she liked him. *A lot.* Despite what Grant said, she could be happy with him isolated out on his ranch. She was sure of it.

Isabelle held tightly to her handlebars to keep herself

from crumbling in the street. Shane might think she had fainted, and that would never do.

"You're pretty taken with him."

She spun around to face Grant in the doorway. "I guess I am. He likes to read poetry." Just because he found Shakespeare a little mystifying didn't mean he wouldn't quote it to win a lady's heart. But he did sound like he would be gone a lot. A ranch was a lot of work.

"I meant what I said. If he hurts you, I'll have words with him and more."

She could picture Grant having "words" with Shane. A laugh popped out from between her lips. "I'm sure you have nothing to worry about."

"I better not. We've been friends for a long time, and I'm not about to let a swaggering cowboy take advantage of you."

"I'm comforted knowing you are there for me in whatever capacity necessary."

"More than anything, I want you to be happy, Izzy."

"I am, Grant. Today has been a wonderful day."

"And where does Mr. Mallory fit into your rendezvous plans with the cowboy?"

Oliver Mallory was a problem. "I'm hoping to change my parents' minds." Correction. Adelaide's baby and Marguerite were the real problems. Oliver had already offered to break things off and take all the blame like a true gentleman.

Her rendezvous with Shane wasn't the only item on her agenda today. There was another man she needed to find. Who? She didn't know. But if she could find out the identity of the father of Adelaide's child, maybe being a rancher's wife *was* in her future.

Ten

ISABELLE BID GRANT FAREWELL TO HEAD over to Waldon's Mercantile. It could often be a den of town gossip. She normally tried to stay out of such circles, but today, a few wayward whispers could prove useful and put her on the right track.

Not bothering to refasten the fabric strips around each leg to keep her skirt from getting caught in the chain, she grasped the handlebars. Placing one foot on a pedal without lifting it through the frame of the bicycle, she propelled herself forward with the other like on a scooter. In this manner, her dress wouldn't be in danger. It wasn't too far to the mercantile.

In front of the bank, she hopped off the pedal and trotted a couple of steps to a stop. Oliver Mallory stood on the other side of the plate-glass window, talking to an elderly man. Surprisingly, no woman had snatched up the banker. He seemed to be a likable fellow. She felt bad for him that he had no idea what Marguerite plotted for him. He deserved better.

Oliver walked the customer to the entrance and held the door open for him. The elderly man walked out, and Oliver saw her and waved. "Good day, Miss Isabelle. To what do I owe this honor?"

Think fast, Isabelle. "I was riding past and saw you through the window. I don't want to keep you from your work."

"That's thoughtful of you. Would you like to come inside?"

"I can't. I have errands to attend to."

"I don't want to keep you. I'm glad you stopped. You have brightened my day."

No. No. No. Don't be nice. Now she felt bad for enjoying her lunch with Shane.

A man came up behind Oliver. "Mr. Mallory, Mr. Gillies requires your signature."

"I'll be right there," he said over his shoulder then spoke to Isabelle. "I must go as well. It was nice seeing you."

"Nice seeing you too." With thoughts of what life might be like with Oliver, she put her bicycle into motion again and continued the half of a block to the mercantile. She leaned her conveyance against the railing and hurried inside.

Franny Waldon had customers three deep waiting at the counter. She worked to tally one order after another, while Franny's father helped a customer across the store retrieve a kerosene lamp off the top shelf.

Isabelle wandered among the shelves while she waited for Franny to be free. She perused the novels and picked up a romance about a woman being forced into an arranged marriage. Too close to real life. She put it back and thumbed through several others. Another was about a woman who ran off with the man she loved against her parents' wishes. Shane Keegan came to mind. Maybe she would run off with him if he asked. The problem was he hadn't asked and wouldn't likely soon enough to rectify her dilemma. Not to mention she wasn't in love with him. Yet.

Oh bother. She put the novel back. Normally, she would have eagerly read them both and loved them, but her present circumstances had put a damper on her romantic dreams.

Mr. Waldon slipped behind the counter with his daughter, and the customers hastened through the line and out the door. Unfortunately, two additional ones entered. Franny shrugged an apology. Isabelle understood. Her friend had a job to do. Isabelle could wait.

But when five more people entered upon the previous ones exiting, Isabelle's patience had reached its limit. She selected five bolts of calico yard-goods to use in her wandering star quilt for her hope chest. Sadly, her hope was to not marry a certain nice gentleman with sufficient money.

That sounded silly. What young lady wouldn't want to have such a husband? Though most women wanted love, many realized they would be fortunate to find a good man to marry regardless of love. Men didn't seem to need love at all. Any wife would do, as long as she could bear him children.

She took her choices up to the counter. If Franny couldn't come to her, she would go to her friend. Fabric needed to be cut. Cutting took time. Would the five selections give her enough time for a chat? She set them on the side table used to cut yard-goods, sort orders, and bundle up purchases. She went back and chose three more calicos, a muslin backing fabric, and thread.

She shimmied over to the trims where another customer stood and fingered a dainty, off-white lace she could use on a dress she had. She glanced at the blue ribbon in the other person's hand. A strikingly familiar blue silk ribbon. One with which special notes for her had been tied. "That's a lovely shade." She looked up into the startled expression of a handsome gentleman with brown hair under a bowler hat.

His brown eyes widened. "This isn't for me. It's for my aunt." He put it back with the other trim and hurried out the door.

She hadn't meant to frighten him off. She took the lace up with her other selections. Plenty to keep Franny occupied while they talked.

The mercantile kept busy with people in and out.

When Isabelle moved up to second in line, Franny waved her over to the table while her father continued to total up orders. "Are you starting a new quilt?"

"I've decided to make my wandering star one bigger." She liked the idea of starting a new quilt though. She didn't have to decide right now. "I'll take a half of a yard of each of the calicos, five yards of the muslin, and ten yards of the lace."

"Ten? This is such a lovely lace. So delicate. What are you planning to do with it?"

"I thought it would make pretty trim on a dress or two."

"Oh, it would. Mrs. Kesner bought some of this to

make a christening gown for her newest grandson."

Mrs. Kesner was one of the wealthiest people in town. A year ago, Isabelle had dallied with the idea of marrying her oldest grandson. Nothing serious, but a passing thought, nonetheless.

"If it's good enough for her, then it's good enough for me." The talk of babies brought Isabelle back to her reason for coming. Adelaide. "I was wondering something. Has my sister ever been in here with a young man?"

Franny measured out a half of a yard of pink calico. "Like who?"

"I don't know. Have you overheard her speaking about anyone in particular?"

Franny shook her head. "No one specific. You know your sister. She talks about a lot of boys, never anyone more than a day or two. She needs to be careful. Actions like that can gain a young lady a reputation she'd rather not have."

If anyone found out about her condition, she would already have that reputation.

"Why are you asking?"

Now, what should Isabelle say? A version of the truth. "Can you keep a secret?"

"You know I can."

Isabelle leaned in and lowered her voice. She didn't want what she was about to say to start speeding around the rumor train. "Marguerite is in contact with a lord back East. She's arranging a marriage between him and Adelaide, but we fear she might have a beau here who could cause a stir. We want to be sure before things are all settled." The baby's father could certainly cause a stir and attempt blackmail if he discovered Adelaide might be pledged in marriage to a lord.

"A lord? How exciting."

"You can't tell anyone. It's not settled yet."

"I won't. I haven't heard or seen anyone special with her, but I'll keep my eyes open and let you know if I do."

"Thank you." Isabelle couldn't ask for more without revealing her real reason for asking.

As Franny cut the next fabric, she smiled. "Someone was in here earlier and said that handsome new rancher

Shane Keegan was at the hotel dining room today, having lunch with a lady."

Isabelle forgot how to breathe for a moment. "Did they say who?"

Franny giggled. "You, silly. How did you wrangle a rendezvous with him?"

People had seen them and were telling others. She didn't relish being the topic of gossip spreading like wildfire. Had Oliver or her parents heard? That wouldn't be good. "I nearly ran him down with my bicycle. He was simply being kind, but don't tell anyone. My father and Marguerite wouldn't approve."

"Why should they care? They're marrying Adelaide off to a lord. I would think in light of that, you would go unnoticed."

Normally she would, but circumstances were anything but normal. Should she tell Franny the rest of the story? Well not the *rest.* "They sort of want me to marry before Adelaide, but don't tell anyone."

"They do? Let me guess. A handsome, swaggering, rugged cowboy isn't on their list."

Isabelle shook her head.

"Are they looking at anyone I know?"

"I'd rather not say yet."

"I understand. What about Grant? You two have always been close. I've imagined the two of you ending up together."

"Grant? He's just my friend." That's all they had ever been and all they ever would be. Except for that time she'd toyed with the idea of there being more.

"Exactly. Friends make the best spouses."

"We're more like brother and sister. Not a spark of romance between us. He would scoff at such a suggestion." As he'd done in school, setting her straight.

"I think of him as a brother too, but he'd be better than marrying a stranger or some decrepit old man. If you need help narrowing down your choices, I'd be glad to lend a hand." Franny wrapped the fabrics in brown paper.

Too bad there wasn't an actual list to choose from. At least then she'd have some say about her future. With but one name, the only narrowing down would be to eliminate the list all together. Isabelle paid and slipped out the door, holding her rather large bundle in both hands. Who could she talk to next? Franny had been her best option.

A buggy stopped in front of the mercantile. "Isabelle."

Isabelle glanced up to see Aunt Henny. "Good afternoon."

"Good afternoon." The older woman set the brake and waved Isabelle over. "Would you give me a steadying hand? My leg hasn't regained its strength."

Isabelle set her package on the boardwalk bench and rushed over to help the older woman.

Aunt Henny's grip was strong even if her leg wasn't. Once safely on solid ground, the older woman grabbed her cane from the buggy floor. "Thank you. I never felt old or helpless until I broke my leg. I shouldn't complain. At least I'm rid of that heavy cast."

Isabelle smiled. "You are neither old nor helpless."

"I hope not, but I feel that way."

Isabelle felt helpless as well, in a different way. Helpless to determine her own future. "May I ask you a strange question?"

"Of course." Aunt Henny had a mischievous glint in her eyes. "Strange are my favorite kind." She had a keen sense about things. Something someone else might not pay any mind to, she could look beyond it to the heart of a matter.

Hopefully, the older woman didn't discern anything abnormal in Isabelle's question. "You haven't seen Adelaide with any young men lately, have you?"

Mr. Lumbard, one of Aunt Henny's regular boarders, sauntered up. "Pardon me, ladies. Henny, I won't be home for supper, so no need to set a place."

"Thank you for letting me know, Job."

The older man stroked his white beard. "You're welcome. Common courtesy. Good day, ladies." He tipped his hat and continued on down the street.

Had he heard Isabelle's question? Didn't matter if he had. He wouldn't know why she asked, just as Aunt Henny wouldn't. "About Adelaide."

"I've seen your sister with plenty of young men. She needs to watch herself. She doesn't want that kind of reputation, but now that I think about it, I haven't seen her with *anyone* lately. Maybe she's finally growing up."

Unfortunately not, and it was her reputation that needed to be protected.

The older woman patted Isabelle's hand. "I've been thinking about you a lot since our last quilting circle."

"You have?"

"I don't think you get all the encouragement you deserve, so I wanted to tell you that your mother would be proud of you."

"She's not. She finds me a huge disappointment."

Aunt Henny gave a knowing smile. "Not Marguerite. Your real mother."

Isabelle's heart warmed toward the older woman. "She would? I can't remember her. All I have is a photograph. Did you know her very well?"

"I did. She was part of our quilting circle. She loved you very much."

Isabelle wished she could remember her. "Was she a lot like Marguerite?"

"Never were two women more different."

"Then how could my father marry a woman so different from her?"

"Don't be too hard on him. Your father found himself in a tough situation. He sank into grieving the loss of the woman he loved and had a two-year-old child to care for. You were so young, and he didn't quite know what to do. He needed help. Marguerite stepped in and cared for you both. She'd been married before and hadn't been able to have a child. You and your father were her chance to have a family. After several miscarriages, she finally had Adelaide. She had at least two more miscarriages after that."

Isabelle had never thought about Marguerite's feelings. "That had to be hard losing so many babies." No wonder she didn't want Adelaide's baby to get away from her.

Aunt Henny took Isabelle's hand. "If she's being difficult, it could be because she knows you and Adelaide are grown, and you both will be getting married in the near future. That can be lonely and scary for a woman who is a mother at heart."

Marguerite? A *mother* at heart? Those two things seemed more like opposites rather than going together. "Then why would she be pushing both of us to the altar?"

"Is that what your mood was about on Friday? Women can be anxious for grandchildren."

"It's more than that. For better or for worse, weddings are in the very near future for both of us."

"How near?" Aunt Henny rested both hands on her cane and shifted her weight.

"Let's sit down." How could Isabelle have been so insensitive? She guided the older woman up onto the boardwalk and moved her brown-paper package of her yard goods she'd set there.

Aunt Henny sat. "Don't think you can distract me with being thoughtful. How near?"

Isabelle didn't like thinking about her looming nuptials. "For me, as early as next week." If she didn't come up with an alternative everyone could agree upon.

Aunt Henny's eyes widened. "I'm sure that's not true."

"Unfortunately, it is. Father has already spoken to Oliver Mallory. For Adelaide, as soon as Marguerite can talk the lord back East into it." Which would be postponed until after the baby was born, but Marguerite would want to have him on the hook. How did she seriously expect to manage it all and have no one find out?

"Arranged marriages? For you both?"

Isabelle nodded. "I shouldn't have said anything."

"I didn't know you were interested in Mr. Mallory."

She hadn't been. "He seems to be a nice man."

"Nice is fine. He is a good Christian man." The older woman narrowed her eyes. "But do you want to marry him?"

No, she didn't, but he was the best solution so far to the problem at hand. "It won't be so bad."

Aunt Henny harrumphed. "Why would your father press for this?"

"Marguerite is. They want me married so they can

arrange the marriage for Adelaide."

"I can't believe that. This is almost the turn of the century. People don't arrange marriages and marry off their daughters in age order anymore."

Isabelle gave a tight smile. "Some do. I should be going. If you need any help getting back into your buggy, let Franny or her father know."

"I will, and don't you worry about these *arrangements*. I'll take this before our heavenly Lord in prayer. He'll sort it out."

Isabelle hoped so. She strapped her bundle onto the back of her bicycle. She had another person to talk to who might have answers. Adelaide's school chum Sadie.

After making her purchases, Henny drove to the Atwoods' and stopped in front of their stately home. One of the more significant ones in town but not the largest. Why did they feel a need to marry off their daughters in a hurry? Made no sense.

The stable hand approached. "May I help you, ma'am?"

"Yes, please." She took his offered hand and climbed down. Before she could reach for her cane, he held it out to her. Now, this kind of service, she could get used to. "Thank you."

"Would you like me to unhitch your buggy and tend to your horse?"

"That won't be necessary. I won't be long." Henny hobbled up the steps and across the wide porch. One could have a dance out here with a stoop so spacious. She tapped the brass knocker.

Sissy the maid answered the door. "Aunt Henny, come in."

Henny stepped inside. Certainly, having a servant answer the door was as much for show as convenience. "Is Marguerite here?"

"In the parlor. Right this way."

"You don't need to trouble yourself. I'll show myself."

Sissy lowered her voice. "The missus likes guests to be announced."

"Then by all means." Henny followed the maid the short distance to the closed pocket doors and waited while she slid them open. "Aunt Henny's here to see you, ma'am."

Marguerite smiled. "Henny, do come in. This is a surprise. Sissy, bring us tea."

Henny held up her hand. "That's all right. I won't be here long enough."

Marguerite would likely ask her to leave shortly once she gave the woman her opinion of arranged marriages.

Sissy left.

Marguerite motioned with her hand. "Do sit down and tell me what has brought you to my humble home."

Henny sat in the chair nearest the door. "I'll get right to it. No sense wasting either of our time with idle chitchat. I hear you're arranging an immediate marriage for Isabelle. Do you think that wise?"

Marguerite's genial smile turned sour. "That girl needs to learn to keep things to herself. But since she didn't, did she tell you why we're taking this drastic measure?"

"She's the eldest daughter and has to marry first because of some lord back East you're trying to arrange a marriage with for Adelaide. Arranged marriages rarely turn out to be happy." Henny understood that all too well. "It's an antiquated custom."

"It's easy to judge when you don't know the whole story, but since she came to you, I'll tell you." Her mouth hung open as though to continue, but she hesitated before she did. "Isabelle's expecting a child."

Henny instinctively gasped. That took the bluster out of her accusations. Isabelle with child?

"We don't know who the father is. The best we could do was to find her a husband who would accept another man's child."

"Mr. Mallory knows?"

"He's a banker. It wouldn't take him long to realize a child was on the way before they married. We thought honesty would be the best."

Henny couldn't believe Isabelle would do such a thing. It was something she might expect of Adelaide, but Isabelle didn't receive the attention she deserved. Maybe she had been lonelier than Henny had realized. "If there's anything I can do to help, let me know."

"If she comes to you again, tell her to stop dilly-dallying over this decision. The sooner she marries, the fewer tongues that will wag."

As much as Henny hated to admit Marguerite was right, sooner would be better than later.

Eleven

OLIVER SAT IN THE ATWOODS' PARLOR with Isabelle's younger sister, grateful Mrs. Atwood had been called away for a kitchen emergency. Something about having peas instead of green beans at supper. He hoped Isabelle wasn't fastidious like that. He had enough of that kind of activity at work. He didn't want it at his house as well. Home should be a sanctuary from such worries.

Adelaide smoothed her hands across her skirt. "What's it like being a banker?"

The younger Miss Atwood didn't seem to take after her mother in that hard-to-please way. She had been quite endearing at lunch with her questions.

"Busy. A great deal of paperwork and keeping track of a lot of numbers."

"That sounds fascinating." She seemed to be a delightful young lady. So full of life and charming.

"Not really. Numbers, numbers, and more numbers." He enjoyed the job but knew most people didn't care for that sort of fastidious work. "It can be a bit boring."

"I don't think so. All those people giving you their money for safekeeping." She seemed genuine. "How do you get them to trust you that much?"

He hadn't thought about it that way. "I guess by building a strong brick building and putting a large impenetrable safe in it." There was more to it than that, but most people wanted the simple answer.

She smiled. "That would do it. Did you always want to be a banker?"

"My father was a banker, and I wanted to be like him."

"I want my baby to look up to his father, as you do yours."

"Excuse me."

Adelaide's eyes widened. "I mean someday when I'm married and have children, I hope my children will admire their father as you do yours."

"The lord back East?"

She crinkled up her nose. "That may not even happen. It would be hard to move so far away from my family. Do you miss your family, Mr. Mallory?"

"I do and I don't. I love them dearly, but I wanted to see if I could succeed on my own and not just on my family's name and reputation. To be like my father is to be independent and succeed."

"Any children you raise will be fortunate to have you as their father."

A peculiar young lady. Something about her was still childlike, needing someone to take care of her. Another part seemed old beyond her years. Almost like an old woman burdened by the years of life.

That made him curious, and he looped back around to her previous comment. "Do you revere your father?" He found Jackson Atwood to be an outstanding citizen. Honest and trustworthy.

"Of course. He's wonderful. I love him dearly. That's why it would be so hard to move far away from him, Isabelle, and my mother."

Mrs. Atwood glided back into the room. "Please forgive me for having to dash out. So many things to tend to in a house this size. I hope Adelaide was adequate company in my absence." She lowered herself into a wingback chair.

"She has been absolutely charming." Preferable to the alternative, but Mrs. Atwood was going to be his mother-in-law soon. Very soon if this woman had her way. Oliver wouldn't rush Isabelle. He would be a shield between his soon-to-be wife and her mother.

He stood. "I should be going."

Mrs. Atwood stood as well. "You can't leave. I'm sure Isabelle will return any minute. Do stay." She seemed to be flustered over her daughter's delay.

He would like to see Isabelle and get to know her better before they married. If he found she would prove difficult to live with, as her mother seemed to be, he would speak to Jackson and call things off. So far, Isabelle struck him as a pleasant and easy to get along with person. He eased back into the chair. "A few more minutes wouldn't hurt."

Shoes clicked in the hallway, and Isabelle floated into the parlor.

He stood. "Isabelle."

Isabelle stopped short, and her eyes widened. "I—I'm sorry for not being here. I wasn't aware you were expected."

"I wasn't. I dropped by unannounced. After seeing you at the bank, I had hoped to spend a little time with you."

Her smile wasn't quite genuine. "I'd like that."

"A buggy ride?"

Her smile softened. "I'd really like that."

Mrs. Atwood beamed as well. "Wonderful." She rang a bell on the side table.

A moment later, the maid appeared with a curtsy. "Yes, ma'am."

"Tell the stable hand to bring Mr. Mallory's buggy around."

"No need. I'll get it." He turned back to Isabelle. "I'll return momentarily." He hurried away, wanting to make sure his buggy was indeed tidy, and nothing had been overlooked.

Marguerite turned on Isabelle. "How dare you not be here when Mr. Mallory arrived?"

"I didn't know he was coming." Was she supposed to sit around all day, waiting on the off chance a man might drop by? Were unannounced visits from him something she needed to expect?

Marguerite scrutinized Isabelle. "At least you're not wearing that ridiculous thing you ride that contraption in. This dress is presentable." She gasped. "What happened to the hem?"

Isabelle gazed down and shook her skirt. "It's only a few wrinkles."

Marguerite inclined her head toward the staircase. "Go up and change."

"There isn't time."

"He'll wait."

Isabelle rolled her eyes. "This is fine. He won't even notice." Shane hadn't noticed or, at least, hadn't mentioned it. Men didn't seem to care about such things. She headed for the door, preferring to wait outside.

Her stepmother followed. "Be on your best behavior. If you do anything to ruin this chance for Adelaide, you will be sorry."

Isabelle might be concerned if she felt Marguerite's threat had any teeth to it. She could threaten to get Father to disinherit her, which she'd take over being forced to marry. But where would that leave Adelaide? To fend for herself? She couldn't do that to her sister.

How had Adelaide managed to turn out so sweet natured with Marguerite for a mother? True, Marguerite hadn't always been this determined. When Father came into money five years ago, Marguerite had changed. She wanted more and more social status and clung to the lower rungs of the upper society ladder. She'd had a taste of a little and wanted more. Now, she was grasping at a title for Adelaide. A title Adelaide didn't necessarily want.

"Worry not. I'm playing my part." *For now.* She wrapped her shawl around her shoulders.

Marguerite huffed. Very unladylike. "Your part? Hardly. I saw you today with that cowboy in front of the hotel."

Isabelle froze with her hand on the doorknob. She'd been seen. By Marguerite no less. Taking a deep breath, she turned with a flourish. "He is not a cowboy. He's a rancher. And we were merely talking. Were you spying on me?"

"The better question is what were you doing with him? No man is going to allow his wife to keep company with another man. You don't want Mr. Mallory to decide he's made a poor choice and reconsider."

At first, that was exactly what she wanted to do, but then she had gotten to know the man and found him likable.

"What if he had witnessed your indiscretion?"

Hardly an indiscretion. "I doubt he did." Isabelle had spoken to him at the bank a few minutes after she'd parted from Shane. She stepped out the front door.

Mr. Mallory wasn't there yet with his buggy. The stable hands were likely helping him hitch it back to his horse.

No reason to loiter on the porch. She walked around the house to the carriage house.

Mr. Mallory glanced up. "Miss Isabelle, this is no place for a lady."

Isabelle pointed to her bicycle. "I come out here all the time. I parked my bicycle over there a few minutes ago."

He smiled. "You are quite an adventurous lady."

How had he intended his comment? "I'll take that as a compliment."

"That's how I meant it. A lady should be more than merely a man's wife but her own person. She needn't stop having interests simply because she marries."

She just might like this man. Not enough to marry, but to be cordial to and maybe even be a friend. "I couldn't agree more, Oliver." Marguerite would have a hissy fit. They hadn't been acquainted long enough to call each other by their first names. All the more reason.

The stable hand draped the reins into the front of the buggy and held onto the horse's halter. "Ready to go, sir."

"Thank you." After helping Isabelle in, Oliver climbed aboard and drove off. As he pulled out onto the road, Tramp ran up to the buggy and trotted alongside. Oliver waved his hand. "Go on. Be gone."

Did Oliver hate dogs? That would be something for her negative column.

"Tramp won't hurt anything." She certainly didn't want Oliver to treat the dog unkindly.

"Is this your dog?"

"Would it be a problem if it was?"

"No."

That was good to know. "He's a stray I feed occasionally." What would he think of that?

Oliver pulled back on the reins. "Whoa."

The horse stopped, and Tramp put his paws up onto the step of the buggy.

"I don't have anything for you." Isabelle held out her empty hands.

Tramp stretched his neck and sniffed then wagged his tail.

Oliver patted his thigh. "Come on, boy. You want to go for a ride?"

Tramp jumped in and up onto the seat next to Isabelle.

Oliver reached over her and petted him then set the horse back into motion. "I had a dog when I was a boy. Called him Rascal."

So, he didn't hate dogs. Something to put in the positive column. "Do you have a dog now?"

He shook his head. "No time for one."

"But this fellow needs a home." Marguerite had flat out refused to allow Isabelle to keep him, saying they didn't live on a farm anymore.

"Wouldn't be fair to the poor creature to be left alone all the time."

Isabelle lifted Tramp's paw and waved it toward Oliver then spoke in a small voice. "But I could keep you company."

Oliver chuckled. "That's what I'll have a wife for."

Isabelle sobered and released the paw. With his tongue lolling out the side of his mouth, Tramp put his forepaws on the front of the buggy while keeping his hind ones on the seat.

Once out on the main thoroughfare, Oliver let out a heavy sigh. "Finally." He jerked his gaze to her. "I mean no disrespect, Miss Isabelle."

"What offense do you believe you've committed?" She couldn't imagine a transgression this proper gentleman could be guilty of, but if he had done something unseemly, that could work in her favor.

"It's your mother. She scares me a little."

Isabelle burst out laughing. "She can be pretty scary.

But she, in all honesty, doesn't have much bite to her bark." If not for Adelaide's predicament, Father wouldn't allow her to push an arranged marriage.

"But she does bite?"

"Think of her more as a mosquito. Buzzing around and irritating but no real threat."

"Except the itch lasts for days?" He chuckled. "I hadn't planned to take you for a buggy ride, but I am glad to have you all to myself. Not quite all to myself." He scruffed Tramp's ears. "I don't mind sharing with this happy fellow."

Her heart leaned a little closer to this man who showed kindness to a lonely stray animal. "Tell me about yourself." When asked, she could truthfully say she did her part to make polite conversation. And she might possibly find some reason her father would accept that this man should *not* be part of their family. But again, where would that leave Adelaide? It always came back to her.

"Not sure what you want to know. I'm a banker, which your sister found fascinating. Not much more to tell you don't already know."

There was plenty she didn't know. She hoped she didn't have to hold up both ends of the conversation. "What do you like to do when you are not at the bank?"

"I read in the evenings."

Oh, this was good. "What do you like to read?"

"Newspapers, stock reports, financial periodicals."

Not so good. It sounded stodgy. She imagined sitting by the fire after they were married, listening to him drone on about such things. That definitely went on the negative side of things. "Do you like to read anything else?"

"Like what?"

"Oh, let's say poetry or Shakespeare."

"I don't see a need for that kind of nonsense."

Another negative. He and Grant would get along well on that subject. "They are a lyrical way to express your emotions to another person."

He shrugged. "I don't understand their appeal. Numbers express things more precisely. No guessing what the number three means."

Numbers? Numbers expressed nothing but boredom, so she needn't worry about him ever giving her poetry and didn't have to fret he might be her secret admirer. "What brought you out to Washington State?"

"I moved to California seven years ago, then transferred up here a little over a year ago."

"Why did you leave Philadelphia?"

He hesitated. "My wife passed away."

"Oh, you were married before?" That meant Isabelle would be his second wife.

"Yes, just over a year."

He had known what it meant to be married for love, and now, he was being forced into it.

Tramp's tail swung back and forth, thumping against her side. She wrapped her arm around his furry body. "You have my condolences." How sad. He'd lost his wife and then remained single for the past seven years. It wasn't going to be so easy now to turn him down.

"She had been ill for a while. It happened a long time ago."

"Did you have any children?" She wanted to know what she was getting into. If he had a child already, he might be more open to raising Adelaide's baby.

"No children." He turned the horse down a side street, which led out of town on a scenic route. "I have a question for you."

"Fair enough. What is it?"

"Why me?"

She tried to sort out his seemingly simple question but couldn't. Had she let her mind wander and missed something? "Why you what?"

"Why did your mother pick me? I know it wasn't you who requested to arrange an engagement between us. I am several years older than you. I sense this wasn't completely your father's idea. He seemed a bit too reluctant when he broached the subject with me."

Oliver was obviously an analyzer, needing the question "why" answered. He wouldn't be easy to prod along with too little information. That could mean trouble for Father and Marguerite's plan.

"What did they tell you?"

"That it was time for you to marry, and your sister couldn't marry the lord until you had wed. Your sister didn't seem overly anxious about getting married. She gave the impression her marriage might not even happen."

Adelaide certainly wasn't ready to marry nor was she in love with a man she'd never met. "My parents are a little old fashioned when it comes to their daughters." If all went well, that would placate him.

"Your mother made you out to be some unmarriageable spinster. I expected you to be... unpleasant in some way."

Thanks, Marguerite.

"But you're not. You're very pleasant. So, why pick me?"

She pulled Tramp onto her lap and stroked his coat heartily to distract Oliver from her pause in answering.

This man had been chosen for his blond hair. Because Marguerite thought he would be desperate enough. That he would be an easy mark. Say nice things to the forlorn man and make him believe he was doing them a great favor, and who else would marry this poor man. Marguerite obviously thought she could get him to bend to her will. The poor sap.

"She chose you because..." She couldn't tell him any of those things. "I'm not really sure why. I don't always understand the way her mind works. Please don't tell her I said that." Hopefully, he would let the question drop.

"All I heard is you are touched your mother thinks so caringly of you. So, why is a beautiful lady like you not already married?"

Beautiful? Another thing for the plus column. He needed to stop doing that, or she might fall for him. "I haven't found the right man."

"If you give me a chance, I'll try to be that right man."

Oooh. Oliver Mallory was a sweet man.

He sat silent for several minutes. "May we speak of the practicalities of our upcoming marriage?"

"Of course, we are to be wed soon." But not if she could help it.

"It's a bit of a delicate nature."

She would rather hear things now to prepare herself as much as possible. Reduce the number of surprises. Enough of those had come up already. "Go on."

"Sometimes, with these kinds of marriages—arranged ones—one party or the other makes assumptions the other does not."

She sensed where this was going, and her cheeks warmed. "You want to know if this will be a marriage in name only?"

"Yes—I mean no." He took a deep breath. "I mean, I would very much like ours to be a real marriage and have children. Do you want children?"

She longed to say she preferred a marriage in name only, but Adelaide's baby would be a little hard to explain. "I very much want to have children." Her own.

He smiled and nodded. "I'll do my best to be a good father."

She cringed. "I have no doubt of that." Why couldn't she simply fall in love with this nice, sweet gentleman? Then the thought of having *his* children wouldn't bother her.

Part way through the drive, a squirrel chattered from the base of an oak tree. Tramp's ears perked up, and he leapt from the moving buggy, barking. The squirrel ran up the trunk and perched on the lowest branch. Tramp continued to bark up at it.

"Should I stop?"

"No. He'll be fine."

A while later, Oliver pulled to a stop in front of Isabelle's house. He got out and helped her down. "If you don't mind, I'll leave you at your door. I would like to end this day on a pleasant note."

Isabelle smiled inwardly, knowing he meant he didn't want to face Marguerite again. "I understand, but I will be asked why I didn't invite you in for supper."

"Tell them I had a prior commitment."

"Something—or someone I should be jealous of?" Had she just flirted with him? She smiled so he would know she was teasing.

"A stack of my usual evening reading material."

When he smiled back, her insides did a little wiggle of some kind. He took her hand and bowed over it. "I bid you good day." He walked back to his buggy.

She stayed outside the door until he drove away as though she were besot with him. Shaking her head, she went inside.

Marguerite hurried into the foyer before Isabelle had the door closed. "Where is Mr. Mallory?"

"He went home."

"Why didn't you invite him for supper? I've had a place set for him."

"He sends his regrets, but he had a prior commitment." Boring numbers.

"Which day have you set for the wedding? You did take advantage of your time together to pick a day and time, didn't you? The sooner the better."

Isabelle could have. Oliver had given her the perfect opportunity when he spoke of children. Maybe that had been his intent. Though Isabelle wanted to put off the inevitable as long as possible, she knew she couldn't do so for too many more days. "We didn't speak of the wedding." Marriage and children, yes, but not the wedding specifically.

Twelve

THE NEXT DAY, ISABELLE PUSHED HER bicycle from the carriage house out to the street. She couldn't imagine what Grant wanted to show her.

Tramp sat, waiting.

As she approached, he raised up on his haunches.

"I was hoping to see you. I have a treat for you." She held out a bread heel. "First this, then something really special."

The scruffy dog gingerly took the crust in his mouth but didn't chomp it down as he usually did. Instead, he trotted off.

"Wait. I have a bone too." She held up the paper wrapped treat.

He continued to a clump of nearby trees where two other dogs stood. He dropped the crust in front of the golden spaniel who consumed it in a single bite. The black Labrador waited patiently.

Isabelle watched. Tramp denied himself food while looking after his friends.

The scruffy stray trotted back over to her. He sat on his haunches again and waved his front paws in the air.

She held up the bone in paper. "If I give this to you, you'll only give it away, and then there'll be nothing for you." She retrieved the cloth-wrapped cheese from her pocket she'd been going to snack on and walked toward the other two dogs. "Come on, Tramp."

He followed at her side, gazing up at the food in her hands.

When she got within a few feet of the Lab and spaniel, they both turned and trotted away a short distance and contemplated her from there. Isabelle could see the smaller of the two was missing one of its hind legs.

"I get it. You don't trust me." Isabelle broke off a

piece of cheese and tossed it toward the Lab.

It jerked back, but the spaniel inched toward the cheese. When it got a whiff of the food, its feathery tail came up and wagged as it ate.

The Lab ventured forward and sniffed the ground where the cheese had been and wagged its tail.

Isabelle threw some cheese to it.

This time the Lab didn't retreat but gobbled the food.

She gave the last bit of cheese to Tramp who swallowed it immediately. She handed him the bone and showed her empty hands. "That's all I have. I'll try to get more tomorrow." She headed off to meet Grant.

When Isabelle pulled up to the White Hotel on her bicycle, he already stood outside. She slowed with the hand brake. Once stopped, she put out her feet to catch herself.

Grant smiled. "You never disappoint."

"Why do you say that? Because you know I've brought lunch?" She tapped the basket behind her.

"No, because you rode your bicycle."

Why would he care about that? She stood to get off.

"Stay where you are." He stepped forward and gripped the handlebars. "We'll get there faster on your bicycle."

She sat back on the seat and widened her eyes. "You aren't planning to ride this, are you?"

"Of course." He stepped one foot over the frame in front of her, straddling the vehicle.

"With me onboard?" A rush of heat warmed her face.

A twinkle of mischief glinted in his eyes. "I can't exactly show you something if I leave you behind, now can I?"

"But you've had only one lesson, and that was under protest."

"As I recall, this wasn't that hard to master. With enough momentum and turning the handlebars to keep our center of gravity over the tires, we'll stay upright. Hang on."

She grasped a fistful of his jacket in each hand and hoped for the best. He made it sound so simple. She hadn't found riding a bicycle difficult, but some people couldn't seem to manage no matter how hard they tried. Her sister for instance. Adelaide had wanted to learn but gave up after a skinned knee in one fall, a scraped elbow in another, and an injured wrist in a third. Isabelle had to give her credit for trying over and over. Her sister had worn long sleeves in the summer until her wrist and elbow had healed to keep Marguerite from scolding her.

With one foot on a pedal, Grant pushed with the other until he could put it on the second pedal. Standing in front of her, he pumped with nary a wobble.

Surprised he rode so well—even with a passenger—she released her captive breath and straightened her legs out to the sides.

She studied Grant from the back. Though a well-groomed man, he didn't have the sophistication of Oliver or the broad shoulders of Shane. But still a handsome enough man.

After about five minutes, Grant slowed and deftly put his feet on the ground. "We're here." He'd stopped in the middle of a block of houses on the opposite side of town from where she lived.

Isabelle looked around. "Here? And where exactly is that?"

He extracted himself from the bicycle. "Come on, and I'll show you."

She climbed off, still unable to figure out what they were doing here. As far as she could recall, she didn't know anyone on this part of the street. Muriel lived farther down. "What's special here?"

He leaned the bicycle against the white picket fence and opened the gate. "This house."

A two-story home similar in size and style to Aunt Henny's stood before her. "Who lives here?"

He climbed onto the porch and retrieved a key from his pocket. "No one right now." He unlocked the door and swung it open for her. "But it might be mine soon."

She stepped inside the empty interior. "Yours? What do you mean?"

"I have finally saved enough money for a down payment." He showed her around.

The main floor had a parlor, dining area, kitchen as

well as a den and small bedroom, likely for a housekeeper. Upstairs had four spacious bedrooms.

"Are you planning to open a boarding house like Aunt Henny?"

"Certainly not."

"Then why do you need this large of a house?"

"To attract a wife. That's why I brought you here to get your opinion. Would most ladies take kindly to living in such a house?"

For years, he'd talked of marrying and having a family one day, but for the first time, he'd taken action. He was serious. Her insides tightened.

"I would think any lady in town would love to live here. But do you really want to attract a lady who is more interested in where she will live than whom she will marry? Do you have any particular lady in mind?"

"I don't know." He studied her a moment. "Someone like... Josie Bragg or Filicia Turner."

"Filicia Turner would never settle for a house like this. She has her sights set far higher than her current station." Much like Marguerite with Adelaide. "Josie Bragg would be content here, but you don't like her. Why would you want to attract either one when you don't care for them in that way? Or are you telling me you *are* interested in one of them?" Her lungs constricted at the thought of her friend being saddled with either for the rest of his life.

"Of course not." He shook his head. "They were only examples."

She touched his arm. "Why go into debt for years for a woman who would marry you for a house?"

He shrugged. "More prospects?"

"When did you start thinking you needed a big house to find a good woman to marry? The right one won't care about the house but care for you."

He studied her for a moment. "You really believe that?"

"Yes, I do. Now, unless you intend to take in boarders, you should reconsider a house so large. I know of a place that would suit you."

He sighed. "Why do I fear what you have in mind?"

She swatted his arm. "There is no reason to fear."

Outside the window, a squirrel chattered at them from a nearby tree limb.

She pointed at the furry creature. "See, even he thinks it's a good idea. Do you have time to look at it?"

He waved her toward the front door. "Lead the way."

Grant drove again while Isabelle gave directions. When he stopped, he hesitated to disengage himself from the bicycle.

Isabelle tapped him on the back. "If you don't get off, then I can't."

He did so, gave her a hand down, and leaned the bicycle against a tree.

Isabelle regarded the weather-worn cottage. When Grant didn't say a word, she shifted her gaze to him. "What do you think? Your down payment on the other house could practically buy this one."

"*This* is what you think of me?"

She studied the little house with its overgrown weeds, faded paint, and loose shutters. "No. Not how the house is now, but what it can become. This is a house you can pour yourself into. You love fixing stuff. You would be offering your future wife not only a home but a piece of yourself. The other one was simply a house with nothing of you in it. You can make this one into a home."

"It doesn't even have a fence."

"You are so handy, you can build one." She hooked her arm around his elbow. "Come on. Let's look inside."

"I don't have a key." He gave her a sideways glance. "Do you?"

She pulled him toward the front door. "We'll merely peer through the windows."

He gripped her arm a little tighter. "Watch your step, that board looks loose and there's a hole." He maneuvered her out of danger.

"The porch is plenty big enough for a couple of rocking chairs."

He grunted.

She cupped her hands to the window. "There is a nice space for a sitting area, an eating table will fit snuggly between it and the kitchen." A variety of debris was scattered across the dusty floor.

"Snug is right. They're all one room." He grunted again. "This won't impress anyone."

She straightened. "When did you get all high and mighty?"

"I just don't see how any woman could be happy here. It needs a lot of work."

"Exactly. That's why you'll be able to get a good price on it. Then you can fix it up and turn it into a home any woman would be proud to live in."

He held her with his gaze. "*Any* woman?"

"Most any woman. It does have three bedrooms. One for you and your wife, and one each for your sons and daughters. Remember the Giffords? This was their home before they moved away. They had such a happy home."

"Small bedrooms."

"Sufficient." She pulled him by his arm. "Let's look at the backyard."

Behind the house didn't appear to be any better than the front. In the yard sat a dilapidated wagon with a missing wheel, a decaying well topper, and a leaning shed attached to a weathered barn.

He pointed at the well. "It doesn't look as though the house has an indoor pump."

"You can change that." She waved her hand toward a patch of bare ground in the distance. "Over there would make a nice sunny spot for a kitchen garden." She turned to face the rear of the house. "You would have so much fun bringing this place back to life."

"Are you sure *I'm* the one you think will have fun?"

"Don't be a grump. Can't you picture yourself coming home from a day's work at the hotel and your wife is waiting for you in the kitchen with supper ready? Children running around at your feet?"

"No. Not in this rundown place."

She could picture it, and it saddened her. Once he married, life would be different. Their friendship would be different. She would no longer see him all the time as she did now. His wife wouldn't permit it.

But wouldn't such be the case for herself when she married? No, she wouldn't allow that. She would make her husband see she needed her friendship with Grant. Would Grant be as convinced? "I grew up in a house like this on our farm. It's not so bad. A good scrubbing, a fresh coat of paint, and some curtains will make it seem new."

"You are an optimist. I love that about you."

She supposed she was. "Why didn't you leave when the rest of your family moved over the mountains to Seattle?"

He shook his head. "Couldn't. Kamola is my home."

"So there's nothing that would cause you to move away?"

He shrugged.

That meant possibly, but he wasn't in a mood to share. She could press him, but history told her she would be wasting her time. Grant would talk when he was ready and not before.

She understood him wanting to have better than he grew up with. "So, you'll buy the other house then?"

"I don't know. The other one *is* expensive, but this one needs so much work."

"It sounds like you're not ready to commit to a house yet."

"I was until I talked to you."

She smiled. "You're welcome."

"For what?"

"Keeping you from making a rash decision you might regret." She didn't want Grant to throw away all of his hard-earned money on a woman he didn't even know. One who would want him for the house he could buy her. He deserved someone who loved him no matter what.

Oliver reread his mother's letter, one line in particular. *I'm sending an agent of persuasion to secure your pledge to return home for Christmas.* His mother was planning a huge event to find him a new wife. She would parade every eligible young lady in Philadelphia before him in hopes of securing her next daughter-in-law and grandchildren. Though his four sisters were all married with children of their own, he was the only son to pass on the family name to his progeny.

Whom would she send? Some people would be more difficult to deal with than others. And when would this person arrive? Before or after his marriage to Isabelle? He hoped after. Easier to discourage them.

If all went well with Isabelle, he could avoid the holiday spectacle.

At the knock on his bank office door, he tucked the letter into his top desk drawer. "Come in."

His assistant, Jonathan, opened the door. "Mr. Jackson Atwood to see you."

"Show him in." Oliver pushed back his chair and stood. What did Jackson want?

Jackson strode in. "Good afternoon, Oliver."

"Good afternoon. Please have a seat."

Oliver waited until Jackson sat before retaking his chair. "What can I do for you?" Not only did Oliver owe this man a favor, which he was in the process of repaying, but Jackson had a great deal of money in Oliver's bank.

Oliver had been loath to owe another man a favor, especially a stranger, lest he abused the hold, but Jackson had proved to be a gentleman. That marriage to his daughter would be the recompense in return had been surprising. He viewed his future father-in-law across his wide oak desk. "What brings you here?"

"My daughter—let's just say she has a certain adventurous streak in her."

A smile pulled at Oliver's mouth. "She is spirited." Maybe too much so to be content with a set-in-his-ways banker.

"She reminds me of her mother in that way."

"Mrs. Atwood?" Oliver found that hard to believe.

Jackson chuffed out a breath. "Not Marguerite. My first wife, Isabelle's mother."

Ah. Things made sense now. He'd wondered how the spunky Isabelle could be Mrs. Atwood's daughter. Jackson must understand what it was like to lose one woman and contemplate marrying another.

"You probably find my request to wed my daughter odd, but believe it or not, I prayed about this. The Lord assured me my daughter would be in good hands with you. When I helped you out of your predicament a year ago, I saw the kind of man you were under pressure. You took the misunderstanding in stride and didn't hold it against any of your accusers. After everything was cleared up, you found it humorous to be mistaken for an outlaw."

"I appreciated all your help and support. Things could have gone very badly for me. But the two favors seem unequal. If anything, I feel as though I'll owe you a second favor."

"Nonsense. This deed outweighs the little I did for you back then. When you have children of your own one day, you'll understand the peace of mind it gives a father knowing his daughter will be well cared for."

"I won't let you down." But what had Jackson come for?

"How are you and my daughter getting on?"

The man was leading to something. Best to go along to see where this road led. "We get on. You've raised her well."

"I fear Isabelle might be a bit reluctant to broach the subject of the wedding date since the two of you don't know each other well."

There it was. "Is she wanting to call it off?"

"Certainly not. Marguerite and I are anxious to move things forward."

"I see." Oliver was anxious to move things forward as well. The sooner he married, the sooner he could call off his own mother. "What are you suggesting?"

"My wife has a lot of details to organize in the preparations. It would be helpful to her to know when to tell people the event will take place."

"How much time are you thinking?" Oliver hoped it wasn't too long.

"Soon."

"You're not thinking this week, are you?" That would be rushing Isabelle too much, but he hoped soon wasn't after the New Year.

"This week would be out of the question with all the festival activities. Perhaps next week some time?"

That suited Oliver. "If that's agreeable to Isabelle."

"Of course, the bride must be agreeable."

Oliver had sensed Isabelle's reluctance and understood. She was young and likely enjoyed her freedom. He would have to reassure her he wouldn't control her to the point of crushing her adventurous spirit. He would encourage her to do the things she enjoyed.

"If you don't mind my asking, why not set your daughters up with trust funds and let them decide whether to marry or not?" He wished his own mother would drop the subject of marriage and grandchildren-to-be.

"As I said. I want to know they are taken care of."

"But wouldn't a trust fund do that?"

"It would see to their monetary needs, but what about their physical and emotional well-being? I don't want them to live their lives alone. If they get sick or injured, I want someone who cares about them to be at their sides. Not in some cold institution with paid servants or nurses who are simply doing a job. A husband and children and grandchildren offer the hope for such."

Oliver sensed this was coming from somewhere deep inside the man. From personal experience? Had Jackson's first wife been alone without her husband sitting beside her when she passed away? Oliver would want loved ones to care for him in his old age. "What day next week? For the wedding?"

"Is there one that would work better for you? We could arrange things for the evening after work if you like. I don't want to be responsible for you being remiss in your duties."

That was thoughtful. "Tuesday or Wednesday?" Isabelle might need more time to get used to the idea. "Or Friday? A nice way to end the week."

"I'll run Tuesday by my wife and daughter and see what they think. We'll let you know." Jackson got to his feet. "I look forward to you becoming a member of my family."

Oliver stood too and shook the older man's extended hand. "I look forward to it as well." Isabelle would keep him on his toes.

After Jackson left, Oliver reseated himself and retrieved his mother's letter. Should he send her a telegram and tell her dispatching her agent would be unnecessary and inform her and his father of his upcoming marriage? After all, a wedding date was nearly set. But something niggled inside him that it wasn't set at all. Until Isabelle had agreed and he felt as though she was committed to their nuptials, he didn't want to tell anyone outside of Jackson's family.

So, he would have to hope the "agent" his mother was sending didn't arrive before he said "I do".

Isabelle pumped hard on her bicycle. Her stepmother was going to be livid at her for being so late. She had tarried far too long with Grant. She hoped her dear friend heeded her words and took the path of reason.

She jumped off without even stopping completely and hurled her transportation against the railing. She gulped in a few gasps to disguise being out of breath.

A gentleman exited the posh dressmaker's shop with a parcel and held the door for her.

"Thank you." She rushed inside and glanced over her shoulder. Was that the same man in the mercantile with the blue ribbon?

"Isabelle, you're here."

She turned to face her stepmother. "I'm sorry I'm late."

Marguerite sauntered over to her with a smile, which looked disturbingly real. "Nonsense. You're right on time."

No verbal reprimand? Certainly, that would come later. What was her stepmother up to?

"We had a few details to go over first." Marguerite

surveyed Isabelle from head to toe, lingering on her Bloomer dress. Surprisingly, she made no comment about it.

Why was her stepmother being so accommodating? Exactly what Isabelle had decided to be, cooperative. It would be better to give the appearance of going along with the wedding plans. Less conflict.

Marguerite ushered her to the sitting area and sat with her on the settee.

Mademoiselle Celeste Dumont sashayed over, speaking with a lilting French accent. "You wear the latest fashion. So practical for your velocipede."

It was good to have at least one person appreciate her attire.

Mademoiselle Dumont waved a hand through the air and over her head. "We have chosen some readymade outfits. But don't let me see you worry over that, just because they have already been sewn up. Each one is an original. Once you choose which you want, they will be altered to fit you so well they will feel as though you aren't wearing anything at all."

Marguerite gasped.

The French woman winked before she sat and tapped her slender index finger on a large, thick book on the table next to her. "Then you can choose from my many designs and my array of European fabrics for the other items in your new wardrobe."

Isabelle would do her best to keep the number to a minimum. Since she hoped to find a solution which didn't involve wedding vows, she wouldn't take advantage of the situation. She would appear indecisive, opting to make her final decisions next week. But for now, she would need to choose a few things or else Marguerite wouldn't let her leave this place. Appear amenable in the beginning, then noncommittal.

"First your wedding gown. Your mother has chosen a most exquisite one. But then all my creations are exquisite." Mademoiselle Dumont clapped her hands twice. "We're ready ladies."

A model glided out wearing a stunning beaded wedding gown and veil. Exquisite, *indeed.* But it wasn't

Isabelle's style.

Both Marguerite and the shop owner peered at Isabelle, no doubt for her approval.

"It's spectacular."

Mademoiselle Dumont leaned a little closer. "But you don't like?"

"I like it very much. I just prefer something that flows and flutters more." Beaded dresses could be so heavy. Weighed down fabric that could hardly move.

Mademoiselle Dumont gave Marguerite a nod.

Marguerite huffed. "I had to try."

"Next." The owner leaned toward Isabelle. "This is the one I chose for you."

The next model glided out in a heavenly confection of layered chiffon that danced with minimal movement. Each layer seemed to waver on an unseen breeze.

Isabelle drew in a quick breath.

"I told you," Mademoiselle Dumont said. "Shall we have this one altered for you?"

Isabelle gazed at the model who appeared to be floating. The beautiful dress almost made her want to get married regardless of who the groom was. "I don't need to see any others." Too bad she would be in a forced wedding when she wore this beautiful gown.

Marguerite inclined her head. "We'll take the other one for Adelaide. She'll be getting married soon as well."

Mademoiselle Dumont beamed. "Victoria, have the girls come out with the other garments and outfits."

In addition to the wedding gown, Isabelle managed to get away with one morning dress, one afternoon garden party dress, an evening gown, a walking suit, and various under garments. She doubted she would have much occasion to wear the evening gown, but her stepmother had insisted. No doubt Marguerite would plan an occasion specifically for that dress.

Thirteen

OLIVER SAT BEHIND HIS DESK SHUFFLING papers. His bank office door opened.

Jonathan poked his head in. "Mr. Mallory, there is a Mr. Young and a lady here to see you."

Young? Who did Oliver know in town with that surname? "Give me a couple of minutes, then show them in." Tuesday was turning out to be a busy day.

His assistant disappeared and closed the door.

This Mr. Young and his wife must be new clients looking to open an account or request a loan. Oliver tucked the past-due loans and mortgages into their proper folders and slipped them in his work-to-be-completed desk drawer.

When the doorknob rattled, he stood prepared to greet his customers.

A man in a fine suit entered with a beautiful lady on his arm.

Oliver couldn't believe it and stepped out from behind his desk. "Ellery! What are you doing here?" He gripped his friend's hand and placed his other on the man's shoulder.

Ellery Young pulled him closer and gave him a couple of healthy pats on the back before releasing him. "I came to see where you've been hiding out. Now that I have, I can't imagine what is keeping you in this out-of-the-way hamlet. You must come back to Philadelphia."

"I'm happy here."

"You're at least returning for your mother's Christmas soiree, aren't you?"

Now it made sense. "My mother sent you, didn't she?" This was her agent of persuasion.

Ellery shrugged. "She wants you home."

The lady stepped forward and held out her hand,

palm down. "Silly men. Your mother sent me to secure your RSVP." She threw a glance at her brother. "You are but my chaperone."

Oliver took her outstretched hand and gave a quick bow over it then released it. Not Ellery's wife, as he had first assumed before really looking at her, but his sister. "Good afternoon, Belinda. It's nice to see you again. Did you bring your husband, Robert?" Last he'd heard, the two were engaged.

She offered him a coquettish smile. "I broke things off with him ages ago. We weren't well suited so never married."

From behind his sister, Ellery shook his head. "Leave the poor man alone."

"I'll do no such thing. Mrs. Mallory entrusted me with this very important errand, and I intend to succeed no matter what."

Oliver mentally groaned. He remembered how persistent Belinda—and other women like her—could be. He didn't miss that one bit.

Ellery stepped forward. "And I intend to keep you free of any female entanglements here or back in Philadelphia. We're staying at the White Hotel. Does their dining room serve decent meals?"

"They do. Nothing fancy, but very tasty."

"Then we'll make reservations for seven o'clock and meet you there."

Though Oliver looked forward to spending time with his friend, Belinda was another matter. "I'll see you at seven." He walked them out of the bank.

On the boardwalk, Belinda made the motions of straightening his lapels. "An evening with you will be well worth the week I endured on a train." She patted the front of his coat.

He stepped back to discourage any further contact. He would put up with her to converse with Ellery. He glanced toward the street.

Isabelle stood frozen in the thoroughfare next to her bicycle, staring at him.

No. He trotted down two steps to her. "This isn't what you think."

"I—I'm not sure what I think."

Ellery came up beside him. "Oliver, who is this ravishing beauty?"

"This is Miss Atwood, my fiancée. Isabelle, this is my friend Ellery Young and his sister Belinda." He hoped Isabelle didn't counter his claim of engagement. Jackson might not have had a chance to tell her the date was set.

Ellery freed one of Isabelle's hands from her bicycle and kissed the back of it. "Very pleased to meet you."

"Pleased to meet you too, Mr. Young."

"We have made a supper engagement with Oliver at the hotel for this evening. You must join us."

Isabelle's gaze flickered between Oliver and his friend. "I don't want to intrude."

Belinda joined them. "Yes, please do come. It will make for a most enjoyable evening and even up the numbers." She looped her arm through Oliver's.

He pulled free. "You don't have to." He didn't want to subject Isabelle to Belinda's conniving.

Ellery dipped his head. "We won't accept no—*I* won't accept no. We're dining at seven. Oliver will call for you at—?" He looked to Oliver for the time.

"Six-thirty? But if you have other plans with your parents, we'll understand."

Isabelle smiled at Oliver. "I'll be ready." She turned her focus back to the Youngs. "It was nice meeting both of you, and I look forward to supper tonight." She pushed her bicycle away.

Oliver ached to explain this whole situation to Isabelle, but in front of his friends wasn't the place or time. He would go a little early to pick her up, explain everything, and give her the option to back out.

Ellery clasped Oliver's shoulder. "*Now,* I can see why you are staying here. But are you sure you want to get tied down again? You don't want to waste your second shot at freedom."

"I'm sure." Though he was prepared to marry Isabelle, he wasn't sure she would marry him.

Belinda touched Oliver's arm. "You aren't seriously going to marry a simple country girl, are you? Did you see what she was wearing?"

"Her bicycle dress? Very practical. I like it." He actually hadn't formed an opinion about it. "Isabelle isn't a simple country girl. She's interesting." And made him feel as though there could be something more to his life than working. "Yes, I am going to marry her. The wedding is set for Tuesday, next week."

"Next week? Rushing things, are we?"

"It's complicated. I'm sort of repaying a favor to her father."

"By marrying his daughter? Does your mother know about this? Of course she doesn't, or else she wouldn't have sent me."

His mother didn't know. There wasn't time. She would have a fit about not being here for the wedding, but she'd get over it once she met Isabelle.

"You can't get married without your parents here." Belinda flapped her gloves in the air. "You'll have to postpone."

"Isabelle's mother has everything set for next week. The wedding will take place as scheduled."

Belinda gave a sly smile. "We'll see about that."

He would need to warn Isabelle when he picked her up that Belinda might be a little testy. *After* he explained what Belinda was doing outside the bank fussing with his suit coat. That there was absolutely nothing going on between him and her.

Anymore.

Isabelle stood in her closet dressing room. She couldn't believe what she was about to do. Dress up for pretentious socialites. She was tempted to remain in her bicycle bloomers to show the Youngs she didn't care one whit what they thought of her. After all, they had already seen her in it. Her appearance couldn't get much worse.

She studied herself in the standing mirror, admiring her practical outfit. Mademoiselle Dumont had approved of it, and she, if anyone, knew fashion. A wave of guilt washed over her. Oliver didn't deserve to be embarrassed by her showing up underdressed to a supper engagement. Even though she still hoped to get out of this marriage agreement between him and her parents.

She flipped through the racks of clothes and draped one...two...three gowns over her arm.

"What are you doing?" Adelaide stood in the doorway between the large closet dressing room and the bedroom.

"I'm trying to decide what to wear tonight. Oliver has some society friends, a brother and sister, in town visiting, and we are all going out to supper. The woman particularly doesn't like me, and I think she plans to steal Oliver away from me."

"Oh, dear. What if Mr. Mallory chooses her over you?"

Isabelle wouldn't mind for herself because her wedding would be called off. But for Oliver, she did care. Miss Young would make his life miserable. He deserved better than a designing woman like her. "If he does choose her, we can do little about it."

"Oh, dear." Adelaide put her hands on her abdomen. "I'll go see what Mother has to say about all this. She'll know what to do."

"No, don't."

But her sister had already hurried from the room.

Isabelle's insides tightened. She imagined Marguerite would have plenty to say. She would likely blame Isabelle for them coming in the first place. She could do nothing about her stepmother nor the brother and sister. She laid her three best gowns in a row on her bed and steeled herself for her stepmother's disapproval.

Marguerite stepped into her room. "Adelaide says we have a serious problem."

Isabelle turned toward her stepmother. "Oliver has some society friends in town. I need to know what to wear to supper." She waved a hand toward her choices. At least she couldn't be accused of not trying.

"I've never known you to be concerned over your attire."

"This is different. Oliver's friends from Philadelphia are here. I could tell by the way that woman stared at me, that she disapproved of everything about me." She'd seen that look plenty of times on Marguerite's face. "They're refined and cultured."

"Now you're interested in all I've been trying to teach you the past five years."

Did that mean her stepmother didn't want to help her?

Marguerite crossed to Isabelle's bed where the three different gowns lay. "Your attempt is commendable. You appear to have listened to some of my instructions." She pointed to the red velvet gown. "This one won't do. It will seem as though you are trying too hard to impress. The key is to look elegant without effort. A natural allure."

She was going to help after all. That left the lavender one with beading and the pink lacy one.

Isabelle joined her stepmother beside the bed. "Which one of these two will give me the air of not trying when, in truth, I am?"

"Though both are stunning and perfect on you, neither are right for tonight."

What? "But you chose both of these. All three." One of the reasons Isabelle had pulled them out—guaranteed approval.

"I know." She sauntered off into Isabelle's dressing room closet.

Isabelle followed.

Marguerite flipped through hanger after hanger not pausing on any gown longer than a second. How could she so quickly deem them suitable or not? She stopped short and removed a hanger from the rod. "This one." She held up a blue confection of ruched chiffon, one of Isabelle's favorites, which Marguerite had previously maligned. Even with the layers of under garments and yards of the lightweight fabric, Isabelle felt buoyant in this dress.

"I don't understand. You've never liked this gown."

Marguerite held it up to Isabelle. "But you do, therefore you'll feel confident in it. Your face brightened already with the thought of wearing it. Definitely the right choice. The blue will enhance your eyes. The other young lady won't be able to compete."

Had Marguerite paid her a compliment? And been

helpful? This wasn't a competition. But Miss Young might think it is.

"Mr. Mallory will have eyes for only you."

"You think so?" Isabelle never imagined a statement like that about a man she didn't love could make her feel special, adored.

"Of course. He won't be able to help himself. We'll have Gwen pull your hair up into a style to bring out your best features." Marguerite's personal maid did wonders with hair.

"Thank you. I didn't expect you to help me so much."

"We can't have that trollop stealing your future husband."

Now it made sense. Marguerite was keeping watch over her own interests, and to do so, she needed to insure Isabelle made a good impression. She didn't mind.

Marguerite's maid twisted and curled until Isabelle's hair embodied sophistication without being overdone or appearing as though she was trying too hard to impress.

Adelaide hurried in. "Mr. Mallory has arrived. He's quite dashing."

Isabelle straightened. "He's early." She tried to stand, but her stepmother put a hand on her shoulder.

Marguerite took a slow breath. "Always keep the gentleman waiting. You don't want to seem too eager. Adelaide, go tell Mr. Mallory your sister will be down in a few minutes."

Adelaide darted out.

Marguerite opened a velvet jewel box to reveal a simple sapphire necklace featuring a single, light-blue teardrop stone surrounded by small diamonds hanging from a gold chain.

"This is beautiful. Are you sure I should wear it?"

"Definitely. A piece of jewelry like this says your family has money, but you aren't flaunting how much wealth."

To Isabelle it said she was flaunting it, but she loved it anyway. After checking her reflection one last time, she rose to her feet. "You don't think I'm overdressed for the White Hotel dining room, do you?"

"You aren't dressing for the venue but for the people

present. It's time."

"I'm ready."

Marguerite crossed the room with her. "Try to remember all the etiquette rules I attempted to teach you."

"I will." Isabelle stopped at the top of the staircase.

Oliver stood at the bottom, smiling at Adelaide talking with hand gestures.

"Your sister really needs to learn to control herself." Marguerite clasped her hands in front of her.

When Adelaide pointed, he turned and gazed up at Isabelle. He did look handsome.

Her breath caught.

"Go show him you are the better choice."

Was that a hint of pride in her stepmother's voice? Remembering Marguerite's warnings from the past, Isabelle took the steps slowly.

It was nice that Oliver seemed to approve of her appearance, but she really wanted the Youngs to approve. She wasn't quite sure why.

Sissy held out Marguerite's blue cloak. Her stepmother's best. Surprised again.

Oliver took the wrap and draped it over Isabelle's shoulders. "You look beautiful."

Smiling, she clasped it around her neck. "Thank you. You are quite dapper yourself."

Once Oliver had escorted her outside and the door closed, she stopped. "I need to talk to you before we go."

"I would like to speak to you as well. It will be warmer inside the closed carriage. We can converse along the way." He held the conveyance's door open for her.

She climbed in and settled on the seat.

He followed, sat beside her, and tapped the side of the interior for the driver to go.

The carriage lurched forward.

Once out on the main street, Oliver shifted in his seat. "You go first."

She wasn't sure how to start. "I was wondering about the Youngs. Are they close friends?"

"Ellery is."

"And Miss Young?"

"She's his sister." His tone held no detectable clues as to how he felt about the woman.

She needed to spit it out. "It's obvious Miss Young is attracted to you. If you feel the same, I don't want to stand in the way of true love."

"I'm glad you brought this up. It's what I wanted to talk to you about. Not true love or any kind of love. She may have feelings for me, but I don't return her affections. I escorted her to a few functions in the past, but nothing serious. Honestly, I'm hoping she will feign an illness this evening. Ellery is an old friend. We've had some good times together."

On one hand, the news pleased Isabelle that this woman meant nothing to him, but on the other, if he was interested in Miss Young, it would have given her a legitimate excuse to get out of the wedding. "Then I'll know to ignore all of her advances toward you."

His eyebrows knitted together. "You believe me? Just like that?"

"Is there a reason I shouldn't?"

"No, but in my experience, women make more of a fuss about another woman being interested in their man. Even if there is nothing to be jealous of."

She didn't exactly think of Oliver as *her* man, but in truth, she supposed he was. "You have given me no reason not to trust you." He did seem like a trustworthy man.

"Thank you. And I trust you."

Without realizing it, he'd heaped guilty coals on her head. Not only had she eaten lunch with Shane, but she should tell Oliver about her secret admirer. She was the one not to be trusted. She hungered to hold on to her freedom a little longer. A dose of silent rebellion against coercion. It wasn't like she would see Shane once she was married, and she didn't even know who her secret admirer was.

"One more thing. Like his sister, Ellery likes to flirt. Don't take anything he says too seriously."

"Thank you for the warning."

At the hotel, Oliver escorted her inside and took her

cloak, hanging it on a rack with his coat. Mr. Young waited alone at a table. Where was Miss Young? Was she to be absent as Oliver hoped?

Mr. Young stood and kissed the back of her hand. "Miss Atwood, you are a vision of loveliness." A flirt, as Oliver said.

"Thank you, Mr. Young. Is your sister not feeling well?" She wouldn't mind if the woman feigned an illness either.

"She's fine. She has a need to make a grand entrance so everyone will take notice."

Oliver held Isabelle's chair out for her.

She sat and reached back to touch his hand on her chair. "Thank you."

Five minutes later, Miss Young swept into the room in a red-velvet gown not that different from one of the ones Marguerite had rejected as overdressed. So, she was trying to impress Oliver. All heads turned toward her. Ellery stood and held out her chair. Oliver stood as well.

Miss Young fluttered her fan. "This is a quaint little hotel in a charming little town. Of course it's not what I'm used to, but I can adapt."

Mr. Young handed his sister a menu. "Don't linger over your decision. I'm hungry, and everything smells delicious."

"One could hardly linger over a menu with so few offerings. I was hoping for duck." Miss Young frowned at her menu. "Hmm."

Isabelle set her menu down. "I'll have the baked chicken."

Miss Young lifted her gaze slowly. "I doubt that's a good idea. I fear this place will overcook it and it will be dried out."

"Thank you." Isabelle hadn't thought about the chicken being dry. Marguerite had trained their cook how to prepare chicken to her liking, and it was always moist and tasty.

"The pork will likely be dry as well. Do you think they could prepare a medium-rare steak without overcooking it?"

Mr. Young huffed. "Just pick something."

"I don't know what kind of standards they have here."

The waitress stopped at their table. "What can I get for you?"

Miss Young blinked up at the server. "Tell me how your chef prepares the chicken."

Hadn't she already determined it wouldn't be fit? So why ask?

The waitress hesitated before opening her mouth.

Mr. Young intervened. "My sister will have the roast beef and red wine. I'll have a steak medium-rare and a brandy." He plucked the menu from his sister's hands and turned both his and hers over to the waitress.

Oliver motioned for Isabelle to order.

That was nice of him not to order for her without asking. Another thing for the plus side where he was concerned. "I'll have the baked chicken."

Miss Young made the tiniest of movements back and forth with her head.

But chicken was what Isabelle wanted, and chicken was what she was going to have.

"Something to drink?" the waitress asked.

"A cup of tea."

Oliver ordered. "I'll have the pork chop and coffee."

Again, Miss Young shook her head very slightly.

Let her disapprove. Had Oliver gone against her advice on purpose? Another plus.

Once the waitress walked away, Miss Young turned to her brother. "Why did you order the roast beef for me?"

"It was the only thing you hadn't complained about yet."

"Well, I'm not familiar with this establishment. I was simply trying to make the best choice under the circumstances."

"And you have. You will have food." Mr. Young faced Oliver. "Tell me all about this town of yours."

"The town has over twenty-five hundred residents, is surrounded by various cattle ranches, and has a teacher's college. It's a nice place to live. Quiet. I like it here."

Miss Young turned to Isabelle. "Have you lived in this quaint settlement your whole life?"

Marguerite wouldn't put up with a person calling Kamola something as mundane as a *settlement*. She liked to think of Kamola as more metropolitan than it was.

"I have lived here my whole life. I was born on a farm outside of town."

Miss Young's smug expression soured. "You mean you were born out in the *wilderness* with no doctors or a hospital?"

"I wouldn't call it the wilderness. There was a midwife. My father never would have gotten my mother into town in time."

The waitress returned, set their beverages in front of them, and left.

"You're a *farm girl*?" Miss Young glanced at Oliver.

Just like Marguerite. Being a farm girl wasn't good enough. And if Marguerite found out she'd admitted such a thing to the Youngs, she'd be aghast.

Oliver sat up straighter. "Isabelle's father is one of the most prominent men in town."

That was sweet of Oliver to stick up for her.

"I suppose this would be the sort of place where a *farmer* would be prominent."

Oliver opened his mouth to defend her again no doubt, but Isabelle rested her hand on his forearm to let him know she would like to speak up for herself.

"We aren't farmers any more. Not since my father inherited a bit of money a few years ago from a relative back East. Though we do still own the farm as a sort of remembrance."

"A little inheritance doesn't make one a member of high society." Miss Young took a sip of her wine.

Oliver couldn't seem to contain himself. "Isabelle's father hails from the Boston Atwoods."

Miss Young choked on her wine, actually spewing some out. She set her glass down and dabbed her lips with her napkin.

Mr. Young let out a small snort.

"I'm going to the powder room." Miss Young brushed her napkin at the front of her dress then stood. She swung around and sauntered out.

Mr. Young let out the laugh he'd been trying to hold in. "That was marvelous, Oliver. I've never seen her flabbergasted like that."

Isabelle had been told the Boston Atwoods were supposedly important but had never understood until now. Etiquette dictated she follow Miss Young and offer assistance if needed, at the very least, support. Chances were Miss Young would rebuff her, but Marguerite would be pleased she fulfilled her social duty.

She pushed her chair back. Both men shot to their feet even though it wasn't necessary. Oliver guided her chair so she could stand.

"I'm going to see if she needs anything." She left the dining room and crossed the lobby to the water closet. She knocked. "Miss Young? Are you all right?" Rustling came from the other side of the door, then it swung open.

Miss Young held her voice barely above a whisper. "Don't think I don't know what you're up to. This fast wedding can mean only one thing."

"What is that?" What a place to have this conversation, in the lobby outside the water closet.

"You've thrown yourself at him so you could trap him into this wedding."

The woman didn't know how close she was to the truth. Though Isabelle hadn't been the one to do the throwing, and her parents had done the trapping. "You think I'm in the family way?"

"Why else would he be marrying you in such a rush? I've informed his parents, and they will put a stop to this."

Oliver's parents? She hadn't thought about them attending the wedding. Surely he had told them. Would they come?

"Don't think for one moment I believe you are related to the Boston Atwoods." She brushed past Isabelle and sashayed away.

Isabelle bit her tongue to keep from throwing a spiteful retort back at her. Their Boston relations went without question. She, her parents, and Adelaide had all traveled to Boston twice. Most of those relatives were as pretentious as Miss Young, and considered Isabelle's branch unworthy to carry the family name.

"Izzy?"

She turned to face Grant. Had he heard her conversation with Miss Young?

"What are you doing here?"

"Oliver has some friends in town visiting."

"Mr. Young and his sister?"

"You've met them."

"Miss Young has been educating the staff in how to bring this hotel up to a *moderate* standard."

"A bit demanding?"

He nodded.

She wished she could escape with Grant and go fishing like they did as children. "I should get back to the dining room."

"Before you go, I want to say you look really pretty." He gave her a strange, tender look she couldn't interpret.

She warmed inside. "Thank you." That meant more to her than anyone else's compliments.

Fourteen

THE NEXT MORNING, ISABELLE FILLED A flour sack with leftover food and scraps wrapped in waxed paper to keep them from making a mess. She'd asked Molly to cook up the chicken parts the family didn't eat like the skin and insides. A half of a dozen slightly charred biscuits went into her sack along with some left-over oatmeal that had congealed into a semisolid state and the remaining cooked peas. All of this would provide quite a feast for the hungry dogs.

Feeding a pack of strays was the last thing Isabelle should be spending her time on with a wedding looming in her immediate future. Focusing on something else helped her to not get too distressed over her own situation.

On foot, she headed out to the trees where she'd last seen Tramp and his friends. Since her bicycle outfit was in to be laundered, she wore her green riding skirt for when she took out her bicycle later. "Tramp. Here, boy." She didn't know if Tramp was indeed a boy or a girl. "Here, Tramp."

The bushes rustled, and Tramp poked his head out from a wild rhododendron bush. The others were nowhere in sight, but she suspected they were near.

Isabelle held up her sack. "I brought you and your friends some food. Where are they?"

She walked around the bush. "Go on. Show me where they are."

Tramp trotted a little way, stopped, and sat in front of her, paws in the air begging for the food.

"Not until you take me to your friends."

She moved in the direction she thought they might be.

Tramp scampered and sat again.

Isabelle pointed. "Show me where they are."

After several minutes of coaxing, Tramp scurried to a bare patch of ground between two fir trees and barked at one of them.

The spaniel first and then the Lab peered out from behind the drooping evergreen branches.

"Howdy, fellows." Isabelle held up the bag. "I brought some food."

Both dogs sniffed the air and stepped out into the clearing, tails wagging.

She tossed each dog a piece of cooked chicken skin, including Tramp, the smallest of the three.

They gobbled down the morsels. An orange striped kitten of about six months appeared between the two leery dogs, sniffed their muzzles, and meowed.

"Well, who are you?"

The kitten turned toward her and hissed.

"You look an awful lot like our barn cat, Marmalade. Is he your papa?"

The cat answered with another hiss.

Isabelle retrieved a piece of the cooked chicken innards and tossed it to the kitten.

It hissed again but inched toward the food, as did the Lab. The feline swiped a paw at the dog who yelped and jerked away.

Isabelle laughed. "It seems as though someone has already tasted the pain of those claws."

The kitten devoured the chicken.

"Not so fast. You'll choke."

Next, a green-headed duck hopped out to join the others. One foot missing.

"You poor thing." Isabelle retrieved a charred biscuit and broke off a piece. She held it out toward the foul.

It quacked and flapped its wings.

It evidently didn't trust her any more than the others. She tossed the bit to him.

With a wagging tail, the three-legged spaniel came closer.

Isabelle sat on a large rock and doled out the food. With each morsel, the ragtag pack inched closer until they were all seated around her with the kitten climbing onto her lap to make sure she wasn't overlooked. When the food was gone, she held out her hands. "That's it. I'll bring you more another day."

Tramp and the spaniel each licked a hand. The Lab sniffed, and the kitten bit Isabelle's finger.

"Ow! That's not something to eat." With Isabelle's outburst the kitten ran off a few feet while hissing. "I don't think all your sputtering is any kind of threat." Reminded her of Marguerite.

The duck sat on the ground, apparently content with his meal. The others all seemed to have space in their stomachs that still needed to be filled.

"I wish I had more. Truly I do." She hadn't planned for the two extra mouths to feed, not that they had eaten all that much being the smallest. "I'll come again and bring more if I can." Isabelle stood and brushed her hands down her green riding skirt.

The Lab and spaniel darted off a few feet, and the kitten hissed.

She should hurry home before she was missed and hustled away with Tramp at her side. "Shoo. Go on back. I don't have any more today."

The scruffy dog gave up and lagged behind.

Close to her house, Isabelle slowed her pace. It wouldn't do any good to have Marguerite testy at her for behaving unladylike.

"Good morning, Isabelle."

She turned to face Oliver. "Mr. M—I mean Oliver. I wasn't expecting you."

"I thought I'd drop by and see if you were available for a buggy ride."

She should agree but was reluctant because it would be one more step toward a future she hoped to avoid. "I'll need to check. I'm supposed to help gather items for the Founders Day festivities. Let me see if I can get out of it."

Oliver walked her to the door and escorted her inside the house.

Marguerite called in a terse tone from the other room. "Isabelle? Is that you?" She appeared around the corner and brightened upon seeing Oliver. "What are the two of you up to?"

Oliver smiled. "I ran into Isabelle outside and invited her for a buggy ride. She says you need her help with some Founders Day preparations."

"Nonsense," Marguerite oozed. "Adelaide and I have it well in hand. Go, and have fun."

Isabelle's emotions jumbled up together, warring with each other. Though grateful to be away from Marguerite, she didn't feel right stringing Oliver along when he didn't know the real reason for her need to marry. And not to marry just anyone, but him in particular. What would he think if he knew the real reason why her parents had chosen him? Because he had the right hair color for their scheming plan.

She sat in the buggy next to him.

Oliver set the vehicle into motion. "Where is your furry friend today?"

Isabelle pointed in the direction she'd come from when he'd met her in front of her house. "I was over there taking him and his friends some food."

"His friends?"

She nodded. "Yesterday, when I offered him food, he gave it to a pair of other dogs waiting in the distance. A black Labrador and a golden spaniel. I felt bad for them to have to share the little bit of food I thought would be for one dog."

"So, they all received enough today?"

She drew in a deep breath. "I'm not sure. There were two *more* to the group this time."

"Five dogs?"

She shook her head. "Only the three dogs—at least for now. The additions were a kitten and a one-legged duck, and the spaniel has but three legs."

"That's quite a multifarious band of animals."

"I think it's sweet they look after each other."

He turned onto the street. "I wanted to apologize for Belinda last night."

"You warned me she might be fractious." Knowing ahead of time the woman would be contentious helped.

"It was more than that. I didn't like the way she spoke down to you. Money aside, you are more of a lady than she has ever been."

"Thank you." Why did he have to continually be nice? If he weren't, it would make it so much easier to dislike him. "I think my stepmother would disagree with you."

"A lady should not be defined by her social standing or clothing but by the way she treats others."

If he kept this up, she might find herself falling in love with this man. She never should have agreed to this buggy ride.

Oliver drove in silence for a couple of minutes, trying to figure this woman out. "I get the impression I'm the lesser of two undesirable duties."

"How do you mean?"

"I don't think you really wanted to go for a buggy ride with me, but helping your mother with the preparations was more distasteful."

Her eyes widened. "Please don't think I view you as distasteful."

"But?"

"But I'm having a challenge getting used to marrying a man I'm not..."

"...in love with?"

She lowered her head. "Yes."

As he'd suspected. This was likely the beginning of the end of this courtship. "I have no delusion you will fall in love with me. I know this wasn't your idea."

"Don't you want love?"

"Though love would be nice, it's not required for a successful marriage. I hope you don't feel as though I'm pressuring you." The last thing he needed was a reluctant wife.

"Of course not. I'm sure in time we'll come to care for each other."

Not what he'd imagined when Jackson first approached him two weeks ago about marrying his eldest daughter. "I can insist upon a long courtship to give you time to adjust to things."

"No. You can't do that."

This girl obviously didn't want to marry him, but at the same time, she didn't want to put it off. Perplexing. "Why don't you marry your friend Mr. Dawson? You're obviously fond of him, and he of you."

"Grant? We're friends. Nothing more. My parents would never agree to him anyway."

"But you already have that closeness you claim we would develop in time."

She sat silent for a few moments, apparently thinking on that. "Grant would never do."

Why? Oliver hoped it wasn't because the young gentleman didn't have much money. If that was her reasoning, that would mean she was marrying Oliver for his money. He'd thought better of her. Dare he ask? "Is your parents' disapproval the only reason you wouldn't marry him?"

"Why are you going on about Grant?"

He might as well see this through. "If we marry, I wonder if I'll have anything to worry about where he's concerned."

She chuffed out a laugh. "No. We're nothing more than good friends."

He knew people like that could be well suited for each other. Ideal, in fact. They already had a foundation of mutual respect on which to build a strong marriage.

Oliver wanted to give that to Isabelle, but she didn't seem to want it for some reason. Though he sensed her parents' eagerness for her to wed him, he also suspected there was more to this arrangement. Maybe this whole thing was a bad idea.

Isabelle pondered the idea of friends making good spouses. She might consider it with someone like Grant, but he wouldn't agree to that kind of an arrangement. If she was going to settle for a marriage without love, then why not with Oliver?

Oliver pressed the catch button on his pocket watch. "I'm going to be late. I'll take you home."

"You don't have to do that. I prefer to walk."

"Are you sure?" He turned the horse. "I'll get out at the bank, and you can take my buggy. I'll send someone for it."

"You'll do no such thing. I have some things to do in town." Had she known the drive would end up this way, she would have asked to attach her bicycle to the back of the buggy. No finagling a way to escape. "I'll enjoy the walk." More time away from home and wedding plans.

"Oh, no." Oliver groaned.

"I want to walk. Truly, I do." It would give her a chance to order her thoughts and pray. And maybe she could figure out a way to come to peace with this new life being foisted upon her.

"It's not that. It's what's waiting for me at the bank— or rather *who* is waiting."

Miss Young stood on the boardwalk under her white lace parasol with a tassel dangling from each point.

He parked in front of the building.

Miss Young's pleasant expression turned sour.

"Let me help you out." He set the brake.

Isabelle could tell Oliver genuinely didn't want Miss Young's attentions. So, when Oliver offered her his hand and she stepped down, she feigned tripping and fell into him. Marguerite would be so proud of her.

As any gentleman worth his salt, his arms came around her and held her upright. "You did that on purpose, didn't you?"

Isabelle glanced over his shoulder at a scowling Miss Young. "And it received exactly the right reaction from a certain lady."

"I believe, Miss Atwood, you have a wicked streak. In the vein of showing a certain lady I'm taken, would you permit me to kiss you on the cheek?"

"Such a display of affection in public would be completely, socially unacceptable." She fussed with his lapels in much the same manner Miss Young had the previous day. "So, please do."

"Definitely a wicked streak." He smiled and pecked

her on the cheek.

Her skin tingled under his touch.

"Are you sure you won't take the buggy?"

"I'm sure." She looped her arm around his. "Now walk me inside."

"Why?"

"For show."

"Are you staking your claim on me, Miss Atwood?"

"Maybe."

He guided her up onto the boardwalk and stopped. "Good morning, Belinda. Where is Ellery?"

Miss Young beamed at Oliver. "Back at the hotel."

Isabelle inched a little closer to Oliver. "Miss Young, how pleasant to see you again."

"And to see you." Miss Young ran her gaze down Isabelle and let it settle on her riding skirt. "You do wear unusual attire."

"Thank you. I take pride in my appearance." Isabelle turned to Oliver and inclined her head. "Shall we?"

Oliver opened the door and let Isabelle enter. "Belinda, tell your brother to come see me. We haven't gotten to catch up." He stepped inside without inquiring if Miss Young had planned to come in. He escorted Isabelle to his office and closed the door. "What now? You realize she won't be put off for long. She'll probably wait."

"But it gives you a small reprieve and the chance to tell your assistant to call you away on something urgent." A trick Marguerite employed when conversing with a disagreeable guest at a social gathering.

He chuckled. "Most decidedly a wicked streak."

"I like to think of it as being helpful." Marguerite would approve of anything Isabelle did to remain between her future son-in-law and any woman who would attempt to steal him away.

"I wish you could stay here all day to keep her at bay."

Strangely, that didn't feel completely unpleasant. It had been nice to help him. "But I should be going. I don't want to keep you from your work."

Fifteen

SHANE RODE HUCKLEBERRY ALONG THE MAIN street of town. Isabelle Atwood strolled down the boardwalk, appearing to be deep in thought. He looked forward to supper tonight with her. But no harm in talking to her now. He guided his horse her direction. "Good morning, Miss Isabelle."

She jerked her head up, then smiled. "Good morning."

That smile could make a man want to do almost anything for her. He reined in Huckleberry and swung down. "Where's your bicycle today?"

"At home. I didn't ride it. I look forward to supper this evening."

"I do as well. And some time, I'd like to show you my ranch."

Her smile widened. "I'd like that. The livery isn't far." She pointed that direction. "I could rent a horse."

He raised his eyebrows. "Right now?"

Her mouth formed into an oh. "I didn't mean to presume."

"No. I'm glad you did." He liked her encouraging enthusiasm. "If you don't have any place else to be, I'll take you to the livery. We can ride on my horse together."

With a sideways glance, she considered him a moment. "I don't think that would be fitting. It's not so far to walk."

He'd expected her to decline his offer, but a fellow had to try. True that riding together could bring a young lady's reputation into question.

He walked beside her, leading Huckleberry. "What brought you into town without your bicycle? Or a buggy?"

"Nothing really. I was fidgety and wanted to get out of the house. What brings you all the way into town?"

A restless woman on a ranch wouldn't be good. "I

needed to send a telegram."

At the livery, he called into the yawning opening. "Amos? You in there?"

Amos's gangly fourteen-year-old son, Beanpole, stepped out of a stall with a pitchfork in his hand. He leaned it against the wall and strode toward them. "My pa's not here right now. What can I do for you?"

"I'd like to rent a buggy."

Isabelle inched forward. "We don't need a buggy. Just a saddled horse."

Bean's eyes widened. "We don't have a lady's sidesaddle."

"I don't' need one. A regular saddle will do."

Shane gazed down at her. "I don't mind renting a buggy." He'd expected to when she agreed to go with him.

"I'd rather ride horseback."

Such an unexpected woman.

He turned to the lad. "Bring the lady what she wants." How would she ride sideways on a regular saddle? This would be something to see.

A few minutes later, Beanpole led the saddled mount outside. "This here is Cinnamon. She's a real sweet girl and won't give you no trouble."

Shane clasped his hands together and held them low enough for Isabelle to step into and get up onto the saddle. She took his assistance and swung one leg over the horse's back. "You're going to ride astride?"

"I do have on my riding skirt."

He stared at her a moment. He'd never met a lady like her. Not at all how he'd assumed her to be a week ago when he'd snatched her off her bicycle. She surprised him at every turn. Life with her wouldn't grow boring.

He mounted and rode beside her out of town. Not knowing what to say, he remained silent.

"What made you decide to become a cattle rancher?" Her lilting voice had a way of scattering his troubled thoughts.

"My uncle died."

"Oh, I'm so sorry."

"You don't have to be. I didn't know him. He had no

children so left his place to me." The only family he'd had, and he hadn't known about him until a Pinkerton had tracked him down for his uncle's attorney.

"Do you enjoy the work?"

"I do."

"Had you worked on a ranch before so your uncle knew you'd be able to run it?"

He shook his head. "I don't know what my uncle was thinking. His attorney offered to help me sell it if I wanted to get rid of it. Since I didn't rightly know what I wanted to do, I figured I might as well try my hand at it. I've done a little of this and that. Could never stick with one thing. Nothing seemed to fit right."

"And being a cattle rancher does?"

"I'm not sure yet. I like it better than anything else I've tried. Maybe it's just the satisfaction in knowing the land is mine. The cattle are mine. Whether I succeed or fail, that's on me."

"But you're doing well?"

Was she fishing to see if he could take care of a wife? "So far. I have a seasoned foreman who has taught me a great deal. Being a wrangler for someone else is a lot different than running a whole operation, so I still have a lot to learn."

Isabelle's horse snorted and reared. When Cinnamon came down, she tried to run, but Isabelle held the reins tight.

Shane maneuvered the now agitated Huckleberry closer and reached for Cinnamon's bridle but missed it.

Her horse stomped and tossed her head and reared again.

Isabelle lost her grip on the saddle horn.

Shane shifted his focus from the bridle to the beautiful lady at risk. As she slid sideways, he leaned toward her and hooked his arm around her waist.

The horse bolted out from under her.

Shane pulled Isabelle to himself with her legs dangling. He took his foot from the stirrup and held it out with his boot. "Can you get your foot in there?" He could lower her to the ground but preferred to keep her close. It wasn't often a cowboy had a legitimate excuse to hold a charming lady close.

She poked her toe in and took some of the weight off his arm.

He pulled her all the way up onto his saddle. Yes, keeping her near was nice. "Are you all right?"

"I'm fine. That's twice you've rescued me from my capricious transportation. Are you going to make it a habit?"

Intriguing idea. He gazed into her enchanting blue eyes. "Would you mind if I did?"

Her answer came out breathy. "Not at all."

What would she do if he kissed her? He ached to know. *Too soon, Shane. Too soon. Remember she's a lady.* "We should go find Cinnamon. She went this way." He goaded his mount into motion.

Isabelle didn't seem to mind being on his horse now that there were no people around to witness them. He would just as soon keep her where she was while they searched.

After about twenty minutes of plodding along, he guided Huckleberry over a rise and reined him in. In the distance sat his ranch—house, barn, corral, and other outbuildings. "There it is." He gazed out over his spread as Isabelle must be seeing it. Dry and dirty, with leaves dying on the tree branches. "It's much prettier in the spring and summer when everything is coming up new."

"It's beautiful with all the vibrant colors of autumn. Yellows, golds, oranges, reds with bits of green hanging on here and there."

He looked again and saw the colors as beautiful instead of signaling impending death and the first howls of winter. He could picture Isabelle on his ranch. She would be like a long-anticipated summer rain, welcomed and refreshing.

Movement to his right caught his attention. Cinnamon stood near some trees, still breathing heavily from her fright.

Shane swung off, leaving Isabelle on Huckleberry. "You stay here." He crept slowly up to the agitated horse.

Cinnamon pawed the ground and eyed him warily.

When he got close enough, he stroked the side of her

neck and grabbed the reins that had tangled around some brush. No wonder she hadn't returned home. "What spooked you, girl?"

She blew out a heavy sigh from her nose as though relieved to have him find her.

He checked the unnerved animal's legs for injury. She appeared to be fine, so he walked her back over to Huckleberry.

Isabelle shifted in his saddle. "Is she all right?"

"She seems to be. Did you see what spooked her?"

Isabelle shook her head. "Will you help me down?"

"Stay there. Cinnamon still needs more time to calm herself. She ran pretty hard." He tied the reins to his saddle horn, put one foot in a stirrup, gripped the saddle horn, and swung up behind Isabelle. It gave him a chance to be close to the pretty lady.

He walked Huckleberry the remaining mile with Cinnamon trailing behind, down to his ranch buildings. He swung to the ground. "Wait there. I'll help you." He knew she could get down on her own, but he wanted to help her. He tied both horses to the hitching post next to the water trough.

She waited for him to come around, held out her arms, and placed her hands on his shoulders. He gripped her waist and lowered her to the ground.

Her words came out breathy. "Thank you."

He stared at her a moment, then leaned forward, and pressed his lips to hers.

She leaned into him and a soft satisfying sound emanated from her throat.

Isabelle's insides danced at Shane's kiss.

He pulled back with a grin. "Pardon my manners. I couldn't help myself. Your beauty drew me in."

That was poetic and romantic. Maybe he *was* her secret admirer. "It's my fault you kissed me?"

One side of his mouth hitched up. "Yes, ma'am.

Can't blame a poor cowpoke with no sense at all in his head."

She struggled not to sigh aloud. He could quite possibly be everything she wanted in a romantic suitor. Oliver popped into her mind, and her elation stopped short. *Careless, careless, careless.* She had let her emotions run wild. She had been overwhelmed and taken in with the beauty and romance of the ride and her surroundings. And the man with her. She could have no future with Shane Keegan.

She was sad that this would likely be the last she would see of him. She would need to cancel tonight's supper with him. She couldn't risk being seen in town with him again. But a small part of her didn't care, maybe even wanted to get caught so she wouldn't be facing a compulsory marriage. "Have you ever been faced with something you really didn't want to do"—a forced wedding—"but knew you had to do it? That you had no choice?"

"We always have a choice. Some are worse than others, while others are more desirable."

Yes, she could choose to let Adelaide suffer a much worse fate than Isabelle marrying a nice gentleman.

The time had come to tell this handsome rancher she couldn't keep their supper engagement or see him anymore. A part of her wanted to hold on to the dream of controlling her own future a little longer, but that wasn't fair to him.

A rider raced into the yard and stopped near the trough. With him came a black and white collie and a tricolored one.

Shane spun around. "Pepper. Roxy. Down." Both dogs immediately lowered their bodies to the ground.

"They're so beautiful. May I pet them?" Isabelle crouched.

Shane nodded. "Come."

The dogs trotted forward and sat in front of him.

The black and white one swung his head toward Isabelle.

When she petted him, he rolled onto his back.

"Pepper, get up."

The dog flipped back upright.

Shane shook his head. "He tries to get away with stuff when there's a pretty lady around."

Had he brought many ladies out here? She supposed it didn't matter.

The rider, a pockmark-faced man, chuckled then leaned sideways on his horse. "Mr. Keegan, we think we spotted those rustlers crossing the north portion of your land. Handley is following them and leaving a trail we can track."

Shane stepped toward him. "Are you sure it's the rustlers?"

"Handley said he'd never seen them in these parts before. He didn't want to approach them until you decide what you want to do."

Shane rubbed his palm across his mouth and jaw, looking between Isabelle and his ranch hand. "I'll take Miss Atwood back to town and return quickly, then we can ride out after them."

Isabelle stood. "No. You go. That's more important. I can get back to town on my own."

"What about your horse getting spooked?"

"Cinnamon will be fine. You need to make sure your cattle are safe."

"I like that you understand priorities on a ranch." Shane untied Huckleberry from the hitching post and handed the reins to the rider. "Saddle fresh mounts for both of us." He turned back to Isabelle. "Are you sure you'll be all right? I feel bad for sending you off on your own. I can take you."

She didn't want him wasting any more time on her when they could have no future and he had pressing matters at hand to tend to. "I'll be fine. The rustlers are north, and I'll be traveling southeast."

"There are other hazards. Like your horse spooking again."

"I'll keep my eye out for anything dangerous." She'd been too distracted by the handsome rancher at her side to notice any hazards on the trail. "Please go."

"All right. Thank you. Let me help you onto Cinnamon." He helped her up, then untied the reins, and handed them to her. "This could take a while. I could be out all night, so I won't be able to make it into town for supper with you."

"Of course not." It was best that way. "I hope you find the men and your cattle are safe."

He bobbed his head. "Be careful."

"I will. You too." She turned Cinnamon and goaded her into a trot.

Her heart sat heavy in her chest as she made her way into town without incident and stopped at the livery. She swung down.

The owner met her. Unlike his lanky son, Amos was round all over but not fat. He took the reins from her. "How did Cinnamon behave for you?"

"She was a darling. However, she did spook and rear then bolted."

"Reared? And you held on?"

"Not exactly. I was rescued before I could land on the ground." He didn't need to know all the details of her in Shane's arms. That would set too many tongues to waggling. "She doesn't seem to be hurt."

"I'll check her over to be sure."

"Thank you for letting me rent her." As Isabelle turned away from the livery, she stilled at the sight of the red-haired man who'd held open the hotel door for her.

He smiled at her, touched his hat, and strolled away.

Before she could think much about the man, Adelaide strolled along the street and captured Isabelle's full attention. Where was her sister going? No buggy, no driver, and no parents. It wasn't right.

Isabelle watched from the other side of the road, when Adelaide was far enough ahead, she crossed to follow her.

If she had no buggy, driver, or Marguerite, she'd likely slipped out of the house unseen. Isabelle knew that trick, but she had her bicycle to take her places when she escaped. Adelaide didn't have that convenience.

If Adelaide was on an unsanctioned outing, where could she be going that she didn't want anyone to know about? Possibly to see the father of her baby?

Isabelle would find out.

The September sun heated through his suit coat. Wouldn't be too many more of these warm days. He needed to copy another poem for Miss Isabelle Atwood. Maybe this time, he would write one of his own. Yes, that would be better. Use his own words to express his feelings instead of someone else's.

He smiled when the subject of his thoughts strode toward him in her green riding skirt and jacket. Though without her usual mode of transportation, she strolled along the side of the road next to the boardwalk. Her attention seemed to be riveted on something across the street. He cast his gaze that way but couldn't tell what had her transfixed.

She walked right past him without so much as a glance in his direction on the boardwalk.

Should he greet her? Call out her name? Not yet. His curiosity to learn what had captured her interest outweighed his desire to speak to her.

Raising up on her toes, she looked around a cluster of four cowboys riding down the middle of the street. Once they passed, she stopped short, moving her head back and forth. She appeared to have misplaced whatever had held her attention.

He glanced up in time to catch a glimpse of a woman in yellow with a wide-brimmed fancy hat rounding the corner.

Isabelle lunged forward to cross, hesitated to allow a wagon to pass, then hurried across the street and took long strides to close the distance between her and the woman. If she wanted to catch her, why hadn't she called out? She appeared to be following this woman in secret for some reason.

What are you up to, Miss Atwood?

He didn't have time for this. He had work to do, but when she disappeared around the corner too, he trotted across the street. At the edge of the building, he paused. What if she were just a few feet from where he stood?

What if she noticed him? What if he lost her?

He took a deep breath, straightened his coat by its lapels, and strode forward.

Isabelle sauntered along the boardwalk midway up the block. The woman she followed was nearly to the next intersection bordering the Washington State Normal School campus.

He moved along at a slightly faster pace than Isabelle. His curiosity rose, and he ached to ask her what she was up to.

At the end of the block, she too crossed the street.

He made it to the corner shortly after her as the other woman turned toward one of the normal college's vast buildings.

He halted. Adelaide? Why was Isabelle trailing her sister surreptitiously? And why was Adelaide going to the college? She didn't attend there.

One mystery solved—who Isabelle was following— and two more to niggle at him.

Obviously, Isabelle didn't want her sister to know she was following her. But why?

Isabelle stopped at the stone steps leading up to the building.

Unfortunately, he didn't have time to learn the answers to his questions. He had work to return to. When she disappeared inside, he swung around and headed back.

Isabelle climbed the stairs of Asher Hall, opened the door, and looked about. She had three options. Straight ahead where stairs led up, a closed passageway to one side labeled ADMINISTRATION, or the opposite side labeled PROFESSOR OFFICES.

Adelaide was nowhere in sight. Why would Adelaide come here? Did her baby's father attend this college? Had her sister stayed down here? Or gone up a flight or even all the way to the third floor. Isabelle marched forward and ascended the staircase.

A long hallway stretched out to the left and right. She went up another flight. It looked much like the second, with doors along each side of the hallway.

She returned to the ground level, entered the administration area, and walked up to the counter. "I'm looking for my sister. She has blond hair and is wearing a yellow dress. She would have just come in here."

The woman attendant shook her head. "No one like that has come in recently."

"Thank you." Isabelle left and went across the foyer to the professors' offices. No one sat at the reception desk. Beyond it, a hallway of offices. Should she go down there? She glanced around and headed in search of someone. Anyone who could help her. Each door stood closed, and she couldn't see anyone through any of the narrow windows.

And what would she do if she found Adelaide and the baby's father? As her sister had said, the man would deny it was his, and there was no way for her sister to prove otherwise.

Isabelle returned outside and waited. What if Adelaide left through one of the other exits? She could be long gone. Isabelle would wait a little while. A few minutes later, her sister rushed out of the building and down the stone steps.

"Adelaide?"

Her sister looked up with a tear-stained face. She wiped her hands across her cheeks. "What are you doing here?"

"I would ask you the same, but I think I already know the answer. The baby's father?"

"He laughed at me and called me a silly girl. Said I could never prove it was his. I can't tell you who he is, Isabelle. I can't."

"I know. Father could pressure him into marrying you."

Fresh tears streamed. "He can't. He's already married, and his wife recently had a baby."

Married? The air choked in Isabelle's lungs. No point learning this scoundrel's identity. It would benefit no one, least of all Adelaide.

"I can't believe I thought I loved him. He's not even a very nice man. I think he only ever told me what I wanted to hear."

Her sister had always been gullible. This wasn't the first time she'd listened to the wrong person.

Adelaide brushed away the remainder of the moisture on her face and straightened her shoulders. "I've cried my last tear for that man."

Isabelle smiled. "Good for you. I'm proud of you."

"But I'm still going to have a baby. I wish I'd figure out what kind of person he was before."

So did Isabelle.

"Isabelle, you are the best sister anyone could ever have. I don't know what I would do without you."

She suspected Adelaide would have been in a lot more trouble and likely at a younger age. Isabelle had thought her sister had grown up enough to look out for herself, so she had become lax in her efforts to protect her. Therefore, Adelaide's predicament was partially Isabelle's fault. She knew better and should have been more vigilant. She had been too caught up in her own folly, riding a bicycle and irritating Marguerite. She had been the childish one, and Adelaide had paid the price. Too late to change things now.

Sixteen

On Thursday, Oliver sat at his dining room table with his breakfast before him and the local newspaper open in his hands. He folded it and set it beside his half-empty plate. The table, which could seat ten before any of the extensions were added, seemed strangely odd today. He'd never thought about his furniture or much about his house. But now he did.

Where would Isabelle sit? At the far end opposite him? Or near him to his right or left? He wanted her near, but with their rushed engagement and soon-to-be-marriage, the distance might be a better choice as it would reflect their relationship.

Would Isabelle like his house? Would she feel at home or like a stranger? He would give her an allowance to make whatever changes she wanted so she could feel like this was her home as well.

Home? This had never felt like a home to him. Just a house. Isabelle would make it a home.

His housekeeper rushed in. "I told them you were eating."

Belinda skirted around Mrs. Fielding. "Good morning, Oliver." She tugged at the fingers of her blue kid gloves.

Ellery came in behind her.

"Mrs. Fielding, thank you. Would you bring my guests plates?" His cook always prepared enough food for his modest staff of three—housekeeper, cook, and stable hand who took care of the grounds as well—so there should still be something ready in the kitchen.

Belinda waved her first freed glove in the air. "Don't bother. We already ate at the hotel."

Ellery kissed the back of Mrs. Fielding's hand. "If you would be a dear, please *do* bother on my account. I'm afraid I was rushed out before I had a chance to half eat my meal."

Oliver's housekeeper smiled at Ellery and left.

"Please sit. I don't have long before I need to leave for the bank."

Ellery held out a chair for his sister then sat after her.

Mrs. Fielding set a plate of scrambled eggs, ham slices, fried potatoes, and toast in front of Ellery.

"You are an angel." Ellery picked up his fork and took a bite of eggs.

Belinda rolled her eyes at her brother. "Oliver, it's been long enough since Francine passed away. You must marry again. It's your duty. To carry on your family's name."

It was too soon in the day to manage Belinda. "I am marrying."

"That girl's not right." She freed her second glove and held it aloft. "She has a secret. I can tell."

He, too, had sensed something was off and had attributed it to Isabelle being young and having wedding jitters. But could her peculiar behavior be due to something more?

"She is hardly worthy of you. She was raised on a farm. You need a cultured woman who can help you rise through the ranks of Philadelphia society."

He didn't much care for society life. A bunch of pomp and circumstance. Puffed egos and fancy clothes covering a host of flaws and insecurities.

"One who knows how to appropriately hostess parties for you."

Again, no interest.

"A wife can contribute to her husband's career greatly and just as easily be a detriment to it. I think we all know which kind Miss Atwood would be."

Oliver slapped his hands on the table and stood abruptly. "I've had enough of your disparaging remarks about my fiancée. If you're not going to speak kindly, please leave my home."

Ellery clapped his hands. "Bravo, my good man. Take the carriage, sister. I'll ride with Oliver to the bank. The hotel isn't far from there."

Belinda huffed. "I never said I was leaving. I'll try to

control myself."

That didn't sound very resolute, but Oliver returned to his seat. "*And* I have no plans to return to Philadelphia."

"Once you tire of this place, you'll return." She opened her handbag and pulled out a telegram. "I sent word to your parents. They are on their way. They will talk sense into you."

"You shouldn't have done that. You had no right. I'll likely already be married by the time they could get here. It will be a wasted trip."

He would like to have his parents at the wedding, but he didn't feel it wise to wait. He hadn't told them himself because the whole affair seemed so tenuous. Still did. Until the bride committed, he held the outcome in an open hand. She might not commit until she said—or didn't say—*I do.*

"You'll have to cancel the wedding. Once they arrive, they will talk you out of this foolhardy decision. They'll never approve of that girl."

Ellery took a swig of coffee. "I hate to say this, but I agree with my sister on calling off this wedding, but for completely different reasons. I found Miss Atwood to be fully delightful—"

"Delightful?" Belinda's voice grated.

"Watch your step, dear sister, or you'll be thrown out. Yes, *delightful.*" He shifted his gaze back to Oliver. "But I think you should stay single. Why get entangled with a woman who will nag you to death?"

Oliver couldn't imagine Isabelle being like that. "Miss Atwood isn't that sort of person."

Ellery swallowed a bite. "Maybe not in the beginning, but they all turn into nags in the end. Save yourself the trouble."

It didn't have to be that way. His first wife hadn't turned into a nag. True, they had been married only a year before she passed away. He shook those thoughts free. No good could come from listening to either one of them. Oliver stood again. "I'm not changing my mind. I need to get to the bank."

Ellery stood as well. "We'll take you in our rented

carriage. It's right out front." He forked a large chunk of ham and shoved it into his mouth.

Oliver didn't really want to ride with them after their comments, but it would be rude to turn them down. It would also save his stable hand the time and trouble of hitching Oliver's carriage and returning it here. His man would still come and get him at the end of the day. "Not one word about my impending marriage or my fiancée."

Belinda tugged on one glove. "You can hardly blame your friends for trying to spare you from inevitable strife."

"Mrs. Fielding?"

His housekeeper returned to the dining room. "Yes, sir."

"Have Foster hitch up—"

Belinda stomped her foot and gave Oliver an icy glare. "Fine. I'll be as quiet as a church mouse."

Ellery nodded his consent as well.

Would either abide by their own agreement? One of the reasons he'd left his home town and come west was overbearing and opinionated people like these who could be so tiring. He didn't miss those circles of people. Isabelle and her family were refreshing and so much easier to be around—even Mrs. Atwood.

Henny stood in her kitchen double-checking the plethora of items she needed to take to the field where the Founders Day Festival would be held. Today, tents and booths would be set up in preparations for Saturday's events. Some people would gather on Friday night for the bonfire and sing-along, but the bulk of the events would take place on Saturday.

Her boarder Job Lumbard, professor at the teacher's college, stood in the doorway, an older man with white hair and beard. "You have a minute?"

Strange. Both of her boarders would have usually left by now. "Of course. What can I do for you?"

"I've debated for the past three days on whether or

not to say anything. I don't like gossip. See no need for it."

"I don't like gossip either. It usually only hurts the people involved. If it's gossip, I'd rather you refrain from telling me."

He fingered his well-trimmed beard. "I'm not sure it is gossip. If someone asks you a question with nothing more in mind than to help someone else, would it be gossip to answer the question if your intent is to help as well?"

A fine line separated help and gossip. "I suppose if it would help someone in need, it would depend on the circumstances. But I don't recall asking you a question you didn't answer."

"It wasn't you who did the asking. Another party asked you a question I might know the answer to."

"I see." Though curious, she didn't want to cross that fine line.

"So, would it be gossip for me to tell you? If you had known the answer, I'm sure you would have told this person."

She worked her mouth back and forth. A difficult dilemma. "Maybe you should give the answer to the person who posed the question."

"I don't feel right about that. I don't know the lady well enough. Not like you do."

A lady? She bit her bottom lip, not wanting to participate in gossip. "What if you told me the question? Then we could decide from there." Terribly thin ice Henny was treading on.

"That seems fitting. On Monday, you were talking to that Atwood girl in front of the mercantile."

She thought back. "Isabelle?"

He nodded. "She inquired about whom her sister might be keeping company with."

Now Henny really wanted to know but needed to be careful. "Will it help either Isabelle or her sister to tell me?"

"I don't know. I'll tell you the facts I know, and you can decide what to do with the information. If you'll let me."

The Atwoods were going through some difficult times

right now, and if Henny could help, she wanted to. "All right. Go ahead." *Lord, forgive me if this is gossip.*

"I've seen the younger Atwood girl at the college in the area of the professors' offices on a number of occasions. I don't know who she was visiting, but I do know she's not enrolled at the college."

"Maybe she's getting information to take classes in the future."

His white eyebrows pulled together. "Several times? Without either of her parents? Unlikely."

That was a little out of acceptable propriety. Adelaide couldn't attend the college without her parents giving their approval, and she couldn't take classes without their financial support. Besides, Marguerite would never consent to her daughter becoming a schoolteacher. Not with a lord waiting in the wings.

Mr. Lumbard dipped his head. "That's all I know." He turned and left with Mr. Tunstall, Henny's other regular boarder who also taught at the college.

"Thank you." Henny wasn't sure what it meant or what she should do with the information.

Someone knocked on her kitchen door.

She opened it to widower Saul Hammond who'd offered to help her take things to the festival grounds. He was such a sweet gentleman.

He furrowed his eyebrows. "Something's got you worried."

"Why do you say that?"

"You have that look. A burden shared is a burden halved."

Saul was a good friend and trustworthy. And perhaps, a bit more. "I've learned a piece of information about a particular person, but I'm not sure what it means." Since she didn't know the ramification of it, to repeat what she'd been told *would* be gossip.

"But you sense it might be important once you figure out the significance."

It was hard to know for certain. She felt as though she'd just been handed the center piece of a large mysterious puzzle. "I think it could be."

Saul donned a thoughtful expression. "I've found

when a matter is troubling me—and I've done about all the thinking on it I can—if I turn my mind to other things, whatever the issue is becomes clearer. Whether that's understanding on my part or a solution."

Henny hadn't exactly done much thinking on it. Hadn't had a chance yet. "You're right. I'll try to set my thoughts aside if I can." She doubted she could. She kept picturing Adelaide at the college but not taking classes. What could she be doing there?

"I'll help you load these things into my wagon." He hefted a small crate of canned fruits to be auctioned. Each of the quilting circle ladies contributed one item or another, some several. Single men eagerly purchased most any homemade food product. With the number of outlying ranches and farms, hungry bachelors were a plenty.

After everything was loaded, she sat next to Saul on the wagon seat and pulled her shawl tighter. The breeze coming down the canyon had put a chill in the autumn morning air and clouds gathered overhead. She had been warm enough while carting everything out to the wagon, but not so now.

Saul drove down one of the main thoroughfares of town.

The Atwoods' carriage sat outside the French dressmaker's shop. Marguerite made grand hand gestures to her driver and pointed. He held several large parcels stacked in his arms. Dresses no doubt. She seemed more distressed than usual.

Henny's talk with Marguerite earlier this week came rushing back. Particularly the news that Isabelle was expecting. She kept replaying it in her mind and realized Marguerite had made a slight hesitation before speaking Isabelle's name. A pause Henny had attributed to the delicate nature of the news. The shape of her mouth had changed minutely. Henny replicated the movements of Marguerite's mouth from the initial letter in Isabelle to the other shape and back and forth. What had Marguerite been going to say? She mouthed her way through the alphabet, and it could be only one letter, an "A", for the other daughter. As of late, Adelaide had been paler than normal and grimacing at food.

"Are you talking to yourself?" Saul asked from beside her.

"Stop the wagon."

"In the middle of the street?"

She patted his hand. "Yes, right here. I need to get out."

"Whoa." Saul hauled back on the reins. "What's wrong?"

"You were right. I turned my mind to other things, and the meaning became clear." That and seeing Marguerite. She climbed down as fast as she could, favoring her weak leg.

"Be careful," Saul called after her.

"I am." Henny hobbled over to the dressmaker shop. As she stepped up onto the boardwalk, she lifted her cane. "Good morning, Marguerite. May I have a word with you?"

Her friend smiled. "I'm in a bit of a hurry."

"I just have a quick question. It's about your daughters." Henny moved away from the carriage and the driver.

Marguerite followed. "What is it? Are you all right? You look positively flustered."

If Henny's deduction was correct, she was flustered all right. "I figured it out." She lowered her voice. "Adelaide's the one who is with child." Likely by a professor who should know better. "Why did you tell me it was Isabelle?"

Marguerite blanched and glanced around before she spoke in a whisper. "I never said Isabelle was in the family way, only that she was *expecting* a child."

Semantics. "Implying it was Isabelle. She's going to raise Adelaide's baby? With Mr. Mallory?"

"Adelaide is hardly up to the task. She's too young for that kind of responsibility. You understand, don't you?"

Adelaide was both young in years as well as being a bit immature, but that could be because Marguerite always told her what to do. The poor girl never had a chance to think for herself.

"You wouldn't want her to be burdened with a child at her tender age. I trust you'll keep this to yourself."

"You know I will."

"Good. Now, I have a lot of wedding preparations to take care of before Tuesday." Marguerite climbed into her carriage.

Henny watched her leave, too dumbfounded to move.

Saul came up next to her. "Are you all right?"

"I'm fine." But how would Isabelle and Adelaide fare through all of this?

Seventeen

A COLD WIND FROM THE NORTH blew down the canyon. A fall storm rolling in had put a decidedly brisk chill in the air. The change in temperature reminded Isabelle winter was on its way, and with it, she would lose the freedom of her bicycle on snowy days. But then she would likely be shipped off for the winter to who knew where with Adelaide. She gripped the handlebars tighter. Would Marguerite come as well? Probably.

A disturbing thought swept into Isabelle's mind. What if Oliver refused to allow her to pack up and leave for several months? That would dislodge a few railroad ties in this out-of-control locomotive. Had her stepmother accounted for that possibility? Of course she had. Oliver would be no match against Marguerite's persuasion. If he proved formidable, Father would insist, claiming it to be part of the favor Oliver owed. Or they might send Isabelle and Adelaide away while Oliver was at work and inform him his wife had already left town on an urgent family matter.

If her family and this whole situation were a runaway train, which part was she? The caboose? No, if she were, it would be easy to detach herself from the rest. She certainly wasn't the engine. But then neither was Adelaide, even though it had all started with her. Marguerite definitely drove this train. Adelaide felt like the caboose, though part of the train, she trailed along where everyone else led. If any of the cars uncoupled from the rest, she'd go with them. So that left Isabelle and Father as the carriages in between the two. Oliver fell somewhere in the middle as well. Trapped, like Isabelle, between Adelaide and Marguerite.

She shook the thought of the unwanted situation to the back of her mind as she pushed her bicycle to the clearing where she'd fed Tramp and his friends the day before. She unstrapped the picnic basket with a hinged lid and removed the sack of scraps from within it. Cook had once again held aside several things for this ragtag pack. "Tramp? Here boy."

The scruffy dog pranced out from underneath a nearby fir tree followed by his friends who kept their distance.

Again, she had many other things she should be doing—like wedding plans—but her stepmother had that well in hand. The only decisions Isabelle was allowed to make were the ones which agreed with Marguerite. Besides, ignoring the whole affair made it seem less real. Disregard it and maybe the entire problem would go away. Now, she sounded like Adelaide.

She set the basket on the ground. "I have a plan for how to get you dogs to follow me. You need to be safe for the winter and out of the harsh weather. I have the perfect place in mind, but it's temporary. I'll get Grant to feed you while I'm away. He won't mind." She could always depend on him.

Maybe Oliver would allow her to keep the animals if she pleaded with him. He'd said no because he wouldn't be around, but after they married—if they married—she would be at home. At least after the baby was born. Maybe Shane could take one or two of the animals. He had a lot of space out on his large ranch. How could she ask him when it would be best if she never saw him again?

She pointed to the kitten and duck. "It's the two of you who might be tricky. You wouldn't consider jumping into my basket all on your own now, would you?"

The duck ruffled its feathers, and the kitten hissed.

"I didn't think so. I guess I'll have to catch each of you in turn." She held out a piece of bread crust to the duck.

He hopped toward her and took the morsel.

The dogs sniffed the air but remained rooted in place.

She held out another piece and drew the duck closer and closer to the lidded basket. She tossed one inside the basket.

He stretched his neck over the edge but couldn't reach the bribe, so he flapped his wings to lift himself up and over the edge. Once inside, he pecked at the crumb.

Isabelle tossed in the rest of the slice, but before she could close the lid to keep him from escaping, the duck hunkered down, satisfied with his surroundings.

Now for the kitten.

She took off her cloak and flung it over the hissing orange ball of fur. She scooped up her cloak and the kitten in a bundle. The kitten quieted and went limp.

Oh, dear. She hadn't hurt it, had she? She pulled back the fabric just enough to take a peek.

The kitten lay contentedly in her arms.

She petted her head, and the furry one purred. "You little rascal. All that hissing was for naught." She tucked her into the basket with the duck, gave her some cooked ham to eat and closed the lid. Hopefully, those two were as good of friends as she imagined. She strapped the basket onto the back of her bicycle, securing the lid.

The dogs were another matter altogether, but she had her plan. Whether it worked or not was something else.

She waved a hambone with a generous amount of meat still clinging to it in front of the dogs.

Tramp rose up on his hind legs for it. The other two stretched their necks and sniffed the air.

"If you want this, you're going to have to follow me." Tied with a rope, the bone dangled from the back of the basket. She climbed on her bicycle and kicked it forward. "Come on, everyone. Let's go." She glanced over her shoulder as she rode.

Tramp trotted a few feet, stopped, and barked. The other two stood even farther back.

No sense to worry about them right now. One problem at a time. Once she got the kitten and duck settled, she would figure out another way to get the dogs. Tramp would be easy enough, but if she left the other two behind, they wouldn't likely fare the winter very well.

She pedaled as quickly as she could to the little bedraggled house Grant had repudiated. The abandoned homestead would suit her purposes well. As the first few cold drops speckled her face, she cycled around to the modest barn, opened the door, and walked her bicycle inside, closing the door behind her.

The gaps between the wall boards allowed enough light in for her to see a bit. The back stall had enough broken lower boards to allow the animals a way to come and go as they needed to. But they would know they had a safe place here.

After unstrapping the basket, she set it on the ground, and lifted the lid.

The kitten and duck lay curled up together. The kitten hissed and jumped out. She zeroed in on the ham bone lying on the ground and attacked it.

When Isabelle tried to move it, the kitten growled and put a claw-extended paw on it while gnawing at the meat.

Isabelle held up her hand. "Fine. Eat the whole thing."

Though the duck watched her, it stayed nestled inside the basket.

Did she have time to go back for the dogs? Only if they cooperated. She could at least try.

She pushed her bicycle to the door and opened it. The three dogs stared up at her in a light rain. She stepped back. "Come on in. Come on."

Tramp pranced inside and shook his whole body, throwing water everywhere, including all over Isabelle. Though the other two looked in, they remained outside.

Isabelle receded into the shadows and stood as still as she could.

The pair of dogs skulked through the doorway, saw Isabelle, and darted over to where Tramp stood by the growling kitten with the ham bone. They shook to dry off as well.

Isabelle gazed out at the rain. She had gotten here just in time but would have to ride home in this if it kept up. She closed the door to keep any of the animals from escaping if they spooked. If only she could get men to do her bidding this easily, life could be a whole lot simpler. "Not quite fair that the little one gets the whole bone. But not to worry, I have something for the rest of you." She sat on an upturned crate and doled out the ham and fat bits, which were scarfed down without being chewed.

Once the kitten had eaten its fill, one of the dogs could have the bone.

Tramp came over to her and nudged his head under Isabelle's hand. She petted him. "I know I have more pressing matters than looking after a few strays, but it's nice to think of someone other than myself. I wish I could stay here with you fellows. Leave all my worries behind and forget the rest of the world exists." How nice that would be.

She blew out a breath and studied the diverse animal pack. "I think it's time I gave you each a name. Tramp, you have one. Duck, you can be Hopper."

The duck, who had gotten out of the basket, shook its head and ruffled his feathers.

"You don't like that name? How about Emerald on account of your green head?"

He shook his head again and quacked.

"You are a picky one." Exasperated, she threw up her hands. "What do you think you are? Royalty? King Arthur?"

He bobbed his head up and down then settled on some straw.

"You think you're something special, do you? Very well, King Arthur."

She determined the kitten was a girl. "Buttercup. Do you like that?"

With a full belly, the feline didn't seem to care and curled up on Isabelle's lap.

She determined the spaniel to be a boy. "I'll name you Trefoil after the pea plant on account of your color and three legs." She pointed to the Lab, a girl. "And you shall be Shadow because you blend in so well."

The barn door opened with a creak.

With a gasp, Isabelle jumped to her feet and spun around, dislodging poor Buttercup. "Mercy." She faced a silhouetted figure in the doorway.

He stepped inside. "What are you doing in here?"

She slapped her hand to her chest and released her captive breath. "Grant, you scared me."

He removed his hat and shook the rain off.

The two dogs skittered away as did the kitten. King Arthur quacked, and Tramp trotted up to Grant.

Grant crouched and petted him. "You have some motley group here. I saw them following you. What is all this?"

"These poor animals have no homes. With winter coming, they'll need shelter. And since this place is abandoned, I figured it wouldn't hurt for them to stay here."

He straightened. "You realize this place belongs to *someone*?"

"But they're not using it right now. I'll bring the animals food until I can figure out another solution. This will give them a place out of the weather."

He shook his head. "You have a soft heart. The hotel usually has scraps from the dining room. I'll see if Hazel will save them for me."

She leapt over to him and gave him a quick hug. "Thank you. I appreciate this *so* much."

He ducked his head. "You're welcome."

Grant always came through for her. The animals might very well get enough to eat with two sources of food.

The rain had ceased, so Isabelle walked with Grant back to the hotel.

"Grant, what do you think our responsibility is to our families?"

"I'm not sure what you mean."

She wasn't sure either. "Should a person do anything their parents ask of them, even if they don't want to?"

He tightened his face the way he did when he was thinking. "If it's within the person's power and it's not illegal, I guess they should. Wouldn't you want to know your family was there to support you no matter what happens?"

Why couldn't he have given her a way out? "Yes." She hated to admit it. She wanted to confide everything to him, but at the same time, she didn't want her best friend to know how low she'd been driven. She left her bicycle outside and went into the lobby with him, stopping short just over the threshold. She should have known better than to come in here.

Miss Young stood at the desk, berating the clerk behind it.

Isabelle touched Grant's arm. "I'll let you get to work."

"Get out while you can. I'd go with you, but this is my job."

Miss Young swiveled around, narrowed her eyes at Isabelle and sneered at her bicycle dress.

"Too late," Grant said. "You've been spotted."

Isabelle could still be rude and walk away without speaking to the woman, but she crossed the lobby instead. "Miss Young, how nice to see you again. I didn't realize you were still in town." She wished the woman would go back to where she'd come from.

"Oh, I'm not leaving anytime soon." Her gaze flickered to Grant. "Does Oliver know about your gentleman friend?"

Grant straightened his shoulders. "We are just that. Friends."

If Grant were a dog, his hackles would be sticking straight up.

"Oliver is very much aware of my friendship with my childhood chum."

The hotel manager stepped out of his office. "Good. Mr. Dawson, I was hoping to find you here. Come into my office." The man turned on his heel and disappeared.

Grant glanced between Isabelle and Miss Young.

Isabelle smiled. "I'll be fine."

He shrugged and headed off to do his boss's bidding.

Miss Young smiled smugly. "I had breakfast with Oliver this morning."

The woman apparently thought to bait Isabelle, trying to make a situation sound like something it probably wasn't. She would like to scratch the woman's eyes out but refrained and changed the subject. "Our annual Founders Day Festival is Saturday. I hope you'll come. You and your brother could enter the three-legged race."

Miss Young gasped then composed herself. "I know something you don't."

"I'm sure you do. Good-day, Miss Young." Isabelle

pivoted to leave.

"It's something about you. Something vitally important to your future."

Don't turn around, Isabelle. Don't take her bait. She swung back around against her own counsel. "I'm not interested." But she was and ached to know what ridiculous thing Miss Young would say.

"You won't be marrying Oliver on Tuesday."

Had Oliver changed his mind in light of this woman's arrival and said something to her? Isabelle should welcome this turn of events, but something inside her flared. Was that jealousy?

Oh, dear.

She couldn't possibly be falling for him, could she? She shook her head to free the absurd idea. Must be her mind playing tricks on her. Her heart getting used to her inevitable future. Or simply that a kind man like Oliver deserved someone more good-natured than Miss Young?

"Did you hear me? You won't be marrying Oliver on Tuesday."

"Is that so?" Her voice came out a little shaky.

"You must postpone the wedding."

Isabelle would like nothing more. "I can't." Marguerite was an unstoppable locomotive.

"Oliver is too much of a gentleman to say anything, so I will. You wouldn't deny his parents the opportunity of being in attendance at his wedding—their *only* son— would you?" She touched her upper chest with her slender fingers. "His poor mother. She would be heartbroken."

His mother? Oh, dear. Isabelle hadn't considered his parents and, obviously, neither had her parents. Would they approve of her? Or try to stop the wedding?

"I've sent them a telegram. They are coming. So you see, marrying Tuesday is out of the question."

For the first time, this wedding was at risk. Legitimately at risk. "We'll see about that." Isabelle sashayed away before Miss Young could make any more disparaging remarks and kept herself from running as she crossed the lobby. Once outside, she breathed a sigh of relief.

"My sister does that to people."

Isabelle spun around to face Mr. Young leaning against the building.

He chuckled. "I didn't take you for the timid type. Oliver is fortunate to have found you."

Though she'd never wanted this marriage arrangement, she found the prospect of Oliver for her husband less unappealing than before she'd gotten to know him. "Did he say anything about our wedding? About... postponing?"

"Of course not. Don't let my sister rattle you."

She hated to admit it, but the woman had. A woman who knew his parents well enough to send them a telegram. A woman whom they probably already approved of.

He pushed away from the hotel front. "The key to dealing with Belinda is to not let her smell your fear. Square your shoulders, chin up, and don't back down."

Was he genuinely trying to be helpful? Or teasing her? Maybe a little of both. "Will Oliver's parents try to stop the wedding? Do they hope he'll marry your sister?"

"Oliver is his own man. He will marry whomever he chooses to. Even if he for some reason chose to call off your wedding—which I doubt very much he would—I find it highly unlikely he would marry Belinda. I would be forced to kidnap him first."

She appreciated his reassurance.

"If you were a shrew like my sister or some spineless creature, I would do everything in my power to keep Oliver from marrying you."

Was that a threat? "I'm not sure how to take that."

"If you are everything you appear to be, then you have my blessing. But if not..." He tipped his hat and strode down the boardwalk.

Isabelle fixed her gaze on his retreating form. Exactly what did he think she appeared to be? She had never tried to hide her true self, so he had seen the real her. She climbed on her bicycle and rode to the bank. Inside, a young man ushered her into Oliver's office.

Oliver stood and motioned toward the chair. "This is a most pleasant surprise. Have a seat."

She sat. Which subject to bring up first? "It's about your parents. I never thought about them wanting to be at the wedding. Should we postpone until they can arrive?"

"No need. I received a telegram moments before you arrived. It had apparently gotten misplaced at the telegraph office on Tuesday. My parents took the first train out of Philadelphia and will arrive on Tuesday morning. They should be here in time."

"I'm happy to hear that." Fear mixed with disappointment. Fear he would cancel the wedding spoiling the plan to help Adelaide, and disappointment he hadn't canceled, which would free Isabelle from this predicament. "Will they try to stop the wedding?"

"I doubt it."

Not a firm answer. It left a lot of room for them to object to his marrying her. "What if they don't approve of me?"

He took her hand and patted it. "You have nothing to worry about. I make my own decisions."

Just what Mr. Young had said, but she did worry. "There is one other thing I think you should know about. I stopped in at the hotel and ran into Miss Young."

"Please don't listen to her, darling. I don't know why she's trying to cause trouble."

Darling? How could the endearment be appealing? It shouldn't be. She pushed it out of her thoughts. "Why? Because she wants to be Mrs. Oliver Mallory."

"That will never happen. Again, nothing to worry about."

"That's good to know, but I wasn't worried. I just thought you should know she made innuendoes about the two of you."

He frowned. "Dare I ask what she said?"

"It wasn't so much the particular words but how she said them. She claimed the two of you had breakfast together, implying..."

He held up a hand. "I know what she was implying. She and Ellery stopped by my house this morning during breakfast. That's all. She didn't even eat anything. I nearly threw her out."

Isabelle smiled. "You did? I would have liked to have seen that."

Oliver smiled as well. He had a warm, endearing smile. "If she continues to cause a fuss, you may have that opportunity."

Something to look forward to where Miss Young was concerned.

He leaned forward. "She believes you are harboring some sinister secret."

The air froze in Isabelle's lungs. "A secret?" Oh, she had a secret all right.

"Don't worry. She's simply trying to stir things up. I understand if you're having wedding jitters. Please don't let how fast everything is happening upset you. I'll give you time to adjust after we're married."

She couldn't afford to take time to adjust. "I assure you I'll be fine. By the time Tuesday rolls around, I'll be all adjusted." At least she hoped so.

He scratched the pen across the paper as it ran out of ink and stopped to redip it. He studied his seventh attempt at poetry. Would Isabelle Atwood like it? It was no Shakespeare but better than flowers and honey.

He had the worst timing. He'd planned to woo her over several weeks. Had many poems selected to send her. Get her so intrigued to know who was leaving her letters she'd be willing to take a chance on him. See that there was more to him than met the eye.

But now, he needed to act fast. This could be his last opportunity to tell her how deep his feelings for her ran. His one chance to steal her away from another. If he didn't tell her now, he would forever hold his declaration to himself. And continue to suffer in silence as he saw her every day on the arm of someone else.

He crumpled another piece of paper and tossed it into the wastebasket with the other half a dozen sheets. He was no good at poetry. The lines didn't make sense together. A jumbled mess. He very much wanted to create his own piece for her, to show her how much he cared, but it was no use. He would never be a poet. The reason he'd copied others' work. He reinked his pen and put it to a clean sheet.

My Dearest Isabelle,
I tried writing my own poem for you, but I'm no good at it. Time after time everything came out all wrong. The same as when I try to tell you how I feel in person, the words get all caught up in my throat like a logjam. So, no romantic musings from another this time and no poem written by me, just earnest words from my heart.

He dipped the pen in the ink again and let it hover over the paper. He'd thought it would be easier to write his feelings rather than speak them, but they got stuck as well. He cleared his throat and swallowed hard to dislodge them. Dare he say how he felt straight away? Or lead up to it? Or explain things to her? Or...?

There is so much I want to tell you. You would probably laugh and call me foolish were we face to face. Could the unattainable be attainable? I know I'm not good enough for you, but I can't help how I feel. I love you, Isabelle Atwood. I want to marry you but dare not ask in a letter. If you would at least entertain the notion, meet me under the old elm by the pond—

When should he ask her to meet him? He'd like it to be tomorrow or Saturday, but with all the ruckus and chaos with Founders Day, she might be too busy. Get waylaid. Or it could slip her mind with all the fuss. Then he'd never know if she meant to come and couldn't, or if she chose not to meet him. Would Sunday work? That might not be any better. Monday? He couldn't wait any longer than that, or else it would be too late. He wished it could be sooner.

...Monday at noon.
If you come, I'll be forever grateful you've given me a

chance. If you don't, I will bother you no more, but my heart will always belong to you and only you.

Oh, bother. *Earnest words from my heart? Forever grateful? My heart will always belong to you?* He couldn't give her something this sappy. She would probably laugh. This was no good. He pushed the paper away from him. He should abandon all hope.

Eighteen

On Friday morning, Henny stood behind a table along one side of the town hall interior with other women from all across Kamola. She circled her hands in front of her. "Gather round, ladies."

Everyone huddled up on the opposite side of the table.

"I'm impressed by the plethora of items for this year's Founders Day live and silent auctions. My quilting circle has donated a quilt as well as a basket of fabric squares to be put into a quilt. The students and professors at the teacher's college have given a slew of books. The ladies' auxiliary contributed several household items, including a wringer washtub. Franny and her father have donated a kerosene lamp from Waldon's Mercantile. Mademoiselle Dumont made this beautiful walking suit." She pointed to the garment on the dress form. "Which includes a fitting. Mrs. Kesner's contribution is generous again this year with a treadle sewing machine and a silver tea service, among other things."

The ladies clapped lightly to honor the wealthiest lady in town.

Henny continued down her list of donations by the various groups, individuals, and families. "And everyone has contributed an assortment of canned and baked goods. This may be our best auction yet. The money raised with this auction as well as from the box social will go a long way to build a gymnasium for the school so the children will have a warm place to run around during the cold winter months."

Oo's and ah's rippled through the group then a few comments rose.

"I wish there had been a gymnasium when I attended school."

"My nose nearly froze off."

"Don't forget how nice it will be for the children when it rains."

"This has been long overdue."

The use for this year's money had been agreed upon by most people in town.

"We need to make a place card for each item naming the donor. The ones in the silent auction will also require a bidding sheet created with a description, its value, and a suggested opening bid at half the value."

"Most things will be part of the silent auction. The sewing machine, the walking suit, the quilt, and a handful of other larger items will be auctioned off live. The food donations need to go on the tables across the room and the others on the tables on this side. As people arrive, direct them as to where to place their contributions. I need someone to put together baskets with various items." After assigning everyone a task, Henny called Isabelle over, having saved her for last. "I could use your help in creating an inventory sheet of everything to be auctioned with a description, value, final bid, and who won it."

Henny guided Isabelle away from the others to a small table at the back with a pair of stools. "I wanted to talk to you privately."

"What about?"

Henny leaned in and whispered, "I know about the baby."

Isabelle's eyes widened. "You do? How?"

"Marguerite told me."

"My stepmother?" Isabelle shook her head. "I find that unbelievable."

"Believe it." Though it hadn't been a direct confession. "I was surprised at first, in more ways than one, but then once I had time to think on it, everything made perfect Marguerite sense."

"So you understand why I have to marry Mr. Mallory?" The girl slumped onto a stool.

"Not exactly. Marguerite told me that you are the one with child."

"What!"

Marguerite sauntered over. "Is everything all right? Do you need any help?"

Henny sat on the second stool. "No, no. We're fine." She handed a sheet of paper to Isabelle and spoke to Marguerite again. "How are the ladies doing who are creating the baskets of various goods?"

Marguerite waved a hand in the air. "They are having a time of it, deciding what to put in each of them."

"Could you remind them to keep track of the value of each item included so we can have an accurate value for the whole basket?"

"Certainly." Marguerite strolled off.

Henny watched her walk away. "I'm surprised she came—both of you came—with all the wedding preparations."

Isabelle used her Marguerite voice. "We can't shirk our civic duties. How would that look to people?" She picked up the pencil lying on the table. "What were those categories? Item, value, and winning bid?"

"And the highest bidder's name." Henny faced Isabelle again. "Don't worry. I know it's Adelaide who's with child."

"How if my stepmother told you I was the one?"

"Everything added up. Adelaide being peaked in recent weeks. You asking if Adelaide had been seen with any young men. The way she's been leaning back in her chair to keep pressure off her abdomen, *and,* most of all, Marguerite not getting after her for it. Last but not least, I believe it would be out of character for you, and I know you would do a great many things for your sister. What I don't understand is, if it's Adelaide who's expecting, why are you the one who has to marry immediately?"

Isabelle bit her bottom lip. "I'm supposed to pretend I'm the one expecting so Adelaide will have an untarnished reputation and will be able to marry the lord."

Unbelievable. "And Mr. Mallory is fine with all this chicanery?"

"That's what bothers me most and has been keeping me from going through with this. He has a right to know, doesn't he?"

"Marguerite gave me the distinct impression he knew. He doesn't?"

Isabelle shook her head again. "He's never said anything to me about it, and I think he would have. He should be told, but it could ruin everything for Adelaide."

Regardless of the outcome, the man should definitely be told. If he found out after the wedding, things could be a lot worse for everyone involved. Not only would Adelaide's reputation be ruined but also Isabelle's and their parents'. No good could come of this. The trouble in Henny knowing all this information was she wasn't the one with the right to tell the oblivious man.

Aunt Henny straightened the blank papers to make herself appear busy. "I take it you don't wish to marry Mr. Mallory?"

"I... I don't know." The distressed girl twisted one hand in the other. "There's more to it than simply marrying him. I don't know what to do. I need to protect Adelaide from any further trouble. I don't know what else to do. Marrying Mr. Mallory seems like the best solution. This whole thing is Marguerite's idea."

Henny had figured as much. The woman meant well but was pressuring her stepdaughter into a marriage she clearly didn't want. "If you choose not to marry him and need a place to live, you can stay in one of my rooms."

"That's nice to know. But I think I might be able to bring myself to marry him." Isabelle finally wrote the categories across the long side of the paper.

"But?"

"But it's not right for him to be uninformed. She thinks because he is a little older, he will be thrilled to have a wife and child. Any wife and child."

"You're right. You shouldn't start off a marriage with lies." *Please let this girl do the right thing and confess the truth to Mr. Mallory before it's too late.*

"I didn't directly lie to him, but I haven't told him the truth either." Isabelle drew lines down the page between the columns. "If I do, he might not marry me. It's not my secret to tell. I would feel as though I would be betraying Adelaide's confidence."

She had a hard decision to make.

"What about the baby's father? Has he been told? I may have a lead on him."

"I had hoped to find him and force him to make this right, though I know Marguerite would never approve."

How true. Few gentlemen would be acceptable to Marguerite, and none without titles. "But now you don't think the father will do what's right?"

Isabelle drooped her shoulders. "He already has a wife *and* a new baby."

"Gracious." Henny put her hand on Isabelle's. Knowing the father was a professor wouldn't be any help at all.

After a sigh, the girl continued. "I believe Marguerite might send Adelaide and me away after the wedding night and later tell Mr. Mallory I'm expecting. I'll have the baby while I'm gone, then return with a little one in my arms and let him believe it's his. I think I'm prepared to marry him and raise Adelaide's child, but it's not fair to Mr. Mallory to not have the option to make the same decision for himself."

"I agree. I also agree the secret of the baby isn't yours to tell." A delicate situation such as this needed to be handled with caution. It would be a whole lot easier if the groom knew all the facts before agreeing to this marriage. "Could you convince Adelaide to tell him?"

"I doubt she would cross Marguerite. She's too frightened and overwhelmed with everything. She just wants it all to go away. I'm afraid this might break her."

"But it won't you?"

Isabelle drummed the pencil on the table. "A lot of women have fine marriages that are arranged for them."

But going into one with such a huge secret wouldn't bode well for anyone. "You had hopes of falling in love." What girl didn't?

Isabelle pursed her lips. "Love doesn't guarantee happiness."

"It helps."

She increased the beat with the pencil. "Mr. Mallory is a good man."

Henny covered the girl's hand to still her nervous movements and stop the clacking. "Even so, it makes you sad to not be in love with him."

Isabelle sat quiet a moment. "I think this is best for everyone."

"My offer stands. If you decide to defy your parents in this, know that you can always stay with me." If Henny'd had someone to offer her similar help in her time of need, things could have turned out very different for her.

"I can't believe you would do that for me."

"I would. For you and Adelaide. And the baby." It would be scandalous, but what was one more scandal in Henny's life?

With the sun having almost set, Isabelle and her father roamed through the crowd gathered for the evening's festivities. The bonfire would be lit momentarily. Grant should be around here someplace. He came every year. She really wanted to talk to him.

After a lot of begging, Father had agreed to escort her. Adelaide wasn't allowed to attend for fear of her secret being exposed, and Marguerite hadn't wanted to come. Both of which suited Isabelle. She had taken advantage of her father's guilt for what he was forcing her to do and coerced him to bring her. She would have preferred to come alone, but that had been completely out of the question without a chaperone. Her reputation had to be protected. Father had been the compromise.

"Father, I'm going to look for Grant by the edge of the grounds nearest town."

He shook his head. "You really shouldn't be looking for one man when you are engaged to another."

"Grant is only a friend, and this engagement wasn't my idea. I won't be long." She strolled off. She needed to talk to her best friend.

Knowing Aunt Henny would give her and Adelaide sanctuary only served to confuse Isabelle. She now had an alternate option, didn't she? Could she get Adelaide to agree to it? Staying with Aunt Henny would mean disgrace for Adelaide, as well as for her father and Marguerite. Secrets were atrocious things. Burdensome to live with and hard to confess. The longer a secret remained concealed, the more damage it would do in the end. If people would be forgiving and not hold Adelaide's poor choices against her, it wouldn't be so difficult of a choice.

Isabelle located Grant walking toward the yet-to-be-lit bonfire. "There you are."

His eyes widened. "I didn't expect you to be here. I almost didn't come myself."

"I'm glad you did."

Grant glanced around. "Where's your fiancé?"

Likely at home listening to Miss Young extolling her virtues while listing off Isabelle's many faults. "I doubt he would come to an event like this. It doesn't seem like his kind of function."

"That's why I didn't expect you to be here since you are engaged to him."

"Well, I am here, and I have something to show you." She tugged on the drawstring opening of her reticule and withdrew a folded sheet of paper. "This was waiting on my bicycle this morning."

He cocked an eyebrow. "Another love poem?"

"No. This one's better. All his own words. He poured out his heart."

"That's better?" He frowned.

"Definitely."

"Are you going to read it aloud to me like the others?"

"I'm not sure." This one was more personal.

"Then why mention it?" He shook his head. "That's like telling someone you have a secret you won't tell them so they will beg to be told. You are a cruel woman."

She supposed that had been callous. She had wanted Grant to be happy for her, to understand, but how could he when he knew nothing of the contents? "He said he loves me and wants to marry me."

Grant stopped short and gaped. "Love? Marry?" He pointed to the paper. "Are you taking that seriously? You don't think it's a lark?"

"He sounds so earnest." And she desperately wanted something other than her real life to be true.

"Then why does he hide behind pieces of paper?"

"I don't know. It's romantic. Maybe he's afraid. It can be scary to tell someone your feelings not knowing if they will return them." She knew the sting of that all too well. She'd poured out her feelings to Grant all those years ago, only to have him pull away from her.

He narrowed his eyes. "How are you supposed to return anything? This is a one-sided communication."

She bit her bottom lip. "He wants me to meet him on Monday at noon under the elm tree by the pond."

Grant studied her a moment. "Are you considering going?"

"Of course."

"Even though you'll be marrying someone else the next day."

"I'm dying to know who he is."

"Izzy, you don't know what kind of man this is."

"I know, but I want to find out about the man behind the words."

"You are hopeless."

"Go with me."

He scowled. "Me? I don't think that would be a good idea. That would put a damper on a romantic rendezvous. If he sees me, he might not show up. No, I can't go."

"You can stay out of sight."

"I have work."

"It's during your lunch. Please say you'll go with me."

He heaved a sigh. "Fine. I'll go."

"Thank you, thank you, thank you."

That evening after Isabelle returned home, Adelaide entered her room with her hands tucked behind her back. "I have a favor to ask of you."

Wasn't marrying a man she didn't want to in order to cover up her sister's indiscretion a big enough favor?

"Well, it's more of a question."

"Ask."

She moved her hands in front of her to reveal a yellow and lavender nine-patch quilt block. "I want to make a quilt for the baby. Would that be all right?"

Isabelle took the block. Her sister never much cared for quilting. The small, tight stitching attested to the care which went into this piece. Not like most of Adelaide's work. Her sister grew impatient while sewing, always wanting to be someplace else. Isabelle glanced up.

"I want my baby to have something from me."

Adelaide appeared to be getting attached to her child. Was that wise? It was good she cared and wanted to have a connection with her baby. Caring too much would make it more difficult for her to give the child up when the time came.

"Of course, you can make a quilt for the baby. It's yours."

Adelaide shook her head. "It's not. I have to think of it as yours. Mother won't let me keep it."

Isabelle's heart broke for her sister.

Nineteen

THE FOLLOWING MORNING, ISABELLE SAT BACKWARD in the carriage next to her father, while Marguerite and Adelaide faced forward across from them. Normally, Adelaide sat rear-facing next to her, but with her morning sickness coming and going still, no one wanted to take the chance that having her sit backward would bring on a wave of nausea. Or worse.

Adelaide's hand rested on her stomach.

Isabelle leaned forward and touched her sister's arm. "Are you all right?"

Adelaide gave a wan smile. "I'm fine."

Marguerite fidgeted with her handkerchief, pulling at the hem. Something she would never do in public. "I'm still not sure about Adelaide participating in the box social. Not in her condition."

"She has taken part the last two years," Father said. "If she declines this year when she doesn't have a suitor, it will be perceived as suspicious."

"I know you're right, but I worry. What if..." Marguerite darted her gaze toward Adelaide and lowered her voice, "...*he* bids?"

Why had she lowered her voice? Adelaide could still hear her. *He* being the baby's father. If he did bid, that could mean all the work to protect Adelaide could be for naught.

Father shook his head. "I doubt he would be so foolish."

Father was right. If the man had already refused to claim the baby, why would he risk exposing himself now? If she were him, she wouldn't attend the festival at all.

Marguerite folded and refolded her handkerchief. "But what if he does?"

"He won't. Don't invite trouble. Leave it be. We'll deal

with whatever comes up."

Marguerite fluttered her handkerchief as she rolled her head to the side to gaze out the carriage window.

Adelaide gave Isabelle a worrisome expression and turned her head the opposite way to look out the other side of the carriage.

It would have been simpler to allow Adelaide—and Marguerite—to remain at home, but that might raise too many questions. To say Adelaide wasn't feeling well would add fodder to the rumors that would fly once Isabelle had a child too soon after marrying. People weren't stupid. She knew there would be whispers about her when she had a full-term baby too soon after a hasty marriage. It couldn't be helped. If the woman married before she was showing, most people feigned ignorance.

Once at the festival grounds, Isabelle carried her box of food for the lunch social auction. She walked with her family to where the boxes would be stored until the bidding started. She and Adelaide each added their contributions to the collection.

People crowded the whole area with a scattering of tables and tents across the three-acre field. Isabelle had tried to convince her parents to let her ride her bicycle so she could arrive early, but they had refused her request. Claiming that with her impending marriage, she needed to behave like a proper lady. Would Oliver insist upon decorum at all times as well? He'd said a lady shouldn't have to give up the things she enjoyed just because she married. She hoped he'd been earnest, and that his words weren't offered simply to mollify her until after they were wed.

She shook her head. She wouldn't think on anything unpleasant today. This would be her last real day of freedom. Starting tomorrow, every minute would be focused on the wedding and the aftermath. Her stomach tightened thinking about it. Nothing would ever be the same again. If only she could stop time. Or run away. Neither were viable options.

"I'm going to find some friends."

Before Isabelle could escape, her father said, "Remember you'll be marrying soon. Don't do anything to bring shame upon you or the family."

A veiled warning about Grant. "I know. I won't." No harm in talking to a friend in public. No shame in that whatsoever. She hurried off before anyone could stop her.

Oliver meandered through the crowds with Ellery and Belinda. Why hadn't he thought to make arrangements to meet up with Isabelle? Now he had the distasteful task of trying to locate her in this multitude.

"I find it strange with your wedding three days away, you aren't with Miss Atwood. If I were her and you were *my* fiancé, I wouldn't let you out of my sight."

How truly unappealing. But her assessment that he should have set up a prearranged meeting place hit the mark. Or better yet, he should have picked her up and brought her here himself.

Ellery pointed. "Isn't that her over there?"

She stood with her friends Miss Waldon and Mr. Dawson, talking. And smiling. She always seemed to be with him. Perhaps Mr. Dawson had escorted Miss Waldon.

He approached with Ellery and Belinda at his sides. "Good morning, Isabelle."

Isabelle made the introductions. "These are my friends Franny Waldon from the mercantile and Grant Dawson. This is Mr. Young and his sister, Oliver's friends from Philadelphia."

Miss Waldon smiled. "We were talking about the three-legged race. The other day, Isabelle challenged Miss Young to enter with her brother."

Ellery perked up. "Sounds fun."

Belinda huffed. "I will do no such thing."

Miss Waldon smiled mischievously. "Don't you want to see if you can best Isabelle and Grant? They have participated every year since they were eight."

"I do not."

"Come on." Ellery elbowed his sister. "It will be a

lark."

"You're a buffoon." Belinda pressed her lips together and glared at Isabelle. "A lady would have no part of such a crude activity."

"It's not crude. It's fun." Miss Waldon turned to Isabelle and Mr. Dawson. "You two are entering, aren't you?"

Isabelle gazed up at Oliver. "Would you mind?"

It was nice of her to consult him.

Before he could answer, Mr. Dawson cleared his throat. "I'm going to have to refrain. I twisted my knee the other day. It's a bit tender, so being tied to someone else probably isn't a good idea."

Oliver appreciated his consideration to back out gracefully. Would the young man still have if Oliver hadn't been there?

Isabelle sighed, clearly disappointed.

Ellery scooped up her hand. "Fret not. I'll be your partner. It'll be fun."

To have Mr. Dawson as her teammate was one thing, but not Ellery. Though Ellery was his friend, he had been known to create mischief. Oliver retrieved Isabelle's hand. "She's my fiancée. If anyone is going to be her partner, it will be me."

Isabelle gazed up at him bright eyed. "Really?"

He had surprised her. Good. But he didn't relish making a spectacle of himself in front of most of the town. Could people trust a banker who made a fool of himself? This seemed to mean a lot to her. "If you really want to participate in this, then I'll do it with you."

She beamed at him. "I do."

The two words he hoped she would repeat on Tuesday.

Belinda batted her eyes. "You can't possibly intend to run amuck with a horde of people."

Oliver gazed down at his fiancée. "I do."

Ellery held out his hands. "It seems I'm still without a partner. Miss Waldon, would you do me the honor?"

She giggled. "All right."

Oliver escorted Isabelle over to the event.

She held up a strip of cloth. "I'll tie this around our

ankles."

He took it. "I can do that."

She hiked the hem of her dress a few inches to expose her boot-clad ankle and scooted her foot next to his.

He tied it. "Is that too tight?"

"No. It feels about right."

He straightened.

Isabelle pointed to where they were joined. "The key is to start with our feet that are tied together first."

She was giving him pointers?

"I've run one of these a time or two."

Her eager expression faltered. "Oh. I'm sorry. I assumed..."

"I was a stodgy old banker? I was young once."

"I don't think you're stodgy."

"But you think me old?"

A worry line creased between her eyebrows. "I didn't say that."

He smiled to let her know he was teasing. "I know I'm older than you, but I'm not so old I can't remember what it was like to be young and have fun."

"I'll keep that in mind."

"Did you and Mr. Dawson always win?"

She shook her head. "Only once. We usually came in third or fourth. The lead teams all got tripped up that year and landed on the ground. We won by default."

"I can't promise you a win, but I'll do my best not to trip you." He hooked his arm around her tiny waist.

She blinked up at him as though unsure before she did the same.

A rush of awareness washed over him. This woman was going to be his wife soon, and he'd be holding her close often. Or would he?

All the pairs lined up. Ellery and Miss Waldon stood three teams down the line from them.

"Where's your sister?" Oliver shifted his toes to the starting line. "She probably would have been a better choice for your partner."

"Adelaide couldn't do this because of the—"

He waited. "Because of the what?"

"Because of the... way she's so uncoordinated. She tends to fall over her own feet." He sensed she might have been about to say something different.

The starting official raised his arm high in the air. "On your marks. Get set. Go!" He jerked his arm down.

All the duos hobbled forward.

Oliver tried to match Isabelle's stride. An important strategy to not out-distance his teammate and not get his tied foot tangled around hers. Though tumbling to the ground with her in his arms could be interesting. Providing neither of them received an injury.

Several teams pulled ahead of them, but they managed to finagle a position in the front third of the pack.

A pair of older schoolboys on the other side of Isabelle staggered along until one tripped the other and fell into Isabelle. Oliver tightened his hold around her waist, pressing her firmly to his side, and lifted her off the ground at the same time he pivoted. The boys landed on the ground in front of them. Oliver swung her all the way around until he faced the finish line once again. He set Isabelle back down. "Are you all right?"

She let out a whoosh of air. "I'm fine thanks to you. Let's keep going."

"We can't win."

"That doesn't matter. Come on."

They ended the race in the back quarter of pairs who were still on their feet. Ellery and Miss Waldon completed in the front half of the group.

After crossing the finish line, Oliver leaned over to catch his breath. Surprisingly, he'd had fun. A glimpse of the enjoyable life to come with her?

"Isabelle! How could you?" Mrs. Atwood glared at her daughter.

"Don't blame her. It was my idea." His idea to keep Ellery from having an arm around Oliver's fiancée.

Mrs. Atwood's demeanor immediately softened. "Well, if it was your idea. She has a way of coercing people into doing things they otherwise wouldn't."

It seemed as though if blame was to be assigned, Isabelle ended up on the receiving end. That didn't seem fair.

He crouched and removed the ligature from around their ankles. He stood and handed Isabelle the cloth. "Let me buy you a lemonade." He didn't wait for an answer but guided her away from her mother. "Thank you for that."

"For what?"

"For the race. It made me feel young again."

"Why do you keep doing that?"

"Doing what?"

"Referencing your age and calling yourself old. I know you're older than me, but you're not that advanced in years."

"I guess I'm acutely aware of our age difference and want you to know I'm not oblivious to the fact. I'm sure you could marry any number of men closer to your own age"—like Mr. Dawson—"but for some reason, you're content with me. I'm having a hard time letting that sink in."

"You make it sound as though I have a stack of marriage proposals sitting at home for me to choose from. I assure you, I don't."

"I find it hard to believe a lady as kind and beautiful as yourself hasn't had even one proposal in her lifetime. Probably many." Probably from men he knew.

"None that count." A flush bloomed on her cheeks.

"Don't all proposals count? What proposals have you had?"

She walked without a word.

Ignoring his question? "Your silence has me curious. Do tell."

She sighed. "When I was six, a school chum told another boy he was going to marry me when we grew up. In truth, he didn't actually propose, so it can hardly count."

A school chum? Mr. Dawson? "Does your young suitor have a name?"

"Mikey Hoffabert. He moved away the following summer, and I never saw him again."

Good to know it wasn't Mr. Dawson. "What other proposals have you had?"

"Why are you so interested?"

Oliver shrugged. "It lets me get to know you better. So how many others?"

"Just one. But it doesn't count either."

"Why not?"

She chewed on her bottom lip before answering. "Because it was written in an unsigned letter. One can hardly accept a proposal from a phantom."

"A secret admirer? You must have found that romantic."

She shrugged. "What about you? How many ladies have you proposed to?"

"None."

She stopped and faced him. "But you were married before. You had to have proposed."

"I didn't."

"*She* proposed to you?"

He shook his head. "Not directly. She just sort of started planning our wedding, asking me about various details. I liked the idea of marrying her, so I didn't stop her. It made it easy that way."

"So, without others intervening, you would never marry." Her voice dipped to a melancholy tone.

"Don't feel bad for me. I believe both my marriages are in God's divine plan. They may not have started out in a conventional way, but that doesn't make them any less right."

"I guess that's a positive way to view them."

"God works in mysterious ways." Like Oliver being mistaken for an outlaw over a year ago, Isabelle's father helping him out, and Oliver owing the man a favor. Mysterious indeed.

Twenty

THE TIME FOR THE MAIN ATTRACTION of Founders Day had come, the box social auction.

Isabelle stood off to one side with half of the ladies while the others waited on the opposite side.

The men bunched together in the middle, vying for the best view of the boxes to be bid on. None wanted to miss the chance to win their sweetheart's contribution and the opportunity to eat with that special lady. Though the preparers of the boxes were supposed to remain anonymous, most people knew which lady had brought which box. Some young ladies would switch boxes with a friend to confuse the gentlemen, but most wanted the fellow they were interested in to know which box to bid on.

Merl Kinnier stood behind the table loaded with decorated boxes in front of the crowd ready to facilitate the bidding. "Everybody, settle down!"

Though the din lessened, a buzz still vibrated from the crowd.

The auctioneer rapped his gavel on the table. "If you all don't hush, you're going to miss your chance."

Standing with her sister on one side of her and Franny on the other, Isabelle scanned the crowd. Oliver stood with her parents on the other side of Adelaide. Grant had positioned himself where he always did, the very center of the crowd. Not front, not back, not either side, but as middle as he could get. And in the front, on the far side, Shane tipped his hat to her. She hoped no one saw. Her cheeks warmed.

Adelaide grabbed Isabelle's hand. "What if no one bids on my box?"

Grateful for the distraction, Isabelle patted her sister's arm. "There's not a chance of that happening.

You know Professor Lumbard bids on every box."

Generally, more men vied for boxes than were available. The men who didn't win one of these meals could eat at one of the food booths.

"He's not so bad. But what if he already has one by the time mine comes up? What if some old coot gets mine? I couldn't bear it."

"Regardless of who wins yours, you'll be fine. Smile and be pleasant. That's all one of the older gentlemen wants. And to have a good meal with a pretty lady."

"I wish I knew who's going to win mine."

Isabelle prayed the father of Adelaide's baby didn't bid. If he was indeed married, no one would benefit. Father was right. The man wouldn't risk exposing himself.

Merl auctioned off several boxes before he picked up Adelaide's. "This looks like a prize lunch, men. I do believe roast beef and apple pie are in some fortunate man's future. "Who will start the—?"

"Two dollars." Professor Lumbard made his customary opening bid. As an older bachelor, he desired only a good meal.

Isabelle patted her sister's hand. "See. Yours won't be without any bids."

A young man bid on Adelaide's box.

Was that the father of her child? Couldn't be. Adelaide insisted he was married, and that young man wasn't.

On the other side of Adelaide, Marguerite gripped Father's arm. "Bid. We can't have her eating with just anyone. It could ruin her reputation."

Father bid the next logical increment, and after being outbid a couple of times, he called out, "Twenty-five dollars!"

The young man dipped his head and slunk away. Father won.

Isabelle's box came up next. Her stomach tightened. Who would win her box this year? Grant had bid and won the past three years. The first year he'd said he hadn't known it was her box, but she suspected he had. The next two years, he'd done it to keep her from having to eat with some undesirable man. Would he bid again this year?

Hopefully, a certain handsome rancher would bid, even if he didn't win. It would be nice to have him make an attempt. If her stepmother had anything to do with it, Oliver Mallory would be bidding on Isabelle's box, and he likely had the means to outbid anyone else if he so desired. She hoped he didn't bid at all. If she was going to be forced to marry him, she would like one last—innocent—rendezvous with Shane Keegan. Then she would let the rancher know she couldn't see him again.

But the biggest question was, would her secret admirer bid? That could be exciting. Maybe she would be able to figure out who he was before Monday. Possibly have lunch with him.

Merl Kinnier held up her box. He put his nose to it and drew in a deep breath. "I do believe I smell roast beef again, with chocolate cake this time. What's my opening bid for this lovely box?"

"Two dollars!" Professor Lumbard offered his usual bid. More often than not, he won one eventually.

"Five dollars!" Shane Keegan called out.

Isabelle's heart leapt. Did he know which was her box?

He looked at her and winked.

He most certainly did.

How exciting.

"I have five. Do I hear—?"

"Six dollars!" Oliver raised his hand. Most bids went up by two bits at a time, not whole dollars.

"Seven!" Grant called out.

How sweet of him. Isabelle studied Grant. Since Oliver's innocent question as to why she didn't marry Grant whom she already cared about—as a friend—she'd thought a lot about him. But with his dark brown hair and brown eyes, he could never pass as the father of Adelaide's child.

"Eight!" Mr. Young this time.

Oliver gave his friend a sideways glance and shook his head.

"Nine!" This came from the edge of the crowd.

Isabelle craned her neck to see who was bidding. A well-dressed man with black hair. He was the man in the mercantile considering the blue ribbon—for his aunt, of course. Had it actually been for her? She'd seen him again outside the dressmaker's shop. Could he be her secret admirer?

"Ten!" Oliver this time. He would likely be the winner as it should be.

"Eleven!" A handsome young man with bold red hair in the middle of the crowd.

She had seen him around town as well. He'd opened the door for her at the hotel and she'd seen him a second time outside the livery. Was he her secret admirer?

Unbelievable that six men were bidding on her box, though Grant really didn't count being her friend, or Mr. Young as Oliver's friend. Hers wasn't any better decorated than anyone else's.

Shane bid. "Fifteen!"

Certainly no one would outbid that. She hoped not.

Oliver stared at Shane. "Twenty!"

Grant shook his head this time. The red-haired man slumped his shoulders, and the black-haired man seemed to be out, as well as Mr. Young.

Shane returned Oliver's stare. "Thirty!"

Thirty dollars for a lunch? Though a little exciting, this was getting embarrassing.

"Thirty-five." Oliver.

She willed Shane to stop. Oliver needed to win and have this done with.

"Forty." Shane.

Each time Shane bid, a thrill danced through her. She *should* be happy when Oliver bid. She would be spending the rest of her life with him.

Which man would back down first? The silent crowd watched these two men.

She wanted this to stop, but she had no control over the men bidding.

"Forty-five."

"Fifty."

Oliver's eyes narrowed at Shane.

What was he thinking? What were either of them

thinking? They both must know that was her box, or why else would they be bidding so high?

Most young ladies' boxes went for five to ten dollars. Boxes belonging to wives were generally bought by their husbands for three to five dollars.

The auctioneer spoke in a soft voice. "The bid is fifty dollars. Do I hear fifty-five?"

Oliver tipped his hat to Shane.

Bang! "Sold to the determined rancher for fifty dollars."

Isabelle's heart leapt, then she glanced at Oliver who looked disappointed. Then she caught Marguerite's glare. Her joy squashed two-fold.

No doubt, Isabelle would be blamed for this, but she didn't care. She'd had nothing to do with the bidding. It wasn't as though she had told anyone which box was hers. She would enjoy her innocent meal with Shane and not worry over it.

Shane strode up to the front to pay and claim his box.

"Would the young lady step forward as well?"

Isabelle slunk up to the front and took Shane's offered elbow. She gave Oliver an apologetic shrug and strolled off with her handsome rancher. Guilt twisted inside her every step of the way.

Shane tilted his head sideways toward her. "I have a confession to make. I knew which box was yours. I watched when you put it on the table."

He'd been watching her?

She smiled inwardly. "Most men do so they know whose box to bid on. Could you imagine what it would be like if everyone left it up to chance?"

"I never thought of it that way. But isn't it supposed to be a secret?"

"It's much more romantic when a fellow knows, and he bids for..." Isabelle bit her bottom lip. She should *not* finish that sentence.

"He bids for the girl he's sweet on?"

She nodded. "Or for the best cook because he wants a good meal."

"Since I don't know about your cooking ability, you

can guess why I bid on yours."

Her inside went all skippy and happy.

"You're blushing."

She put her hands on her hot cheeks. How embarrassing.

"I bid to make up for cancelling supper plans on Wednesday."

"You didn't have to do that."

"I wanted to." He pointed. "That looks like a nice spot over there."

She appreciated the change in subject.

He spread out a wool blanket and held her hand while she sat then lowered himself. "Do you want to unpack the food? Or should I."

"It's your box. You paid for it." A hefty sum at that.

He untied the ribbon and removed the lid. He pulled out the corked bottle of lemonade, a roast beef sandwich, apples, cheese, hard-boiled eggs, crackers, a slice of chocolate cake, and two cookies. A little of everything.

"I didn't know what you—or whomever—would like. I figured if you wanted the sandwich I'd eat the cheese or eggs."

"It all looks delicious. I'll have some of each. We can split everything."

"Sounds perfect."

He handed her half of the sandwich.

After a couple of bites, she stopped. "Aren't you going to ask me if I made this?"

He shook his head. "I didn't buy your box to find out if you were a good cook. Remember?"

She bit her lips to keep her smile at bay. She liked that he was sweet on her. "Did you catch the rustlers?"

He shook his head and swallowed. "They disappeared into the mountains. They could have gone any direction."

"Do you think they'll return?"

"My experience says if someone gets away with something once, they'll try again."

"You know what could help you with that?"

"What?"

"Another dog or two to guard your spread."

He chuckled. "I don't think so."

"But there are these three stray dogs who need a home." If he would take just one of them, that would help. Probably not Trefoil with his three legs.

"The two I have know their job. Having untrained dogs might upset the balance. But thanks for thinking of me." He took a bite.

"What about a barn cat?"

"Got three."

"A one-legged duck?"

"To eat?"

"No."

"Then I don't have much use for it."

She'd tried.

Halfway through the meal, he looked at her pointedly. "If I ask you a question, will you give me an honest answer?"

A trick question. "Either way I answer, you won't know if I'm telling the truth or not. If I say yes and that's a lie, then anything else I say would likely be as well. But if I said no and that was indeed the truth, then likewise you wouldn't know if I told the truth."

He cocked an eyebrow. "You are a manipulator of words."

"Simply pointing out the downfall of that particular question."

"Were you waiting for me to ask it? Your answer seemed rehearsed."

"Not waiting for you in particular to ask. Many years ago, I made the mistake of asking that very question to a friend." Grant had always liked playing with words.

"So, you could never trust anything that friend said?"

"On the contrary. He's the one person who will always speak truthfully to me. I'm sorry for teasing you. What's your question? I promise to answer honestly. Provided it's not too personal."

"The banker Mr. Mallory. Is he your beau?"

Her insides tightened. A question with no right answer.

"I ask, because he seemed awfully eager to win your box."

"Beau implies we have a mutual affection for each

other.”

Shane raised his eyebrows. “And you don’t?”

“He’s a nice enough fellow.” The time had come to tell him the truth and cut him free. “My parents wish me to marry him.”

“Your parents?”

She nodded.

“And what do you wish?”

“I wish to choose for myself and marry for love.”

“Then you should.”

Father and Marguerite strolled up to the edge of the blanket, and Father spoke. “The donation auction will start soon.”

Marguerite gave a smug smile. “You don’t want to miss that.”

Isabelle knew they had come to check up on her and let her know she needed to part company from Shane.

Shane stood and held out his hand. “Mr. Atwood, good to see you. I will make sure your daughter gets back to the festivities.”

Father shook his hand. “See that you do.” He and Marguerite strolled off.

Shane sat back down. “They aren’t too happy I won your box.”

No, they weren’t. Isabelle shrugged. “My stepmother doesn’t like not having control.”

“And you enjoy testing her on that?”

She put her fingertips on her upper chest. “I had no control over whom purchased my box.” But she had been elated he’d won. If she had to be forced to marry Oliver, she could at least have this pleasant encounter to savor for years to come.

“Will you marry Mr. Mallory if they press the issue?”

“I don’t know. I may not have a choice.” She kept going back and forth thinking she would marry him and that she wouldn’t.

“What if you had a choice?”

But she didn’t. Not really. “What do you mean?”

“I know we haven’t known each other long yet, but I think we get on well together. I won’t lie to you and say I love you, but I do like you and think you are the sort of girl I *could* fall in love with. I don't mean to be too forward, but I fear if I don't say something now, you'll get stolen away from me before I have a chance."

What *was* he saying?

"I'm heading out on a cattle drive in two days. I'll be gone for a month or two. I'm afraid someone will sweep you off your feet while I'm gone."

Someone like Oliver. Or her secret admirer.

"When I return, I'd like to court you properly with the intent of marriage."

Her insides leapt for joy, and she opened her mouth.

He put his fingers on her lips. "Don't answer now. Think about it while I'm gone. Give me your answer when I return. But I wanted you to know my intentions so you didn't wonder."

His warm fingers made her lips tingle.

She pulled his hand away. "I would like nothing more than to wait for you to return and see if we suited one another, but that won't be possible. It wouldn't be fair to give you hope while you're gone. My parents intend for me to marry Mr. Mallory on Tuesday. The chance of me stopping them is about as likely as catching a bolt of lightning."

"Do you love him?"

"There hasn't been time."

"But you'll marry him anyway?"

"Being a woman, I don't have much say in the matter." She wished she did.

"I could talk to him and convince him to wait."

"It's my parents who would need to have their minds changed, and they won't." Adelaide depended on her marrying right away.

He sat silent for a moment. "I appreciate you being honest with me."

Why did she sense there was more?

"I've been forewarned. Now, I'll warn you. I'm going to hold onto the hope that, you being a smart lady, you'll figure out a way to postpone your wedding. If when I return you're married, I won't bother you. But if you aren't, for whatever reason, may I call on you?"

So romantic. She desperately wanted to say yes. "I

guess I couldn't stop you. But like I said, the chances are nonexistent."

"Anything could happen."

Anything *could* happen.

Twenty-One

Oliver strolled along a line of festival booths with Ellery and Belinda at his side. After backing out of the bidding on Isabelle's box lunch, he'd planned to go home and eat. Until he remembered he'd given his small staff the day to enjoy the festivities. No one remained at his house to prepare him anything, and his culinary skills ill-equipped him to do so for himself.

He needed to get something to eat and contemplated his food options from the booths. He preferred to be alone but couldn't neglect his duty to his visiting friends. "This booth has prepared sandwiches wrapped in waxed paper. A booth farther up has pickled eggs, cheese, and crackers. Another one, nothing but desserts. I'm going to get a ham sandwich here. What do you two want?"

Belinda crinkled her nose. "I don't eat anything with my hands. It's vulgar."

"Then you will go hungry." Ellery pointed down the line. "I want to try those pickled eggs. I'll meet you back here." He headed off.

Oliver wished Ellery had taken his sister with him. He stepped up to the table but spoke to Belinda. "Are you sure you don't want one?"

She wiggled her gloved fingers. "Not with my hands." She hooked her arm around his. "Why don't we go to the hotel and eat in their dining room? It will be much more civil, and the food there wasn't so bad."

He freed himself from her grasp. "I'm getting a sandwich." He purchased a ham one. He would *not* go off and willingly be alone with Belinda. That would give the wrong impression to Isabelle and her family. As for Isabelle off with another man, she hadn't had a choice in the matter. His fiancée picnicking with another man was another reason not to leave the festival. Who was this rancher to Isabelle that he had bid so high?

Oliver unwrapped his sandwich and took a bite. He would like to think Isabelle didn't know the man, and his bidding had been happenstance, but he suspected otherwise.

Ellery returned, licking his fingers noisily. "Pickled eggs are delicious."

"Don't be boorish." Belinda grimaced. "They sound horrid." She turned to Oliver. "Your fiancée should be dining with you. That she went off with that ruffian tells a lot about her character. None of it good."

Oliver swallowed a bite. "He's hardly a ruffian. Besides, she didn't have a choice, and this is a fundraiser."

Ellery brushed his hands together. "Why *did* you stop bidding?"

He'd wanted Isabelle to have this one last freedom before marrying him. It had seemed the right thing to do. "It was becoming a spectacle."

He couldn't believe Mr. Keegan was having lunch with his almost wife. If left up to Jackson and Mrs. Atwood, Isabelle would already be married to him, but he didn't get the same impression from her. If she wasn't willing, he wouldn't marry her. But if she wasn't willing, why not say so and be done with it? He'd given her the opportunity.

He'd been tempted to outbid the man, but the cowboy hadn't seemed to know when to quit. And Isabelle's eyes had lit up each time the rancher had bid. He would speak with her later about it. If one little, innocent lunch could turn Isabelle off him, best to know now.

Oliver finished his sandwich and tossed the wrapper in the waste bin. Adelaide Atwood stood away from the din of activity with a thin fellow in a brown-striped suit. Oliver paused. Who was he? A young girl like her could easily be taken advantage of. As an almost member of the family, it was his duty to look out for her. A strong need to protect her drove him forward. "I'll be right back." He headed in her direction. "Miss Atwood?"

The man jerked around, ducked his head, and

hustled away. He couldn't have been more than a few years younger than Oliver.

As he reached Adelaide, she wiped her hands across her cheeks.

"What's wrong?"

"Nothing." She sniffled.

"You're obviously upset. Who was that man?"

She blinked several times and straightened her shoulders. "No one."

That man wasn't *no one*, but she obviously didn't want to talk to Oliver about him. Maybe he would bring this man up to Isabelle as well.

Sitting on a blanket in the meadow where many other couples and families ate, Henny placed the leftover food into the lunch box. "Saul Hammond, why do I have the sneaking suspicion you knew exactly whose box you were bidding on?"

He smiled. "I don't know what you're talking about. I'm just a fortunate fellow."

She narrowed her eyes at him. "No. You did something sly, and I'm going to figure out how you knew."

He chuckled.

Enough silliness. "How are Lily and Toby settling in over at your house?" Lily and her five-year-old son had come to Henny at the beginning of the summer, battered and scared, running from a terrible past. A few weeks ago, after things in the young mother's past had gotten resolved, she and Edric, Saul's son, married.

"As well as can be expected. Lily is working hard to be the perfect wife and mother. She needs to worry less."

"Edric's not pressuring her, is he?"

Saul shook his head. "I think she's still living in her old life some of the time with the fears of her past. She'll be fine in time."

"And Toby? Is he doing well? Do your granddaughters like having a brother?"

"Estella and Nancy love having him. It's like they've been given a brand-new toy. He seems to enjoy the attention his sisters give him."

"But?"

"He does all right with Edric most of the time."

"But not with you?"

"He has a lot to overcome where trusting people is concerned. He'll come around."

Henny sensed there was more. "And you?"

"Can't hide anything from you."

"As you shouldn't. What is it?"

"I feel like a spare gear that's left over after fixing a clock or a mechanical device. I would go somewhere else to let them all settle in as a family, but I'm not sure where. Everything seems to be working, but I'm out of place."

"It'll take a while for all of you to figure out what your new roles are." Henny's attention caught on Adelaide and Mr. Mallory.

The girl shook her head and hurried away.

"Oh, no."

Saul looked in the same direction. "What is it?"

"There's something I need to do." She shifted to stand.

Saul beat her to his feet and helped her up.

"Thank you."

"What's going on?"

Henny grabbed her cane. "I can't explain right now. I'll catch up with you at one of the booths. I hope you don't mind."

The expression on his face said he felt like that spare part again.

She would make it up to him later. Right now, a young woman needed her help. And she didn't like the way things were adding up.

Henny hobbled along on an intersection course with Adelaide, but the girl walked faster than Henny had anticipated. "Adelaide?"

The girl kept walking.

Probably hadn't heard her. "Adelaide!"

She turned this time with tear-stained cheeks.

Henny held up the hand without the cane. "Could you help me, dear? This leg is giving me fits." She longed for the day her leg was strong once again.

Adelaide nodded and wiped her palms across her face but didn't erase all evidence of her mood. "Are you enjoying Founders Day?"

Henny hooked her arm with the girl's. "I am. I had a nice lunch with Saul Hammond. How about you?"

"Yes. It's a nice day for it. Where are you heading?"

"Right here will do nicely." She stopped under a fir tree.

Adelaide glanced around. "There's nothing here."

"Precisely. I needed to speak to you without risk of anyone overhearing our conversation."

The girl's eyebrows pinched and creased in worry.

Adelaide had every right to worry if Henny's suspicions were correct. Professor Lumbard's information had led Henny down the wrong path. Now, how to start? She supposed being direct would be best. "I saw you talking to Oliver Mallory. Is he the father of your baby?" That would not bode well for Isabelle to have her husband the father of her sister's child. It would make an already complicated situation, more convoluted.

Adelaide's mouth dropped open. "What? I'm— What makes you think—? I don't know what you're talking about."

"Dear girl, I know you're with child."

Adelaide's shoulders sagged as though relieved. "Who told you?"

"I added a few things together and figured it out. Your mother and sister confirmed my suspicions. But don't tell them I told you I know."

"I won't. Mother would be furious."

Henny needed to get to the bottom of this. "You seemed upset after talking to Oliver Mallory. So, *is* he the father?"

Adelaide shook her head.

Was the girl telling the truth? Possibly it was a professor after all.

"Then who's the father?"

"I won't say. It doesn't matter."

"Does the father know?"

The girl nodded.

He was likely older and took advantage of her naiveté. Good thing Henny didn't know this man's identity, because she would want to wring his neck.

"Adelaide, you can't expect Mr. Mallory to raise another man's child without his consent. He's going to figure it out."

"Mother hopes he doesn't realize it's not his."

"He'll know. When his wife isn't in the family way and suddenly has a baby, he'll know. There's no way he won't."

"Mother plans to send Isabelle and me back East right after the wedding to take care of a sick aunt. But there won't really be a sick aunt. When we return months later, Isabelle will have my baby. I'm sure he'll believe it's his."

Henny was sure he wouldn't. "Two problems. One, what if Isabelle becomes in the family way at the same time you are?"

"That's why Mother is sending us away the day after the wedding."

"For Mr. Mallory to believe it's his, there must be the risk she could become with child."

"We all hope she doesn't."

Hope? Henny feared this would all end badly. "The other thing is you will likely have a full-term baby which Isabelle is going to have to claim as one who was born months early. Your baby will be too big to pass off as hers." At the very least, he would think Isabelle had already been expecting and that was the reason for the hasty marriage.

Her bottom lip quivered. "But it has to work. I don't know what else to do."

"I'll speak to your mother."

"No! You can't. I'll be in trouble if she finds out I told you."

"Sweetie, you're already in trouble." Henny understood a little of what this girl was going through, and there was no good way out of it. "It's not fair to do this to another person without their knowledge. He deserves to know ahead of time."

"What if he won't go along with it? What would I do then?" Adelaide shook her head. "You can't tell him or Mother or anyone. Promise you won't tell them. Promise."

"It's not mine to tell, but you should. I told Isabelle the three of you would be welcome in my home."

"Three?"

"You, Isabelle, and the little one."

"But then everyone would know about my baby." Her eyes widened. "And what I did. I couldn't. I just couldn't." Adelaide swung around and ran off, stumbling on her way.

The poor girl. She was too young and scared to realize some people would figure it all out, as Henny had done, whether they said anything or not.

Isabelle dallied on the fringe of the activities alone so she could savor the lingering bliss of her time with Shane. She couldn't believe he'd asked to marry her. Well, not exactly asked, but inferred it. She'd wanted to say *yes* if for no other reason than to thwart Marguerite's plans, but that wouldn't help anyone, let alone Adelaide.

If everything was different and she wasn't expected to marry Oliver to help Adelaide save face, would she want to marry Shane Keegan? A part of her did. It would be so romantic. A whirlwind romance. Like a fairy tale. Another part of her prodded at reason. She hardly knew the man. Did she really want to commit the rest of her life to someone she didn't know? Wasn't that what she was planning to do with Oliver? She didn't know him any better than Shane. If she chose Shane, she would need to wait until he returned, but that would be too late for Adelaide. She wouldn't mind waiting for Shane—not to marry, but to get to know him to see if she might like to marry him. But if she intended to help her sister—and she did intend to—Shane was out of the question—now and in the future.

The man with red hair, who had bid on her box lunch, wandered off toward the tree line. Where was he heading? The only thing of interest that direction was the pond with the old elm tree. She froze. The place where she was to meet her secret admirer in two days. Could he be...? Maybe. She wanted to follow him and find out, but she had been away from her family and Oliver far too long already. They might be getting worried, and Marguerite would be angry at her absence. She would find out who her secret admirer was soon enough. No sense causing more trouble for herself than she already had.

She pointed herself back toward the festivities. Her step faltered.

The black-haired man in the suit who had also bid on her box caught her attention. He gazed right at her, smiled, and touched the brim of his bowler hat. Perhaps he was her secret admirer. On Monday, she would find out.

"Isabelle?"

She sucked in a startled breath and turned to face Oliver. "Yes."

"Did you have an enjoyable lunch with Mr. Keegan?"

Did she hear a tinge of jealousy? She had done nothing wrong. Except to act more thrilled than acceptable to have lunch with the handsome rancher. "I did. Mr. Keegan was a perfect gentleman."

"I'm glad to hear. May I speak with you?"

She wanted to say no. She'd been having a wonderful day so far and didn't want to spoil it by letting reality invade. He would likely grill her on every moment of her lunch. To refuse would be rude. She might as well get it over with. "Of course. What about?"

"Two things, really. I'm not sure which to start with."

If she thought there was anything she could say to dissuade him from speaking about either subject that was obviously weighing on him, she would. "I suppose you should just pick one."

He remained silent a moment. "I think I should address Mr. Keegan first."

She really wanted to say no now. "Mr. Keegan and I

are no more than acquaintances."

"You seemed rather pleased he won your box lunch."

She had been. It would likely be the last chance she would ever have to spend time with him. "What lady wouldn't be flattered to have so many men bidding for her box?"

"This was more than that. I could have outbid him."

She'd suspected as much. "So, why didn't you?"

"I'm not sure. I guess I felt you—he needed to win. If you agree to marry me, it needs to be because you want to. Not because you feel you have no other options. Mr. Keegan seems taken with you."

But she didn't have any other viable options except Oliver. Not really. Was he backing out? Had she ruined her chance to help her sister? Her stomach tightened. "I—I..."

"It's all right. I am quite fond of you, but there is our age difference, as I've mentioned before. A young lady such as yourself probably dreamed of marrying a young man, not an old coot like me."

"You're not old nor a coot." She'd made him feel bad. Not her intention. How could she fix this? She'd selfishly wanted to have lunch with Shane without considering anyone else's feelings. "I'm sorry. I never meant to hurt you. I don't like being pressured into this."

"The last thing I want to do is pressure you. If you want me to tell your father I've changed my mind, I will."

Oh, dear. She *had* ruined things with him. "No, please don't."

"A long engagement perhaps?"

A luxury she could ill afford. "I'm prepared to marry you on Tuesday." Mostly. "What was the other thing you wanted to talk about?" Any subject had to be better than her looming future with a man she didn't love.

"It's about your sister."

Little did he know, Adelaide was still part of the same subject, that the two were intricately entwined. "What about her?"

"A little while ago, I saw her talking to a man."

Isabelle didn't know why he was telling her and what it mattered, so she shrugged.

"When I called out to her, the man rushed off. She was quite distressed. Crying."

The gravity of what he'd described sunk in. "Who was he?"

"I don't know. I didn't really see him before he left."

Isabelle knew who he was. The baby's father. The trouble being, she didn't *know* who he was. "What did he look like? Hair color? Height? Build?" Even if no chance existed of this scoundrel doing the right thing, she still needed to put a face to this cheater so she could keep him away from her sister.

"Sandy-colored hair, about my height, thin and wiry."

That didn't help very much. "Do you think you could recognize him among all the people?"

"I don't know. Why don't you just ask her?"

If she thought Adelaide would tell her, she would. "I'd prefer to talk to him first."

"Like I said, he hurried off."

"Would you be willing to try?"

"If you'd like me to."

"Thanks." She looped her arm with his.

After a half an hour of strolling around among the crowds, the quest proved futile. "I'm sorry to have disappointed you."

"You didn't disappoint me. I appreciate you trying so hard. I'll ask Adelaide about him." Not that she expected any different results.

"I think the live and silent auctions have already begun. Shall we head to the town hall?"

"That's a great idea. That man could be there." She strolled with him toward the building.

"I suppose he could be. Why are you so determined to find him?"

"As you said, he upset my sister." She hurried up the steps before he could question her further.

She stopped inside the door and rose up on tiptoes. "Do you see him?"

He scanned the crowd. "No, but it's hard to see everyone from here."

Marguerite and Father spied her and came over. Marguerite smiled. "There you are. Your father was about to send out a search party for the two of you. You've missed the live auction portion. But not to worry. Your father won the bid on the milking cow. Our wedding present to the two of you. You'll need a lot of milk once the little ones start arriving. I've also put a bid on a baby's layette for you."

Isabelle widened her eyes. "Isn't that a little premature?"

"We look forward to grandchildren. I expect the first of many within a year. I have an intuition about these things." Marguerite turned to Father. "We should check the bidding sheet. We don't want anyone to snatch it out from under us." She addressed Isabelle again. "Do you know where your sister is? She got separated from us after we ate."

More than likely, Adelaide snuck away the first chance she got. "I haven't seen her."

Oliver shifted beside her. "I saw her less than an hour ago. She had been talking to a man and ran off upset. Isabelle and I were looking for him without any success."

Father's eyes widened. "Who was he?"

"I don't know."

Isabelle wished this conversation to end before Oliver got suspicious. "Perhaps she went home."

Father gave a solitary nod. "I'll go see."

Marguerite took his arm. "I'll go with you. If she was upset, she'll need her mother." She put her hand on Isabelle's. "Be a dear and see to it we win the layette, no matter the cost." Her parents left.

Isabelle hoped they found Adelaide.

He watched Isabelle from across the room of the town hall with the man she would marry. Between the banker Oliver Mallory and the ranch owner Shane Keegan bidding for her lunch, he hadn't stood a chance. He'd hoped to get to eat with Isabelle Atwood.

He glanced at the quilt draped over his arm. At least he had this that she'd worked on.

The pair moved through the crowd. He did the same, keeping them in sight. They stopped at a table. Isabelle wrote on the bidding sheet and smiled.

Her smile touched him as it always did, warmed his heart and made everything seem right. But not so today with her fiancé at her side. What was she bidding on that made her so happy? When the pair moved away from the table, he investigated.

Her bid seemed quite high. The basket by the sheet held tiny clothes and knitted booties, hat, and small blanket.

Baby things?

His insides twisted.

Soon after Isabelle had gone to bed that night, her door cracked open and light from the hall splashed across the floor. "Adelaide?"

Her sister's small voice held that little girl quality from when she was young. "Can I sleep in here with you?"

"Of course." Isabelle held open the covers.

Adelaide crawled in. "Thank you."

Should Isabelle confront her sister about what Oliver had seen? She heaved a sigh.

"What is it? I know that sigh. It means you have something important on your mind. Is it about getting married Tuesday?"

Something she tried not to think about. "Oliver saw you talking to the baby's father today at the festival."

Her sister stilled. Not even her breathing could be detected

How could Isabelle word this to sound as though she knew the identity of the man so her sister would accidentally tell her his name?

"Does Mr. Mallory know about my baby?"

Isabelle hadn't thought of that. "No. But he saw the

man. Sandy-colored hair. Thin. I can get him to tell me, so you might as well." That was the best she could do.

"He said he doesn't believe it's his, and he would deny it. Who would believe me when people know I've kissed boys at the kissing tree?"

Her sister was right. With no way to prove the identity of the father, the whole shame and burden fell on the woman. Men like him could do as they pleased with nary a consequence. "He shouldn't be able to get away with this. His wife should know what kind of man she's married to."

"For what purpose? To ruin her life as well? If you were happily married, would you want someone to cast doubt on that?"

When had her sister started thinking like a grown-up? "Yes, I would. Then I'd have the choice of whether or not to stay with him. It's one thing to be blindly and falsely happy, to be living a lie, it's another to knowingly settle for that life. I would like to have the choice. Don't you long to have a say in your future?" Isabelle yearned to have a say in hers. The reason she'd courted danger by meeting with Shane Keegan.

She had two choices. The easy path of going along with Marguerite's plan where everything works out for everyone. Except Isabelle. Or the more difficult path where she waited for Shane to return to see if she could possibly have a future with him, which would leave Adelaide without a safe place to land. Her sister would be worse off than Isabelle if she married Oliver.

Lord, what should I do? The more I think about it, the more I don't want to go along with Marguerite's plan. Couldn't I help my sister in other ways?

If people found out about Adelaide's condition, her sister would have no future. She'd be marked as a harlot and no man would ever want to marry her.

If Isabelle married Oliver, both of them could have a future. Granted, Isabelle's wouldn't be the future she'd always dreamed of, that she would fall in love and marry that man. She could be content married to someone like Oliver, and Adelaide could have a good future as well.

"I'm sorry I wasn't there for you. If I had been paying

better attention to you, I could have prevented all of this." But could she have?

"I don't know about that. You couldn't exactly have followed me around everywhere. I do appreciate you helping me make my mistake better. Making it go away. I don't know what I'd do without you."

Isabelle hugged her sister. "I'd do almost anything for you. You're my little sister." The day Adelaide had arrived in this world, she'd whispered in the tiny, wrinkly baby's ear that she would always protect her. And that's what she intended to do.

Twenty-Two

During church on Sunday, Isabelle's parents announced her and Oliver's impending wedding. She had failed in stopping the plans and wished she could have stayed home this morning.

She recalled her dream from the night before. She had stood at one end of the aisle between the chairs set up in their parlor with Oliver waiting for her at the other. Though she couldn't move her feet, she ended up at the front with him. She spoke no words but was suddenly pronounced his wife. Like Oliver with his first wedding being led to the altar without protest, so too was Isabelle. But hadn't he fallen in love and ended up happy in spite of how that marriage began? Could she be happy as well?

The closing hymn brought her back and pushed aside the last vestiges of her lingering dream.

She proceeded outside with her parents and Oliver and stood with them to accept good wishes from everyone. Her heart weighed heavily in her chest. She must face her future. No more pretending a wedding didn't loom imminently. It had been announced in church. She would be marrying Oliver on Tuesday. The time had come to accept that.

Franny scurried up to her and looped her arm around Isabelle's. "May I steal my good friend away?"

Father gave a nod. "That would be fine."

Marguerite frowned. "Be quick about it. We have a lot to do."

Isabelle strolled off with her friend. "Thank you for rescuing me."

"Oh, that's not why I did it." Franny glanced over her shoulder. "Have you heard about Grant?"

Isabelle shook her head. "What?"

"He's leaving."

"Why shouldn't he? Church is over."

"No. He's leaving Kamola. He's moving to Seattle."

Isabelle's insides wrenched into a knot. "What? That can't be. Kamola is his home."

"I couldn't believe it either, but it's true. The hotel manager was in the store yesterday, and he told Pa he'd be looking for a new desk clerk to replace Grant. That 'the boy couldn't resist the lure of the big city any longer.'"

Isabelle struggled to breathe. No. She wouldn't believe it. Grant would never move. She studied the clusters of people. "I don't see him."

"He's by the church steps, talking to the pastor."

"Thank you." Isabelle pulled her shawl tighter and hurried over.

Grant couldn't go away. He wouldn't. She wouldn't let him.

He turned to depart and sank his hands deep into his pants pockets.

"Grant!"

He lifted his gaze but didn't offer his usual smile. "Congratulations. Looks like it's official, soon-to-be Mrs. Oliver Mallory."

She bristled at the name and ignored his comment. "Is it true? Are you moving away from Kamola?"

He bobbed his head. "'Fraid so."

"But this is your home."

"My folks have been pestering me to move to Seattle with them ever since they left. They have a printing shop. I'll have a good job there."

"What happened to buying a house and staying?"

"I think leaving might be best."

"What about finding a wife? I'm sure if you bought the first house you showed me, you'd find the right girl in a trice. I'm sorry I ever discouraged you." If she had known advising him against the big house would give him the freedom to abandon his life here, she would have pushed him to the bank herself.

"There doesn't seem to be the right lady in town for me. I figure I'll have a better chance in Seattle." Though he tried for a positive tone, she could hear the melancholy.

Tears blurred her vision. "What will I do without you?"

"You'll do fine like you always do."

No, she wouldn't. "When are you moving?"

"Once the hotel finds someone to replace me."

"I'll miss you."

"Naw, you won't. You'll be too busy with your new husband and then you'll have children. You won't have time to miss me."

"I will. Please don't go." She blinked rapidly to clear her vision.

"Don't you have wedding plans to attend to?" He inclined his head. "Your fiancé and family are waiting for you. Goodbye, Izzy." He turned and strolled off with his hands still deep in his pockets.

How could he just go? She wanted to call him back.

She heard people approach from behind, and Marguerite spoke. "It's best this way."

She turned to face her stifling family.

Her father nodded. "There are more opportunities in a larger city for a young man. He'll do well there."

Isabelle shifted her glare between her father and stepmother. Neither one of them had wanted her to be friends with him now that she would be marrying Oliver. "Did you do this? Did the two of you convince him to leave?"

Her father frowned. "Of course not."

Marguerite tilted her head. "The boy has good sense. Now come along. You're overwrought."

"I'm sorry, Isabelle." Adelaide's eyes glistened with tears, and she blinked several times.

White-hot anger exploded in Isabelle's chest, and she gritted her teeth. "You should be. This is all your fault. When are you going to grow up and be responsible for once? Why must I suffer on your account?"

Marguerite narrowed her steely-blue eyes at Isabelle. "Keep your voice down and watch your tongue."

Father gave her a warning look. "This isn't the place. We'll discuss this at home. Come along."

Isabelle glared at each member of her family. "I hate

all of you. I never want to see you again." Oliver stood behind them with Mr. Young and his sister and had heard her outburst. She didn't care. She turned and walked away. She couldn't stand to be around them right now.

"Where are you going?" Marguerite's shrill voice reached out to her like a bramble bush, snagging at her to keep her from running. "We have plans to complete and decisions to make."

"No!" Isabelle gripped two fistfuls of her skirt fabric, hiked it up, and ran. She hoped no one tried to stop her or followed her. She didn't slow until she reached the forlorn homestead she'd tried to convince Grant to purchase.

Panting, she studied the sad place with its sagging buildings, weathered wood, and overall neglect. *This* was what she thought of her best friend? No wonder he'd balked. He worked hard and deserved that big, beautiful house. Why had she shot down his dream?

An answer whispered at the edge of her thoughts. *Because you thought that house would steal him away from you.*

Had she?

Maybe.

But the opposite had been true.

A horse clomped down the street, pulling a buggy.

She hurried through the yard and dashed into the barn.

Tramp barked once as a warning, wagged his tail, and trotted over. King Arthur quacked and flapped his wings from a nest of straw. The others were nowhere in sight.

She crouched and petted the scruffy little dog. "I'm sorry. I haven't brought you any food since Thursday. You poor fellows must be hungry. Where are the others?"

The kitten sauntered out from the nearest stall, stretching her back legs behind her, followed by Trefoil and Shadow.

Buttercup and the two dogs sniffed each of the five empty tin plates.

"Where did those come from?" It had to be Grant. No

one else knew the animals were here. He had been feeding them for her.

She plopped down on an upturned crate. If Grant moved away, she would never see him again.

She pictured the spectacle she'd made of herself in the churchyard. A person could take only so much of others telling them what to do. Demanding blind obedience with no regard for her feelings, hopes, and aspirations. She didn't really hate her family, only their actions. If they hadn't made all these plans for her, Grant wouldn't be leaving. How could he think she wouldn't miss him? Her heart missed him already with a deep ache. Who would listen to her problems? Or her dreams? She was losing her best friend.

Tramp came up and nudged her hand.

She petted the scruffy dog's head. "The time has come for me to weigh my options." Because she *did* have options. "To really weigh them. Maybe you fellows can help me decide."

Buttercup jumped up onto Isabelle's lap. All three dogs sat as though they had been ordered to do so. King Arthur remained nestled in his pile of straw.

Now that her audience was ready, she began. "Option one, Mr. Mallory. He's a kind, Christian man. I can picture myself content with him. If he had evil or malicious tendencies, I would have seen hints of that by now. Wouldn't I?" She looked from one animal face to another. "No opinions whatsoever?"

A sigh escaped. "He's a good man, but I don't think I will ever fall in love with him. There just isn't any spark between us. How could there be when I'm being forced? Maybe if things were different I would have fallen in love with him, but not now. Can I live my whole life with no hope of love?"

Still no response.

"Option two is Shane Keegan. I like him. A lot. But could I fall in love with him? I told him I would likely be married by the time he returned. To which he thanked me for warning him but said he would hold onto hope until he returned and knew for sure. What am I supposed to do with that?"

She studied her feelings for the rancher a moment. "Honestly, my attraction for him isn't very deep. He represents adventure and freedom to make my own choices. Is that a reason to hold out and hope he will eventually fall in love with me? And me with him?" Surprisingly, that didn't appeal to her as much as it had a week ago. She realized the truth in Grant's comment that she would get bored stuck out on a ranch, even one as beautiful as Shane's. He might be gone often leaving her alone.

Tramp remained sitting in front of her. The other two dogs laid down by the feeding dishes a safe distance away.

"That leaves my secret admirer. A man too shy to tell me his feelings to my face. I always dreamed of having a secret admirer. What girl doesn't? A whimsical romantic notion." She had enjoyed the letters. But what kind of future could she have with a man too fearful to face her? She removed his latest missive in his own words from her reticule and reread it. "He does want to meet face to face. Maybe he isn't so shy after all."

She held up the paper. "Three perfectly good options. True, none are perfect. But I could live a decent life with any one of these men. What do you think? Whom should I marry?"

Trefoil and Shadow lowered their heads onto their outstretched front paws. Buttercup had purred herself to sleep on Isabelle's lap, and King Arthur had become bored and tucked his beak into his wing feathers.

She looked at Tramp. "It appears everyone else has abstained. What about you?"

Tramp picked up one of the tin plates in his mouth and brought it to her.

"So, your vote is food." She couldn't blame him and took the dish. Grant probably hadn't had a chance to feed them today.

Grant.

She choked up again at the thought of him leaving.

Marguerite's words came back to her. *No man is going to allow his wife to keep company with another man.* True. So no matter who she married, Grant would no longer be a part of her life. She couldn't imagine that. She covered her hurting heart with her hands.

Her vision blurred, and a tear slipped down her cheek. She wiped it away and studied the glistening moisture on her fingers. She couldn't lose Grant. He was the one man she cared most for.

She...

She...

She sucked in a breath. She loved him. All her suppressed feelings from her school days rushed back and washed over her. She'd lost him then because of her feelings for him and had worked hard to regain his friendship. Since then, she'd kept any romantic notions toward him carefully tucked away even from herself. She hadn't been willing to risk losing him again. She would have rather been his friend than nothing at all. Her actions proved that she longed to spend as much time with him as he would allow. Now, as a woman, she knew what she wanted. *Who* she wanted.

If she married anyone else, she would lose him. If she told him how she felt about him, she *might* lose him again. But she might not. Maybe she could convince him to stay. Explain to him how friends could make a good marriage. Maybe he would even be willing to help her raise Adelaide's baby. She could picture him agreeing to it. She would have enough love for the both of them. That could work but would be selfish of her. He should have a life of his own with someone he could fall in love with. It would hardly be fair to saddle him with her problems the way her family had done her with Adelaide's.

How could she get Marguerite and Father to agree to that arrangement? She couldn't. They would agree to Oliver or no one. If only Grant had blond hair, he could be a contender.

She growled, and Tramp whined. Why should Adelaide get a grand future with a lord and money and happiness, while Isabelle had to settle for second—or third best? It wasn't fair.

She wouldn't do it. She would refuse. "Sorry, Adelaide. This is your mess. You live with it." Isabelle was through doing her family's bidding. She would stay with Aunt Henny until she figured out what to do. Or, she would follow Grant to Seattle.

Lord, I'm not *going to marry Oliver. I can't. I deserve to marry for love. Don't I? And I love Grant.*

At least, she was pretty sure what she felt for him was love.

Protect your sister niggled at the edges of her mind.

That's not what she wanted to hear. *That's not fair. Why should I be punished for her transgressions? I'll help her another way. She and I can go away until she has the baby and arrange for Marguerite and Father to adopt the little one.* Now that was a solution everyone might be able to support. If her parents adopted the child rather than tell everyone Marguerite was expecting, that could work.

But what would God have her do? She feared the answer.

For God so loved the world...

"I know You sent Your only Son to die for us—for me."

For he hath made him to be sin for us...

A thought crept into her mind she wasn't going to like and tried to keep it away. She took a quick breath. "No. No. No. I won't. I don't want to." Tears streamed.

...who knew no sin...

She shook her head but couldn't deny the truth. "No one should be punished for someone else's transgression. That's exactly what Christ did for me. But I'm not Jesus. I'm not that good."

For God so loved the world...

"I know it wasn't fair You paid for my sins. But what am I supposed to do?"

Let Me love your sister through you.

Her resistance waned. "You paid a much higher price than You're asking me to pay by marrying a nice man I don't want to marry—to protect and help my sister."

But wouldn't having Father and Marguerite raise Adelaide's baby protect her sister from the shame and ridicule of her indiscretion? The impression from God was Adelaide needed protecting from something else. But what?

This didn't make sense. She felt that in order to protect her sister, she needed to proceed with the marriage plans to Oliver.

She used to think she had her life figured out, a comfortable routine. Now, her emotions ran wild, her thoughts scattered and fractured. She wanted to return to those simpler days of less than two weeks ago. Before everything changed. Before her world had broken apart. She longed for the time when she had the option to remain single the rest of her life and forever have Grant as her friend.

Now that she knew her true feelings for him, she could never be that carefree girl again.

Holding the air captive in her lungs, she listened for an alternate solution. None came. She slowly released her breath and, with it, any future she might have had with Grant.

Sobs racked her for several minutes, allowing her to mourn the loss.

Then reining in her emotions, she took a deep breath and dried her face.

She would marry Oliver Mallory. For God. And for Adelaide.

She whispered into the stillness. "I'll protect you, baby sister. No matter what."

The rest of her resistance melted away, and a peace washed over her.

Twenty-Three

OLIVER STOOD IN HIS PARLOR, GRIPPING the fireplace mantle. He played the morning's events in his mind once again. Isabelle had been so upset. He'd never heard her speak in such a manner. She blamed her family. He could only ascertain she held them responsible for forcing this marriage to him. Why hadn't she simply told him she didn't want to marry him? He'd told her he wouldn't insist if she wasn't agreeable. In light of this development, he could safely assume the wedding was off.

Behind him in the room sat Ellery and Belinda. He hated that his friends had been witness to his public embarrassment.

"This is for the best." Though Belinda seemed to be trying for compassion, her voice cut through the silence like a stabbing knife. "I told her the two of you wouldn't get married. I could see this trouble coming."

Oliver had known it too, deep inside. How he'd allowed himself to hope, he wasn't sure. But he had hoped. Maybe he was indeed finally ready to marry again. He'd told himself he never would, but this disappointment told him he *had* wanted a wife and children. A desire he'd thought died with his first wife. He'd been foolish to think a week and a half would be time enough for a young girl to settle on a husband she hadn't wanted.

Ellery clasped him on the shoulder. "I'm sorry. I liked her."

Oliver liked her as well, but he'd always known this wedding wasn't her idea. Everyone had been pushing her into it. Including him. This reversal of events was no surprise.

"She wasn't right for him." Belinda's grating voice again.

No, it was he who wasn't right for her. He turned around and stared hard at Ellery. "If you don't mind, I'd like to be alone."

His friend gave a single nod. "Come, Belinda. Let's head back to the hotel."

"Go on." Belinda lifted a hand. "I'm staying. Oliver doesn't know what he wants. He shouldn't be alone at a time like this."

Oliver didn't relish throwing her out, but he would if she refused to leave on her own. He gritted his teeth. "Please leave."

Ellery gripped his sister's arm and pulled her to her feet. "We're going. No arguing."

Belinda sputtered as her brother physically escorted her out.

Once the pair had left, Oliver sat and raked his hands into his hair. Something he never did, but it seemed fitting for some reason. What should he do now? Let the whole thing drop and melt into the past? Or try to convince Isabelle to reconsider with a long engagement?

A moment later, his housekeeper interrupted. "Sir, there's a young lady—"

"No. I don't want to see anyone." Especially, not Belinda.

A familiar, sweet voice said, "I won't take long."

Isabelle?

He lifted his gaze, and as he rose to his feet, he smoothed down his hair. "I wasn't expecting you. Come in. Have a seat." Her red, puffy eyes attested to her tears in the churchyard not having abated quickly. "Mrs. Fielding, would you bring us coffee?" He turned to Isabelle. "Or would you prefer tea?"

Isabelle lowered herself onto the settee and dipped her head toward his housekeeper. "Nothing for me. Thank you."

Mrs. Fielding left.

Oliver sat in a chair opposite Isabelle. "I know why you're here. This wedding was never your idea, and you're calling it off. I understand. I hold nothing against you."

She gave a nod. "I appreciate that. First, I must

apologize for my outburst after church. I learned some distressing news and didn't handle it well. Please forgive me."

"No need. Forgiven." He liked that she admitted her shortcomings. "Unexpected news can throw any of us off balance."

"Thank you."

"Is everything all right?"

She blinked repeatedly and nodded again.

He wanted to ask her what the comments she'd made meant, but it was best to let that fade away. Was that all she'd come to say? Not likely. She'd said *first*. Should he coax more out of her or wait? "If you'd like, I can tell your parents the wedding is canceled. I'll reimburse them for all the expenses."

"I'm actually here for the opposite reason. It's true that the wedding was never my idea, and I've been reluctant. If the wedding is indeed canceled after today, it will be wholly my and my family's responsibility."

She wasn't making any sense.

"I must admit I'm a little confused by your presence here. You don't sound like you came to call off the wedding, but it might be canceled? By you? Are you going to put some sort of stipulation on our marriage I might not agree with?"

She shifted in her seat. "Sort of. My father told you I must marry before my sister will be allowed to."

He nodded this time. "I understand the need for a man to see his daughters are well taken care of."

"It is more than that. You are a very nice and kind man."

He sensed he might not like what she was about to say. "I'm not under the delusion you love me, but I do believe I can make you happy." Why was he trying so hard to convince her? He should let the poor girl go.

"You are so sweet. You deserve better than me and my family."

"It's you who deserve better. I am more than willing to have as long of a courtship as you would like." Unlike his thoughts earlier, he knew he wasn't falling in love with her after only a week and a half, but he was attracted to her and would work hard to love her in time. He was sure of it.

She gave him a tight smile. "Unfortunately, a long courtship isn't possible. My family hasn't been honest with you. I would like to rectify that. Would you accompany me to our house? There is something you need to know before agreeing to marry me. After you learn it, you may not want me for your wife. But if you still do, I'll proceed with the wedding without further delay."

What had she and her family lied about? He shifted in his seat. "Can't you just tell me now?"

"I'm afraid my whole family should be present."

"Very well. We'll go."

He called for his carriage to be hitched up and drove to her house.

Oliver and Isabelle were greeted in the foyer by a smiling Mrs. Atwood. "Welcome. Come in."

Her cheery mood seemed to falter as she led them into the parlor. She could obviously feel the uncertainty he and Isabelle brought in with them, that mixed with a tension he sensed already in the room.

Mrs. Atwood sat on the settee next to Adelaide whose blue eyes were red and puffy as her sister's had been earlier. Whatever was going on had upset both sisters greatly. Isabelle sat in a wingback chair as did Oliver. Jackson stood by the fireplace.

What was going on here? He felt like a condemned man walking to the gallows while silent bystanders averted their gazes.

Mrs. Atwood pulled the edges of her handkerchief through her fingers, around and around the piece of cloth. "We are so pleased to see you. To see the two of you together." Perhaps a little too pleased, and her actions belied her words.

Isabelle cleared her throat. "First, I need to apologize for my outburst earlier after church. I said things I shouldn't have. I don't hate any of you. Please forgive me."

Jackson's stern expression softened. "Of course, we forgive you."

Adelaide and Mrs. Atwood nodded their agreement,

and that white embroidered cloth kept moving in the elder woman's hands, faster and faster.

Oliver wanted to rip it from her grasp but settled for shifting in the chair. The weight of the unknown made him nervous, but why did everyone else seem to be on edge? "Isabelle said there was a matter I needed to know before she and I could marry."

Mrs. Atwood narrowed her eyes. "Did she now? I can't imagine what she could possibly mean."

Isabelle gazed at her sister. "I will marry Oliver—"

Mrs. Atwood sucked in what appeared to be a breath of joy.

Oliver sensed more was to come and didn't breathe. Isabelle was finally going to agree to their marriage.

"*On* one condition. He is told the full reason you want him to marry me."

Full reason? More than the eldest needing to marry first? She'd said they hadn't been completely truthful with him. He leaned forward. "You're not ill are you?" He couldn't take another wife dying soon after they wed.

"No, *I'm* not ill."

"Isabelle," Mrs. Atwood warned through gritted teeth. "This isn't necessary. We can discuss this at another time."

Isabelle glared back at her stepmother. "It is necessary. Mr. Mallory is a good and kind man. He deserves to know the truth. Tell him or I will."

"Truth? About what?" Oliver felt even more like a man being taken to his execution. He got to his feet and pinned his would-be father-in-law with a demanding stare. "Jackson, what's this about?"

The man cleared his throat. "We've had a few difficulties." He looked in Oliver's direction but not directly at him. "You marrying my daughter will help us tremendously."

What was the big subterfuge in that?

Oliver turned to Isabelle for confirmation. She shook her head. He appreciated her wanting him to know the whole story before marrying her. "Unless someone tells me what's going on, the wedding is off." Not that he'd ever felt it had truly been on.

"Look what you've done, Isabelle." The cloth in Mrs. Atwood's hands moved more quickly. "Why do you have to be so selfish?"

"I'm the selfish one?"

Oliver didn't see Isabelle as being selfish at all.

Adelaide cleared her throat. "Mr. Mallory—"

"Hush, Adelaide." Mrs. Atwood gripped her daughter's hand. "This will pass."

Adelaide jerked her hand free and stood. "Mr. Mallory." Her voice squeaked. "I'm going to have a baby."

The room fell silent. No one seemed to breathe. The ticking of the clock was the only sound, and it seemed to grow louder and louder with each passing second.

Mrs. Atwood uttered a nervous laugh and gave her handkerchief a little wave. "She means that someday she'll have a baby. Not now. Don't pay any attention to her."

Jackson averted his gaze toward the window.

Isabelle gave Oliver a nod that Adelaide's declaration had been the point of this meeting.

"I don't understand what that has to do with my marrying Isabelle?"

Isabelle stood next to her sister and glared at her stepmother. "Go ahead, *Marguerite*. If you want this so much, tell him the truth. If he agrees, you'll have everything you want."

Mrs. Atwood narrowed her eyes at her stepdaughter but remained quiet. She almost appeared chagrined.

Oliver studied each person then settled his gaze on the one individual in the room who wanted him to know something.

Isabelle squared her shoulders. "As I said, I think you are a kind and good man."

He wished she would stop saying that. Made him feel like a prized horse to be sold off.

"And I *will* marry you. *But* you have the right to know that in taking me as your wife, you will get more than you bargained for. My stepmother is trying to arrange a betrothal between Adelaide and a lord back East."

He knew that.

"Adelaide being with child complicates that. The plan

is for you and me to wed immediately, and I pretend to be expecting. When my sister has her baby, we pass it off as ours. So not only would you be gaining a wife, but a child several months later."

Adelaide's baby was the reason Isabelle would never agree to a long courtship.

Oliver shifted his gaze from one person in the room to another. No one denied Isabelle's claim. They wanted him to pass off another's child as his own? He studied Adelaide a bit longer. She had a pale, miserable expression. Isabelle favored her father with dark hair and Adelaide her fair-haired mother. Similar to his own.

Now, he understood why he had been the fortunate sap chosen—or not so fortunate—his coloring matched Adelaide's. If the baby turned out to take after her, no one would question the little one was his with the *mother*—Isabelle—having dark hair. "What about the child's father?"

Isabelle thinned her lips. "He's not in a position to claim it."

She was the only one willing to tell him the whole truth. It made him respect her all the more. But could he go along with this deception? Accept another man's child? He focused on Jackson. "I can't believe you were a willing participant in this kind of pretense."

Jackson appeared remorseful. "Granted, I may not have handled this situation in the best manner, but I was looking out for my daughters. Trying to do the best I could for them."

Unbelievable. "Maybe for one daughter. But what about the other?" Oliver shook his head. "Isabelle, I appreciate your honesty."

"But?"

They all waited for him to decide their futures. This was not a light decision.

He studied Adelaide. The poor girl stood huddled in Isabelle's arms. "I need time to think." He strode out of the room and of the house then climbed into his carriage.

Isabelle rushed down the porch steps. "I'm sorry for all the trouble we've caused you."

He glanced at the house then back at her. "All this

subterfuge is the reason you were reluctant about the wedding, wasn't it?"

"Partly. I always dreamed of marrying for love. I didn't like being forced. But I meant what I said before. I *will* go through with the wedding."

"Love? That's why you asked me about marrying for love." He studied Isabelle's earnest face. "Can you truly give up on marrying for love?"

"I would be marrying for love. A different kind of love."

"Love for a little sister?"

She nodded.

"I'll let you know."

Jackson exited the house and stood behind his daughter. "Isabelle, go inside."

"I would be proud to be your wife." Isabelle retreated as far as the top step of the wide porch.

Jackson closed the gap between himself and the conveyance. "Can we discuss this man-to-man?"

A discussion long before now would have been nice. "I can tolerate a good many things, but deception and lies aren't among them."

"I wouldn't expect anything less. When you have children of your own, maybe you'll understand that a father will do almost anything to protect his children. I have failed Adelaide as a father. I'm trying to do what's best for her now."

"What about Isabelle?"

"She's strong. She always has been. Unlike Adelaide who's too young to handle the responsibilities of being a mother. I *am* sorry for all we've put you through. I prayed about all this and believed bringing you into our family to be the right course of action. I would be honored to call you son-in-law."

There was a time when Oliver would have been honored to call Jackson family. "You aren't the man I once thought you to be."

"I'm not the man I once thought me to be either. I beg you to pray on this and reconsider." Jackson stepped back from the carriage.

Oliver gave him a nod and drove off. He neither wanted to pray about this nor think about it ever again.

He wanted to put the whole mess behind him. Maybe even move to another town to start over.

Isabelle watched Oliver's carriage roll away. She didn't know which she wished for most. For Oliver to marry her and help her raise Adelaide's baby, or to never see him again so she might have a chance with Grant.

She walked back inside with her father.

Marguerite stood in the foyer with her hands on her hips. "Look what you've done. You did this on purpose to get out of your duty to this family. You've ruined everything."

Isabelle supposed it appeared as though she'd sabotaged everyone's efforts, but that hadn't been her intent. "He may still agree to the wedding." God had assured her that telling Oliver the truth was the right course of action. He had to come around. She needed him to follow through with the plan for Adelaide's sake. To ease her burden.

"You are naive. Go to your room." Marguerite turned her back on Isabelle.

"Gladly." Isabelle hiked up the staircase, lighter than she'd felt since this whole fiasco started. Honesty had set her free of the burden of the concealed truth.

It had been a risky move to begin with, counting on Oliver to not expose Adelaide after the wedding and to go along with the ruse. Sending Isabelle away for months right after they married wouldn't have likely worked without Oliver's consent.

She believed Oliver would come around and agree to raise Adelaide's child. That was why the Lord had impressed upon her to tell Oliver about the baby, wasn't it? She hoped she hadn't ruined everything as Marguerite had said.

A little while later, Adelaide entered her room. "I brought you something to eat." She held a plate out in front of her covered with a cloth napkin. A peace offering?

Isabelle took it. "Thank you. I'm sorry I may have spoiled this for you."

"I'm glad he knows. I feel freer."

As did Isabelle. The weight of lies and deception had been lifted from her. She sat in the window seat and motioned Adelaide to join her. The plate held cheese, sliced apples, and bread with butter. She was starving. She hadn't eaten since breakfast.

"I hope Mr. Mallory comes back and marries you. He's a very nice man. I really, really want him to raise my baby. I think he'll be a good father."

"I hope he comes back as well." Isabelle crunched on an apple slice and held a second one out to her sister.

Adelaide took it but didn't eat it. "What if he doesn't? What will I do then?"

Just like her sister to always look for others to solve her problems.

"I don't know, but we'll figure it out." Maybe Grant would agree to help them. She'd always been able to count on him. But first, they must wait on Oliver's decision.

Twenty-Four

ON MONDAY MORNING, OLIVER SAT BEHIND his office desk at the bank. He studied the ledger. Everything seemed to be in order. He slammed the book shut.

Everything wasn't in order.

How could Jackson Atwood have planned to let him marry his daughter without divulging the whole story? Would he really have pawned off his illegitimate grandchild on Oliver without his knowledge? Another man's offspring? The poor thing wouldn't even be raised by either of its true parents. At least Isabelle was the baby's aunt. If he'd been told from the start, he might have agreed, but not after being lied to and played for a chump.

The family had been in an impossibly difficult position, but they should have been up front with him from the beginning. And what about Isabelle? She was to be made to bear the burden of her sister's indiscretion. He wanted to whisk her away from her family. They didn't deserve her. But she didn't love him. He was no fool. She deserved to marry someone she loved as she'd always hoped. The problem was, he thought he might be able to fall in love with her. She deserved better.

Visions of his mother's Christmas soiree loomed before him. Dozens of eligible ladies paraded before him, each one vying for his attention.

He should take Isabelle up on her offer to marry him just to spare himself the embarrassment of a huge Christmas event. That would hardly be fair to Isabelle. And what about Adelaide? What would she do if he refused to marry Isabelle and raise her baby? He did want to help the sisters, both of them. But was marriage really the best solution?

Oliver's nine o'clock appointment entered with the

opening of the bank. The man was prompt. "What can I do for you?"

Professor Inger sat across the desk from him. "I need a small loan."

Oliver pulled out the man's file and flipped through it. "You're already late on your mortgage payment. The third time this year alone."

The man fidgeted in his seat. "I know. I ran into a few problems."

Oliver didn't trust people who squirmed. "If you can't meet your current obligations, why should the bank lend you more?"

"I promise I'm good for it. I'll be receiving a tidy sum from a relative in the next month or so. I'll pay it back then and catch up with the mortgage."

Oliver narrowed his eyes. He had seen this man with Adelaide at the Founders Day Festival. The one who had put tears in her eyes. Anger boiled inside him. Like tumblers in a lock falling into place, he knew. "You're the one."

"The one?" The professor stilled. "I don't understand."

"You took advantage of a young lady, and when she became with child, you discarded her." No wonder Isabelle had been so eager to find him.

The man swallowed hard. "I—I don't know what you're talking about."

Oliver thinned his lips. "Adelaide Atwood."

The man's light complexion paled. "How did you find out about that?"

"The question you need to answer is do you want your wife to find out?"

"My wife? There's no need for that. That girl meant nothing. She threw herself at me."

Not likely. But even if she had, he should have known better. Older *and* married. The reason the father of Adelaide's baby wouldn't claim it.

Oliver stood and leaned forward on his desk. "You have two choices. Either, your wife learns of your dalliance and the bank takes your home, or you sell your house, pay off the mortgage the bank holds, and move to a different town, preferably in another state."

"I-I'm sure we can come to some other sort of agreement."

"I'm sure we can't." Oliver detested men like him who did whatever they wanted, took no responsibility, and reaped none of the consequences. This one wouldn't get away with what he'd done so easily. If the man had been unmarried and Adelaide amenable to the idea, he would see to it he did the right thing by her. Since that wasn't possible in this case, making sure he stayed out of her life was the best Oliver could do.

Oliver sat back down. "I need to know your decision right now."

"Give me a day or two to think about it."

"If you don't have a For Sale sign in your yard by tomorrow morning, I'll be speaking to your wife."

"I'll—I'll take care of it." Professor Inger stumbled to his feet and scurried out.

Oliver would give the man a little longer, but not much.

A few minutes after the professor left, a knock sounded on his door.

Not having quite calmed down, he wanted to ignore it but couldn't shirk his duties. "Come in."

Jonathan, Oliver's assistant, poked his head around the slightly opened door. "There's a lady here to see you."

"About what?"

"She said it was personal."

Isabelle.

"Send her in." Anyone else he would have turned away. She had, at least, had the decency to see to it he learned the truth before it was too late. Another thought froze the air in his lungs. He hoped it wasn't Belinda. He should have asked first.

The door swung wide, and Adelaide Atwood stepped across his threshold. "Thank you for seeing me."

Never would have guessed it would be her. He stood. Had he known, he might not have allowed her entry. But since she was here... "Have a seat."

With head held high, she glided in and sat in the chair opposite his desk. She didn't look to be expecting.

He sat as well. "What can I do for you?"

"I came to apologize for my family. Well, not everyone. Not Isabelle. None of this is her fault. You must believe that. My parents, well, mostly my mother's to blame. Obviously not for my condition, but all the marriage stuff. She never would have approved of—" She put her hand on her stomach, seemingly uncomfortable with the line of dialogue she'd ventured down. She shuffle-shifted in the chair. "Anyway, I've come on my sister's behalf as well as my baby's."

She somehow seemed older than he'd previously viewed her. Was it because she sat straighter? Or because she spoke responsibly? Or because she wasn't hiding behind her sister and parents? He preferred this version.

"Please don't blame Isabelle. She didn't want any part of this. Not to marry you. Not to deceive you. Not to lie to you. She had little choice. My mother pushed this. It's hard to say no to my mother."

Surprisingly, he didn't blame Isabelle. He took some of the blame himself for being so willing to enter another easy marriage that he'd questioned none of it. Someone had offered him a beautiful bride, and he'd eagerly agreed.

"I have obviously done things I shouldn't have." Her lilting voice drifted around the room like a ballet. "Being the wonderful sister and person she is, Isabelle was willing to do this for me. To help me."

"Your suitor, the lord, does he love you enough to accept your baby?"

"Oh, he's not my suitor. I've never met him. Mother has written him a letter on my behalf. She hopes for an introduction. I'm sure she'll be able to convince him to marry me due to our money and status, but not if I have a baby."

"Do you want to marry this man?"

"I won't know until I meet him."

"But you wish to marry a titled man?"

"My mother does. I don't really care as long as he's a good man. Like you."

Mrs. Atwood had lofty goals for her daughter which Adelaide didn't share. She was supposed to marry a lord so her mother could have a title in the family.

"I was wondering if you had come to any kind of a decision about marrying my sister tomorrow."

He'd thought of little else while striving not to think about it or make a decision.

"I'm not here to convince you one way or the other. I just want to know what my options are. I laid awake most of the night thinking on this and have a couple of solutions I'm pleased with, but it's safe to say no one in my family will approve. But I don't care. I want to make my own decision in this. If you'll help me."

He should say no. What kind of solution could she have come up with? No good could come to him in helping her. Jackson Atwood had sway in this town. If Oliver went against the man, things could become challenging for him.

Adelaide folded her hands in her lap. "I can see you are contemplating my request. It's a big decision whether or not to offer me assistance, with us being the Atwoods and all. I'll wait quietly while you mull it over." She was rather adorable thinking she was in control of her life. If her mother got wind of anything she was up to, this young lady would be locked in her room for the duration of her life. Or at least until the baby was born. And because Mrs. Atwood would disapprove, he would be a willing participant in Adelaide's scheme. Or at least listening to her fanciful options.

"I'll listen, but I make no promises." He hoped he didn't regret this.

"If you choose not to marry my sister, I'm going to go away and have my baby. I'll give it to a nice couple who can't have children who will love it and raise it."

A bit idealistic. "Where will you go?"

"Boston. I have relatives there. I can stay with one of them."

"You've written them? They would take you in, keep your secret, and not inform your parents as to your whereabouts?"

Her optimistic expression faltered. "I don't know. They might. But what if they don't? I could go to Europe then. No one knows me there."

Did she not see the many errors in her plan? "How would you get there? Who would you stay with? How would you pay for anything?"

"That's why I need your help to arrange things for me."

Him? He'd gotten sucked into this family's schemes once unknowingly. Dare he do it willingly? She did ask for his help. He couldn't let her head off on her own without some sense of what she was going to do. The least he could do was help her think through her course of action. "Have you considered what it will be like to travel a week by train in your condition and then weeks on a rocking ship to cross the ocean? If you didn't have sickness from your condition, you would certainly have seasickness."

"Oh." She blinked several times and covered her one hand on her stomach with the other in a protective manner.

Good. She realized the foolhardiness of her ill-planned idea.

"Then I'll go someplace closer like Seattle or California."

"Where will you stay? How will you support yourself?"

"My family has plenty of money. In this bank. You can get me however much I'll need."

"That's your father's money. He has complete control over it. I can't just give you money from his account without his permission."

"Why not? I'm an Atwood, so it's my money too."

"That's not how it works. It's not *your* money. It's your father's. Without his authorization, I can't do anything with his money. Not even give you a small amount."

"Then what am I supposed to do? Allow my parents to force you and Isabelle to marry and raise my child?"

She seemed to have a strong desire to spare her sister an injustice, just as Isabelle had wanted to protect Adelaide from her consequences. And Oliver wanted to help them both.

"I can think of far worse fates than marrying your sister."

"You aren't suggesting you've changed your mind about marrying Isabelle, are you?"

He wasn't sure what he was suggesting. What other way could he help but to go through with the wedding to Isabelle? "I'll send for my carriage and drive you home."

Her bottom lip poked out in a most adorable manner. "I don't want to go home. They'll make Isabelle and me do what they think is best."

"You can't stay here."

"Will you take me to Aunt Henny's? She offered to help me."

That he could do, and happy to turn this young woman and her problem over to someone who might actually be able to help her.

Twenty-Five

ISABELLE STOOD OFF TO THE SIDE in the parlor with Father and her stepmother, watching the production.

Marguerite directed the moving men where to relocate each stick of furniture, some off to the side while others disappeared to other rooms. "You were right, Jackson. We never would have had this help if we'd gone ahead with the wedding last week. Nor would we have been able to rent some of the town hall's chairs to fill out the number of seats we need."

Incredible. Her stepmother completely ignored the events of yesterday, going about as though there *would* be a wedding tomorrow. Pretending all was well.

At this point, Isabelle hoped the efforts weren't in vain. Marrying Mr. Mallory would still create the least amount of turmoil.

Marguerite waved her hand toward the grand piano the movers had situated in the front corner of the room. "Isabelle, go sit at the piano. I need to see if it's at the right angle for when your sister is playing. I don't know where she could have gone. It's so unlike her to run off."

Hopefully her sister hadn't decided to do anything foolish—well, more foolish than she already had. Her stepmother had no clue about her daughter. Adelaide snuck off all the time. As did Isabelle. "I'm sure she'll be back soon."

Isabelle went to the piano. The sooner the staging was concluded the better. Not that she had anything else to do. She had originally planned to negotiate her own escape for her rendezvous with her secret admirer, but in light of her revelation about Grant, that was moot. But she wouldn't mind getting out of the house and away from all the fuss. "Father, are you going to speak to Mr. Mallory today and see if he's come to a decision?"

Isabelle wanted to know what her future held. Would she be marrying Oliver? Or did she have the freedom to speak to Grant of her feelings?

"I had thought he would call first thing this morning, but since he hasn't, I'll head to the bank right after lunch."

"May I come with you?"

"I don't know if that's a good idea. I would like to speak to him man to man."

Unfortunately, the men held the prerogative to decide her fate. "But he thanked me for being honest with him. That has to mean something."

Sissy, their maid, entered the parlor.

"Miss Atwood, Mr. Mallory is here to see you."

Marguerite spun around and spoke softly. "Show him into Mr. Atwood's study. And close the doors to this room. He shouldn't see any of this. How did he seem? Happy? Ill-tempered?"

"He seemed fine." The maid left before Marguerite could question her further, sliding the pocket doors closed behind her.

Marguerite pinned Isabelle with a stare. "Oh dear. Your dress. Not one of your better choices. Go up and change into your pale-yellow gown. You never wear that one."

Ugh. And she never would if she could help it. Isabelle disliked the dull dress.

"Use the servants' stairway from the kitchen."

"I'm fine the way I am. I don't want to keep him waiting." Isabelle moved toward the exit. "May I go, Father?"

Father crossed to the doors. "Let me go first. You follow in a couple of minutes." He left the room, and soon his voice drifted back to her.

Though she couldn't distinguish his words, he seemed to be doing most of the talking.

Isabelle stepped toward the doorway.

Marguerite put out a hand. "Not yet."

"It's been enough time."

"A moment longer."

Isabelle heaved a sigh and marched forward. She

hoped Oliver would be pleased to see her, or at least neutral. In truth, he should be upset with them all for stringing him along as they had done. Wanting to know what her future held one way or the other, she opened the doors a crack and slipped out.

The two men remained in the foyer rather than the study.

Father stood in an open stance with arms loose and feet apart. "We appreciate your willingness to talk with Isabelle."

Oliver had his arms folded and his lips pressed together. "Which is whom I'd like to see." When he saw her, his arms fell to his sides and his mouth curved up slightly. "Isabelle."

"Oliver. I'm glad you've come."

Marguerite trailed behind Isabelle. "We are so happy you're here. All the plans are still in place. Say the word, and tomorrow will be the most spectacular day of your life."

His eyes narrowed. "I want to talk with Isabelle."

"Of course. Don't let us stop you." But her stepmother didn't leave. She had an impish smile which said all her dreams were about to come true. The dreams of using her stepdaughter to cover up her own daughter's indiscretion so she could marry Lord What's-His-Name.

"If you don't mind, I'd like to speak with Isabelle alone." Oliver held out his hand to her. "Will you take a carriage ride with me?"

Marguerite fluttered. "You don't have to do that. We'll leave you alone in the study."

"If we are to speak of weddings and such, I'd prefer to do it... elsewhere. If you don't mind, Isabelle."

Yes, away from prying ears that would listen at the closed doors. She didn't fault him for that.

Marguerite beamed. "Of course, she would love to accompany you. Sissy, get my good wrap for her."

The maid draped the expensive cloak around Isabelle's shoulders. She would prefer to refuse and wear her own but wanted to escape with as little fuss as possible. And the fact that Oliver was willing to talk had to be a positive thing for Adelaide. She hoped. Regardless, she would know her fate.

He escorted her out and into his waiting carriage, then ordered his driver to go before speaking to her.

Isabelle's stomach flipped one way and then flopped the other. She hadn't yet been able to read Oliver's mood. "I wish to apologize again for my outburst at church and for keeping the plans about Adelaide's baby from you. I needed you to know what you were getting yourself into before we married, and we both did something we might regret."

"I appreciate you telling me. It says a lot about your character. Honesty and trust are important in a marriage."

That they were.

"I'll admit I was angry at first that your parents would trick me into this arrangement, but after pondering, I realized they did what they did because they love their daughters. I have a hard time excusing them for only considering Adelaide's wellbeing and not yours."

"Adelaide does seem to need more guidance than any of the rest of us. As I said yesterday, if you're willing, I'll marry you."

"The fact you would consider this for even one minute tells me a lot about you, your character, and your love for your sister. She's fortunate to have you."

"Adelaide doesn't mean to cause trouble. She doesn't seem to be able to think farther down the road than today. By the time she realizes her actions today will have consequences tomorrow, it's too late. She is getting better as she gets older. She's one of those people who takes longer to grow up than others, but I'm sure she'll get there."

"And you are one of those level-headed people who grew up long before others."

"I guess so. I've always looked out for her. I assume your coming means you've reconsidered marrying me?"

"Yes. No." He stopped and restarted. "I'm here at your sister's behest. She came to the bank."

"That's where she went. I feel better knowing she's safe. I had hoped she wasn't off doing something... well, something foolish."

"I'm glad you think her coming to visit me wasn't in error." He rubbed the back of his neck. "I've agreed to a plan Adelaide suggested. I need your level head to talk me out of it."

"About us getting married?"

"No. About Adelaide and myself marrying."

"What!" When she had sensed she needed to protect her sister, she'd assumed it was from Marguerite. Was Oliver the one she needed to protect Adelaide from? "She agreed to that?"

"Yes. I know it sounds unconventional, but I think it could work."

"Whose idea was this?"

"Hers."

"This is what I was saying about Adelaide. She doesn't understand what she's doing until it's too late." Evidently, her sister needed protecting from her own ill-thought-out ideas.

"That's why Aunt Henny urged me to get you."

"Aunt Henny? She's in on this?"

"No. Not really. Adelaide wouldn't let me take her home. She insisted on going to Henny's boardinghouse. She said she would help her and let her stay there."

"Aunt Henny did offer us refuge. I can't believe Adelaide would suggest the two of you marry?" The idea had some merit but was it sound? Once Adelaide thought about this, she might regret another rash decision. But it did offer Isabelle a glimmer of hope.

Oliver turned in the seat enough to half-face her. "Adelaide and I both agreed you shouldn't have to bear the burden for her mistake. I was prepared to tell you that I won't marry you. Not because I didn't want to have you as my wife, but because I didn't want you to be pressured into something you didn't want. Though I did consider marrying you and raising the child. To save face, Adelaide proposed to marry me. She said if I was willing to take on her baby with you, she should be the one to marry me. I found myself agreeing."

Another potential wife he hadn't proposed to. "Do you know what you will be getting yourself into?"

"I believe I do. I'll get a beautiful, charming wife, who

I've found to be sweet and caring, as well as the guarantee of a child. After spending time with her, I kind of like your sister. She makes me smile. I want to make her happy. And she said she cares for me. We would have no secrets between us. Looking back, I guess I might have felt a connection to her from the start. I thought it was simply because she was your sister. Maybe that's why I had secretly hoped for a long engagement to put things off."

He sounded sincere. Another small spark of hope added to the other.

"But I want you to talk to her. Make sure she really wants this. That she realizes she will be spending the rest of her life with me. I don't want her to feel as though she has to marry me, that she has no other choice. Ideally, I would take the time to court her properly, but I want to spare her any more embarrassment and shame than she'll already receive. If not by marriage, I will help her in any way I can."

"What about Lord What's-His-Name?"

"She doesn't want to marry a man she's never met."

What a relief. The idea of Adelaide blindly marrying a man Isabelle knew nothing about and her sister being too far away to help if this lord turned out to mistreat her, never sat well with her. "You are a nice man, and Adelaide is fortunate, but I'll need to speak to my sister about all this before agreeing to anything."

"That's why I came to get you. We thought to go through with the wedding as planned tomorrow but swap out brides. I know your parents wouldn't be happy about it and might try to stand in the way of us getting married. Your mother has big plans for Adelaide. But would they interrupt the ceremony in front of all the guests?"

"If Marguerite knew, she would most definitely interrupt and then ship Adelaide off as fast as she could to a convent to have the baby to shield her precious daughter from scandal."

"I'm glad you confirmed that. Adelaide said the same. I had a hard time believing it."

Marguerite *was* hard to believe at times. She had her moments of being kind and caring, but she had definite ideas of who her daughter would be. An unwed mother was not one of them.

"So, do you want me to talk to our parents on your and Adelaide's behalf?" Isabelle doubted that would do any good.

"No. We want you to stand up with us."

"If I agree to this wedding, I would be honored."

"What will we tell your parents?"

"Let's worry about that later. I'll think of something." The something that popped into her head was a someone. Grant. Her heartrate sped up at the thought of him. She needed another person with a level head. Between herself, Grant, and Aunt Henny, they would figure out the best solution.

"By the way, I figured out the identity of the man who upset Adelaide on Saturday. He came into my office this morning."

"He did? Who is he? No. Don't tell me. It's better if I don't know. I might try to strangle him. But I should probably know so I can protect my sister from him."

Oliver put a hand on hers. "Don't worry about him. I took care of it. He won't be bothering Adelaide ever again."

"Oh, Oliver. What have you done?"

He chuckled. "Nothing that warrants that kind of concern. I convinced him to move away with his family immediately."

Isabelle felt a wave of relief that this man wouldn't be bothering Adelaide again, and that her sister would have a man like Oliver to look out for her. "I appreciate you doing that."

"I'm glad to help."

As the carriage rolled toward the White Hotel, Isabelle lifted her hand. "Stop. Pull the carriage over."

Oliver banged on the side of the conveyance for the driver to stop. "What? Why?"

The vehicle stopped.

Isabelle jumped out. "I'll be right back."

Grant had always been the person she went to when she needed advice, when she wanted to share good news or needed a shoulder to cry on. Grant was always there for her. No matter what. She couldn't imagine her life without him in it in some manner. Her best friend. The one she wanted to spend her life with. Her heart beat faster as the clear realization hit—firmly this time. The one she loved. She would do her best to convince him of that and ask him to give her a chance, to see if he could fall in love with her as well. But first, she needed to deal with Adelaide's problem.

She hurried inside the hotel. Disappointment washed over her at Grant not being behind the desk. "Where may I find Grant Dawson?"

"I think he's in his room, getting ready to go out. Some special errand. Would you like me to fetch him?"

"No need. I'll get him. Thank you." She headed through the back hallways and knocked on his door.

Grant opened it, in the process of donning his suit coat, and a wide-eyed, shocked expression settled on his face. "Izzy? What are you doing here?"

He had indeed been on his way out.

Her heart thudded hard in her chest as though it were trying to escape and reach him.

"Izzy?"

She shook her head to order her thoughts. Adelaide first, then Grant. "No time to explain. I need you to come with me."

"It's too early to go meet your secret admirer."

"It's not him." That mystery held no appeal now. He had lost his chance by being too secretive. Her heart belonged to another. "Please come. I'll explain on the way."

He followed her out his door and to the front where the carriage waited.

She climbed in, and Grant followed her. He stopped half sitting down, staring at Oliver. "What's he doing here?"

Oliver raised his eyebrows. "You didn't fill him in?"

"No time. Tell the driver to go." She turned to Grant. "Sit."

He did. "Are you marrying him"—he pointed to Oliver—"right now?"

She resisted the urge to lean against him. "No. Adelaide might be. But our parents can't know until we figure everything out, and we need you to help us do that."

"Adelaide?" Grant relaxed back into the seat.

She needed to disclose the truth about her sister to him. She didn't want her best friend to think poorly of her. "You're going to learn soon enough. The reason I agreed to marry Oliver and the reason my sister might is because Adelaide has gotten herself into a bit of trouble."

He shook his head. "That doesn't even make any logical sense. What possible kind of trouble could be solved by you marrying Mr. Mallory?"

She lowered her voice to barely a whisper. "She's expecting."

He didn't speak. He didn't move.

She couldn't tell if he was even breathing. "Did you hear me?"

"I heard. If your sister is the one... who is... you know... why were you going to marry him?"

"Adelaide's lord—or rather Marguerite's lord. My sister couldn't marry him if she has a child. I was supposed to pretend the baby was mine, so she could have my stepmother's happily ever after."

"So, your parents knew about this plan?"

"Their idea."

Grant sat silent for a minute. "So why did you pick him?"

"I didn't. Our parents did."

Grant nodded. "I still don't understand why he was chosen? Why not someone else?"

"He has the right hair color."

Grant squinted at Oliver a moment. He gave a sardonic laugh. "Why am I not surprised your parents were going to saddle you with her problem? You should have refused. Made your sister deal with her own mistake."

"I thought about it, but she's my sister. I needed to help her and protect her."

"You always did look out for her. So now he's going to marry her?"

"Maybe." And if she did, that would free Isabelle to follow her own heart.

Oliver sat silently during her recitation of the details to Grant.

Grant lowered his voice. "What about you-know-who? Aren't you meeting him soon?"

"I can't. My sister comes first." Adelaide always had come first for Isabelle. And *you-know-who* was inconsequential now.

"Him who?" Oliver leaned forward to study both of them.

"No one," Isabelle said at the same time Grant said, "Her secret admirer."

Isabelle gave Grant a hard stare. "It's nothing. I'm not even interested in a man who can't tell me how he feels to my face." It had been a fanciful dream, but that was all. She needed to live in reality. One where Adelaide might be marrying Oliver, freeing Isabelle to follow her own heart.

"You've had an unknown suitor while we were courting?" Oliver asked.

"Only a few notes. And it's not like I could have stopped them or anything."

"He proposed," Grant added.

That wasn't helpful.

Oliver's eyes widened in what appeared to be amusement. "The proposal in an unsigned letter from your phantom was recently?"

Grant frowned. "Phantom?"

Oliver chuckled. "Your reluctance makes more sense. You had another marriage offer besides mine."

"Two actually." What possessed her to admit that? "But neither of them matter, so let's drop it."

"Who's the third?" Grant asked. "Not the cowboy?"

"Rancher." This conversation had gotten way out of control. "And yes, Mr. Keegan proposed, sort of. He alluded that when he returns from his cattle drive, he'd like to court me with the intent of marriage, but that's immaterial now. I'm not marrying any of them, not the rancher, not the banker, and not the phantom. Can we get back to the subject at hand? Adelaide."

Both men settled back in the seat and remained stone silent.

Isabelle replayed her enthusiasm over the notes from her secret admirer. How had Grant put it? *Oversentimental musings written by some confused, lovelorn sap.* She was the sap and oversentimental. Oh that she could take it all back.

Twenty-Six

At the boardinghouse, Aunt Henny hugged Isabelle when she entered and led her into the parlor where Adelaide sat with the preacher.

What was he doing here? Weren't they supposed to be discussing this option, not implementing it?

He stood. "Adelaide tells me that instead of tomorrow, there is to be a wedding today?"

Adelaide shrugged. "The preacher stopped by to look in on Aunt Henny. This must be a sign from God."

Isabelle wasn't too sure about that. "Adelaide, may we speak in the kitchen?" She glanced at Oliver. "Would you entertain the preacher while we confer?"

"Of course. That's why I brought you here."

The preacher shifted his gaze from one person to another before retaking his seat.

Grant and Aunt Henny followed Adelaide into the kitchen.

Isabelle peered squarely at her sister. "Oliver says the two of you want to get married."

"We do."

"*That* is a huge step and commitment."

"One you were willing to take on my behalf."

"That's beside the point. You don't have to marry him if you don't want to. You and I can go away until after the baby is born."

Adelaide smiled and bit her bottom lip. "I want to marry Mr. Mal—Oliver. It's time I took responsibility for my own actions. I can't explain how happy it makes me to decide for myself what I'm going to do rather than have Mother ordering me about all the time."

Was her sister finally growing up?

"I *want* to marry him."

Grant cleared his throat and spoke in a chipper tone.

"Sounds like a great idea. I think you should let her."

Isabelle tilted her head sideways at him. He was supposed to be the voice of reason. She looked to Aunt Henny.

The older woman shrugged. "I hate to say this, but you can't really stop her. If you say no, she'll just run away with no way to support herself or the baby."

Adelaide took Isabelle's hand. "Please let me do this. I think I'm falling in love with him."

Her sister couldn't possibly. "How? When?"

"When he was being so kind to you. I had to see if I could care for him and think of him kindly, knowing he would be raising my baby."

Isabelle's head said this had to be *the* most preposterous idea, even more ridiculous than her own hurried wedding plans to the man. But her heart said Adelaide would be happy with Oliver, and he would take good care of her little sister. "If you're sure, then I won't stand in your way."

"I'm sure. I get to keep my baby this way. I know Oliver will be a good father to him or her."

That seemed to be what Adelaide wanted most, to keep her child... and it sounded as though love might grow between the two. At least they both were open to the idea.

Isabelle's hope grew and her new dream of building a life with Grant crept closer and closer. "Then let's have a wedding." She hoped she wasn't agreeing just to have a chance at the future she wanted for herself.

Marguerite was going to be livid, but she would adjust. Eventually.

An ache niggled in Isabelle's chest for her father not being able to be here. They couldn't very well tell him without Marguerite knowing, and she would put a stop to it. This was what God had impressed upon her when she sensed Him telling her to take care of her sister. She was doing so by allowing her sister to make her own decision about whom she married and helping her to keep her child.

Isabelle took her little sister's hand. "If you're sure, then let's go do this."

Adelaide nodded. "I'm sure. It's so strange, but I am."

She walked her sister back into the other room. "There's going to be a wedding." She looked pointedly at Oliver. "That is if you are sure."

A smile stretched Oliver's mouth, and he got to his feet. "I'm sure." He removed a diamond and sapphire ring from his pocket and held it up to Adelaide. "I bought this for your sister. Do you mind?"

Adelaide touched it. "It's beautiful. I love it. I don't mind at all. Since God knew all along *we* would be the ones getting married, you actually bought it for me and didn't know it."

As Adelaide and Oliver said their vows, Isabelle looked past the bride and groom to Grant. His smile for her made her insides twitch and dance. The flickers of hope within her ignited into a roaring fire, warming her all over. Grant was a good man. The best. She trusted no one else with all her secrets. But one secret she hadn't told him yet, because it had only recently come to light.

She glanced over at Aunt Henny who gave her a knowing smile and a nod. Could the older woman read Isabelle's feelings for Grant? And did she approve? She hoped so.

The preacher pronounced the couple husband and wife. Oliver gave his bride a chaste peck on the lips.

Adelaide frowned. "You're going to have to do better than that."

Oliver raised an eyebrow. "I'll take care of that later."

"Later?" With a mischievous smile, Adelaide put her hands on Oliver's cheeks, rose up on her tiptoes, and kissed him fully. Oliver's eyes stretched wide. She lowered herself with a sigh. "That's better." She turned to Isabelle. "Now your turn."

"My turn for what?"

"To get married. You and Grant."

Isabelle's heart leapt to say yes, but instead she sputtered out. "What?"

"While Oliver was gone to get you, I realized that when Mother learns what I've done, she's not going to want to let Lord Blaine get away. She'll settle for you marrying him. You know she will."

"But—but I can't marry Grant." She needed to talk to him. She needed to convince him to give her a chance.

Grant gave her a nod. "If it keeps you from being forced to marry and move across the country, I'll do it."

He would? "I thought you were moving to Seattle?"

"I'll stay in Kamola."

He would make a sacrifice for her?

That's not what she wanted. She wanted to marry Grant, but she didn't want him to be forced into it. She wanted him to have a choice. She wanted to give him time to fall in love with her. "No. I won't do it. I'm tired of everyone trying to force me into marrying this man or that. And I'm not going to make my best friend marry me to thwart Marguerite's schemes."

Grant studied her. "It's because of your secret admirer, isn't it? You want to meet him first?"

"What? No. I don't care about him." She needed some time alone with Grant.

"But you liked his poems."

"That's beside the point. It was empty frivolity. Can we maybe talk about this someplace else?"

Adelaide touched her arm. "Isabelle, you have to marry Grant. I won't let you leave until you do."

"No. No. No. I'm not going to marry Grant."

His expression went from confused to hurt. "Even if it keeps you from marrying someone you've never met? If this is about me moving to Seattle, I already said I wouldn't go."

"No matter how right it might seem, I'm not going to be pushed into marrying for the wrong reason. And *this* is the wrong reason."

Grant took her hands and a thrill raced up her arms. "Isabelle, please reconsider. Think about your future. Do you want to spend it all the way on the other side of the country?"

"Of course not." Everyone needed to stop pressuring her. If she said yes to them, it would force Grant into something he didn't want.

The preacher lifted his open Bible a little higher. "I have other church members to visit. Is there going to be another wedding or not?"

Grant held up a hand. "Give us a minute." He escorted Isabelle into the kitchen. "What kind of a friend would I be if I let Marguerite send you away and marry you off to a self-important lord. Or is this about the *cowboy*? Do you want to wait for him to return?"

Isabelle smiled. The way he said "cowboy" sounded like jealousy. Whether it was or not, she would hold onto that.

"He's not right for you. I am."

A rush of warmth swirled through her at his declaration. "You are? Why do you say that?"

"Because... I... love you. I've always loved you. I'll make you happy. I promise. You wouldn't be forcing me."

Isabelle dared not breathe lest his words not be real. "You love me?"

"Yes, I do. I know we're supposed to only be friends, but I've been in love with you for a long time."

"You have?" He'd been deceiving her? "Why didn't you ever say anything? Why did you allow me to believe you had no romantic feelings for me? Why weren't you honest with me?"

"I planned to after we finished school and I had a little savings. Then your father came into all that money, and I knew I'd never be good enough for you."

"Not good enough? How could you think that?"

"If I wanted your father's blessing, I'd need to prove I could take care of you."

He had nothing to prove to her. "Say it again that you love me. Did you mean that? Or did you say it to appease my conscience?"

He took both her hands in his and caressed the back of them with his thumbs. "Isabelle, I truly love you. Why do you think I took you to look at that house? I wanted to know if you'd like it, if you could see yourself living there. It's not nearly as grand as your house, but I had hoped you could be happy there. You didn't think I could afford it or that I should buy it."

"How sweet. And in return, I showed you a rundown place. I'm sorry for that." She leaned forward and kissed him on the mouth.

"Wh—what was that for?"

"Because I love you too. I can't believe I didn't realize it sooner. The closer the wedding to Oliver came, the worse I felt. I couldn't imagine not seeing or talking to you every day."

"You love me?" He pulled her close and kissed her.

She melted into his arms, and she never wanted to leave.

He retreated a few inches. "Since we love each other, let's marry right now, so no one can take you away from me, but if you want to wait, I'll do that instead. Knowing you love me, I can wait forever."

"No more waiting." She'd already waited far too long. "I don't want to deal with Marguerite trying to talk me out of it." Not that she could, but she could be very exhausting.

"What about the *cowboy* and your secret admirer?"

She wanted to correct him about Shane being a rancher, but it didn't matter. "I don't care about either of them. I want only you."

"I can't give you an opulent house, fancy clothes, or servants, but I can give you my heart and promise to always love you."

"I'll take it. That's more than enough." When she turned to leave the kitchen, her sister stood in the doorway and clapped.

"I'm so happy. I always thought you two made the perfect couple. I could see you were meant to be together."

Isabelle had thought so too.

She stood next to Grant in front of the preacher, and her legs wobbled a little with the anticipation.

The preacher smiled at them. "I've watched your friendship grow over the years. I can't imagine any couple more suited for one another."

She beamed, unable to believe this was real, and her heart danced inside her.

Less than two weeks ago, she hadn't a care. Since then she had three—no four marriage options. Oliver, Shane, Grant, and her secret admirer. She glanced at Aunt Henny's mantle clock. Two minutes to twelve. The unknown man likely stood at the old elm tree by the pond this very minute. Waiting for her. Too bad someone couldn't go in her stead to let him know to direct his attentions elsewhere.

"Is there anyone here who knows of any reason these two shouldn't be joined in holy matrimony?" The preacher chuckled. "Sorry. I have to ask that."

"Wait." Grant pointed to the clock. "You're thinking about him, aren't you? You need to know who he is."

A deep crease formed between the preacher's eyebrows. "Him? Is there someone else?"

Isabelle shifted her gaze between the man she loved and the minister. Who to answer first? The preacher, first. "No, there is no one else." She turned to Grant. "Yes, I had a fleeting thought, only because it's noon. But no, I don't need to know who he is. I don't care if I ever find out. You are all that matters."

Grant swallowed hard. "But?"

"But nothing. All right, I thought it would be nice if someone could go and tell him I'm not coming, today or any other day. He'll figure it out. If he leaves me any more notes, I'll burn them without reading them."

Grant smiled. "I hope you don't." From his jacket pocket, he retrieved a rolled-up piece of paper tied with a familiar blue ribbon and handed it to her.

The same ribbon as on her other secret-admirer letters. "Where did you get that?"

"I wrote it, like all the others."

"You're my secret admirer?"

He nodded.

She took the scroll. "But you always put them down."

"I was so nervous you would figure out they came from me. I never imagined you'd read them to me."

"Why didn't you just tell me how you felt?"

He ducked his head. "Maybe we could talk about this later. After we're married. Unless you no longer want to marry me."

"No. Of course I want to." Grant being her secret admirer was absolutely perfect. She hooked both of her arms around one of his and turned back to the preacher. "I'm ready."

If she hadn't been so upset and overwhelmed by Adelaide's troubles and all the wedding plans, she would have figured out he was the one. That might have been what Grant had planned and hoped from the start. That would be like him. Another word game.

After Grant and Isabelle exchanged vows, the preacher looked to Grant. "Do you have a ring?"

Grant shook his head. "I haven't had time. I'll get one later."

"I have something." Isabelle held up the final secret admirer letter he'd given her and slipped off the ribbon. "Use this."

As Grant repeated the ring portion of the ceremony, he tied the strip of blue silk around Isabelle's finger. Perfect.

When the preacher pronounced Grant and her, husband and wife, Grant didn't seal the ceremony with a chaste kiss, he gave her a preview of what life with him would be like, and she tingled from head to toe. She couldn't wait.

After the I-do's, Adelaide hugged Isabelle. "Thank you."

"For what?" Had Isabelle missed something in her euphoric state?

"For everything. For being willing to marry a man you didn't love to help me. For marrying Grant so I don't have to face Father and Mother alone to tell them what I've done."

Isabelle sucked in a breath. "Oh, my. We have to tell them right away, don't we?" The words God impressed upon her heart yesterday, came back to her. *Protect your sister.* She put her hand on Adelaide's arm. "I'll go. You stay here with *our husbands.*" She giggled, liking the sound of that. Her husband, her best friend.

Grant took her free hand. "You're my wife. If you're going, then I'll be at your side. I know you're an independent woman—it's one of the things I love about you—but I'll hear no arguing on this. Shall we go?"

Isabelle's eyes watered. "When did you become so bold?"

"Since you declared your love for me. You have freed me from my bondage of silence."

Words from a poet's heart.

She hugged her new husband. "I do love you. Thank you." She turned to her sister. "We'll return in a little while."

Adelaide took her other hand. "I can't let you go alone. I'm a wife now too. I'm going to be a mother, so it's high time I stood up to my own mother." She darted a glance at her new husband. "You don't mind, do you?"

Oliver smiled. "I'm very proud of you, *and* I'm coming with you. With all of us together, we will provide strength to each other."

He had never smiled or gazed at Isabelle the way he did Adelaide. Was that a twinkle in his eyes? Them marrying each other had been the right decision.

The foursome squished into the carriage, and Oliver's driver took them to the Atwood manor.

Once through the doorway, Isabelle's stomach knotted in anticipation of Marguerite's five kinds of angry, but Isabelle needed to be strong for Adelaide.

Though Marguerite smiled broadly, Isabelle could read the uncertainty in her expression as her gaze flickered from person to person to person. "You're back. Did you get everything settled about the wedding?"

Oliver stepped forward. "We certainly did."

"It will be a beautiful ceremony tomorrow." Marguerite's voice faltered as Adelaide moved out from behind Oliver. "Adelaide, you're home."

Father joined Marguerite. "Don't worry us like that."

Isabelle gave Oliver a nod. "I should do this." She cleared her throat as she faced her parents. Her heart wrenched upon seeing Father. He hadn't been at her wedding as she'd always imagined. He hadn't given her away. "I'm sorry, Father."

His gaze darted between Isabelle and Grant beside her then smiled. "Don't be sorry."

Did Father know?

Marguerite narrowed her eyes at Grant. "Something is going on here. I demand to know what."

"I've gotten married." Isabelle looped her arm around Grant's. "To my best friend and the man I love, Grant."

Marguerite narrowed her eyes.

Adelaide, who already held onto Oliver's arm,

shuffled up next to Isabelle. "So have I. To Mr. Mall—Oliver."

Marguerite gasped. "No. I won't allow this. You must have just done this. We can have it undone."

Adelaide took Isabelle's free arm, creating a solid wall of determination. "We won't."

It did Isabelle's heart good to stand united with her sister and Grant. And Oliver.

Grant covered Isabelle's hand on his forearm, warm and reassuring. "We brought *our wives* here to let you know of our marriages and to allow them to collect a few things."

Marguerite glared at him. "You can't. We won't let you."

Father shot his wife a sideways glance. "What's done is done."

"Jackson, you have to stop them. This will ruin everything. What about Lord Blaine?"

"Hush now and leave it be. Our daughters are obviously happy."

"You can't mean that."

"I do. Adelaide won't have to bear the shame of what's she's done. I'll hear nothing further on the matter." He held his hand out to Oliver.

Oliver hesitated then took it.

Father clasped his with both hands. "Thank you. When I felt God had chosen you to marry my daughter, I guess I misunderstood *which* daughter He wanted me to entrust to you. The Lord works in mysterious ways. Welcome to the family."

Oliver gave a nod. "Thank you."

Father shifted toward Grant and extended his hand. "A number of times, I thought you might ask to court our Isabelle, but you never did. I'm confident you'll make her very happy. Welcome to the family."

Grant shook it. "I wasn't sure you'd think I was good enough for her."

"Quite possibly no man will ever be, but you are as close as good enough gets. Remember, I was but a humble farmer."

Isabelle hugged her father. "Thank you." She'd rarely

seen him stand up to his wife that way.

Father continued to study Grant. "I'm considering building a hotel. This town could use another one. Maybe you could give me some insight into the running of one." He pointed toward the staircase. "Girls, go on up and gather what you need. We'll have the rest of your belongings packed up and brought to you."

Back in the carriage, Isabelle and her sister sat in the middle with the men squished against the outsides.

Adelaide sniffled.

Isabelle took her hand. "What's wrong?" She didn't regret her decision already, did she?

"I've ruined everything." Adelaide turned toward Oliver. "I know why *my* parents weren't at our wedding. That was by *my* choice. But *your* parents didn't get to be there. I'm so sorry."

Oliver smiled. "Don't worry about it. They'll be here tomorrow."

"Will they be upset?"

"Disappointed, but it will all be fine."

Isabelle hoped his parents were the accepting kind.

"What if they don't like me?" Adelaide usually won over most people.

"I promise they will like you. They want me happy. And I am happy." Oliver kissed his new wife on the forehead. He didn't seem worried. But then he was a man with fewer restrictions and a broader range of acceptable behavior.

Grant cleared his throat. "Mr. Mallory?"

"Call me Oliver. We're brothers now."

Grant smiled. "Oliver. May we borrow your carriage?"

Oliver lifted his chin. "Ah. Have you told her?"

"Not yet."

Isabelle looked between the two men. "Told me what?"

Grant's smile widened. "You'll find out soon enough."

Oliver held Adelaide's hand in his. "We'll go to my house and then you can take the carriage. One other thing, ladies. While you were upstairs gathering your things, we agreed to return to your parents' house tomorrow for the wedding festivities which will now be a reception."

Isabelle supposed that should have been expected. As long as she had Grant at her side, she didn't mind.

After dropping off Oliver and Adelaide, Grant asked the driver to take them to the hotel.

Isabelle snuggled closer to her new husband. "Why did you need the carriage? They could have easily left us at the hotel with my things."

"You'll see. It's a surprise."

At the hotel, Isabelle stood to descend from the carriage.

Grant held up his hand. "Don't get out. I'll be right back." He hurried off.

Isabelle stood hunched over for a moment longer with her mouth hanging open. Why would he want her to stay here? He must need to tidy his room before she saw it. But why couldn't she wait in the lobby?

She stepped down out of the carriage as Mr. Young and his sister strolled up to the hotel entrance.

"Is Oliver in there?" Miss Young peered through the open carriage doorway. "Where is he? This is his carriage, isn't it? He's not at the bank. They said he left with a young woman."

"You're right. He did leave with a young woman. It seems you were right that Oliver and I wouldn't marry *tomorrow*."

Miss Young's expression turned smug. "You expect me to believe that the two of you eloped?"

Isabelle thought about that for a moment. She *had* eloped, and so *had* Oliver. "That's right. We eloped."

Miss Young gasped.

Her brother chuckled and slapped his thigh. "Good for the two of you."

Now for the best part. "But not with each other."

Both siblings' expressions turned confused.

Isabelle reveled in their perplexity a moment before she continued. "Oliver married my sister, and I married Grant Dawson." She held up her left hand and proudly displayed her blue-ribbon wedding ring. "So you got your way. I didn't marry Oliver."

"I don't believe this, any of this." Miss Young spun around to face the hotel. "Ellery. The door."

Mr. Young obeyed, and the pair disappeared inside.

Quite a satisfying exchange.

Waiting in the lobby suddenly held no appeal, Isabelle climbed back into the carriage and sat. As she did, the paper in her skirt pocket crinkled.

She removed the tube—the final missive from her secret admirer who wasn't a secret any longer—and unrolled it. The words of all the previous notes meant more to her now that she knew they came from Grant. What had he been going to say to her in this one?

My Dearest Izzy,
Since the day I met you, I knew you were special. You were kind to everyone, even a little boy with spectacles and untamable hair who others teased.

He'd since tamed his hair, but she'd liked his unruly mane. It had been free and wild, not confined by social norms

I couldn't help but fall in love with you. I planned for years just how I would court you.

That was Grant. He patiently and meticulously worked out every detail of something so nothing would go wrong.

But I didn't plan for your family to become wealthy overnight. My timing had been as bad as an early autumn blizzard before crops were harvested. I knew I could never measure up. So, I started avoiding you to let my heart heal. But you were still so nice to me, so I began to hope and plan again. I almost had everything in place when your parents arranged for you to marry Mr. Mallory. Instead of teasing you for weeks or even months with little notes, I had to accelerate my plan, but it was still too late. Even if I could talk you out of Mr. Mallory, you'd become enamored with the rancher.

She laughed and covered her mouth with her fingers. He'd finally referred to Shane as a rancher. Oh, how she must have hurt him talking about Shane the way she had.

I hope you are happy in your new life.
You will always hold my heart.
Farewell.
Yours always,
Grant

A tear slipped down her cheek. She pictured herself arriving at the elm tree by the pond to find this attached to the tree and no secret admirer, no Grant. She would have abandoned her own plans to help Adelaide and run to him.

Grant returned with a suitcase in hand and attached it on the back with her own, then spoke to the driver. He climbed aboard with a mischievous grin.

"Aren't we going in the hotel?"

"Nope."

"No? What are you up to?"

The carriage lurched into motion. "Be patient, Mrs. Dawson, and you'll see."

Mrs. Dawson. She liked—no loved the sound of that. "Patient? I'm not very good at that." She knew he was up to something and apparently Oliver knew about it too. She hadn't realized the two of them were friends. But they weren't, or else Grant wouldn't have to have been told to use Oliver's first name. "How long must I be patient?"

He chuckled. "Likely longer than you're capable of."

She fingered the scroll in her pocket. "If you don't even like poetry, why did you go to all that trouble to send the poems to me?"

"I did it for you. I thought you would like them, and I was right."

"Why not just tell me how you felt?"

"I've loved you ever so long and hoped to court you and marry you one day, but then your father inherited all that money, and I knew I wasn't good enough for you."

"Please don't say that. You know that's not true. You've always been good enough. More than good enough."

"I doubt your parents would agree. I figured if I could earn enough money, they would see I could provide for you. That I could take care of you."

"Is that why you wanted to buy that big house? To impress me? To impress my parents?"

"I knew you'd gotten used to finer things. I wanted to give you those."

She scooted closer. "You have given me the finest thing of all. Your love. I don't care where we live, as long as I'm with you."

The carriage stopped.

He motioned toward the ramshackle homestead. "Then you can see yourself living here with me?"

She gazed lovingly at the sagging porch, broken corral, and weathered buildings. "I certainly can. Are you going to buy this one?"

"Already bought it. Welcome home, Mrs. Dawson."

Isabelle sucked in a breath. "This is yours?"

He climbed out and gave her a hand down. "Ours."

"A place of our own? I thought we'd have to live in your room at the hotel. When did you do this? I learned only yesterday you planned to move away. And now this?"

He removed their suitcases from the back and bid the driver farewell. "I bought it on Wednesday. After you showed it to me on Tuesday, I prayed about it. I could see what you saw. I couldn't stop thinking about this place and the picture you painted. I went in to see Oliver on Wednesday. I felt rather deceptive because I was planning to steal you away from him. I'd hoped to woo you, but when I saw how happy you were to have Mr. Keegan win your box lunch, I didn't think I stood a chance. I couldn't live in the same town with you married to someone else."

"Thank you for all of this." She hugged him.

He set their luggage on the porch.

She stared in awe. "The hole in the floor is fixed."

He nodded. "That was the first thing that had to be done. There's more. Come." He led her to the barn. When he opened the door, Tramp waited on the other side, tail wagging. He crouched and petted the scruffy dog.

Because of the gaps between the weathered boards, plenty of light illuminated the interior.

Grant pointed to the farthest stall. "That one on the end needed several exterior boards replaced. I found some lumber in the loft and patched it."

Isabelle had seen that when she'd been in the barn the other times. "But that was how the animals could come and go as they needed to."

He held up a finger. "I'll get to that. The next one will be for the milking cow we'll get some day. Next to that will be for our future horse." He led her to the first of four stalls where the golden spaniel tentatively poked his head out but backed up as they approached.

Inside the enclosure, the spaniel trotted over to the blankets where the Labrador, the kitten, and the duck lay snuggled together. The spaniel laid down with them.

"You made them a bed. You're going to let them stay? They look happy."

"If we're going to have animals, we need to take care of them."

"Are you sure? That's a lot of mouths to feed."

"Hazel at the hotel has promised to collect all the dining room scraps for me." He pointed to a three-foot square of heavy canvas attached to the outside wall. "I cut a large square out of the wall for the animals to go through. The fabric helps keep out the cold and weather. I'm going to come up with something better. Perhaps a swinging door the size of the hole attached at the top."

How clever.

He turned her toward the exit. "Let me show you the inside of the house."

Back on the front porch, after unlocking the door, he scooped Isabelle up in his arms and carried her into the house. "I can't believe you're my wife."

"Nor I that you're my husband." As he lowered her feet to the floor, she kissed him.

He held her tight for a moment then released her. "Let me get our suitcases." He brought them in and closed the door. "As you'd said last week, this place doesn't need as much as it first appeared. The inside is in pretty good shape. I've done some cleaning, but I'm sure you'll want to do a better job. I got some cast-off curtains from the hotel which are still in good shape we can use until you decide what you want in the windows."

Isabelle touched the blue and tan striped fabric hanging at the windows. An old wooden crate in the corner held discarded wood pieces, crumpled newspaper, a broken chair back, and an assortment of debris. Things which had been scattered across the floor last week when she'd peeked through the window.

In the kitchen sat a small, worn worktable and the seat portion of the chair the back had come from in the other room. It still looked solid enough to sit on.

"I have—*We* have one pot, three dented tin cups—I gave the pie tins to the animals—two forks, and a dull paring knife, which I'll sharpen."

"A completely stocked kitchen."

He guided her upstairs and showed her the three empty bedrooms, ending with the middle sized one which wasn't quite vacant. A stack of blankets and pillows sat on a straight-backed chair and a mattress lay on the floor against one wall. "I thought we'd take this one. It's not the biggest, but it has the best view."

She peered out the window, which overlooked a meadow with a pond then turned back toward the room. "It's perfect."

She headed over to the chair and fingered the double-wedding-ring quilt on the top of the bedding pile. "This is the quilt my quilting circle donated for the Founders Day auction. You bought it?"

He lifted the corner of it. "Your hands worked on this. I wanted to take a little piece of you with me to Seattle."

How romantic.

"I had originally planned to move in here and fix things up while I tried to convince you to marry me, so things aren't quite what I wanted them to be for you. We can work on it together." He spread his hands out. "Even so, does everything meet with your approval?"

She stepped into his embrace. "Very much. And what makes it perfect is being here with you."

His arms closed in around her. "The rose is red, the violet's blue, the honey's sweet, and I love you."

"Now that I know you sent me those poems, I expect to receive more. A lot more."

He flashed a big smile. "I still have a few in mind. I told you I could still surprise you."

He had at that. She looked forward to more surprises with him.

Rising up on tiptoes, she kissed him.

He kissed her back.

Perfect, indeed.

Twenty-Seven

THE NEXT MORNING, ISABELLE STOOD AT the basin in the kitchen, washing the breakfast dishes. She drew in a deep, satisfying breath. She couldn't believe she was married to Grant.

He slipped up behind her and wrapped his arms around her waist. "What are you thinking, Mrs. Dawson?"

Mrs. Dawson. That sounded wonderful. She would never grow tired of being called that. She leaned back against his chest. "That I'm so very happy and wish we didn't have to go to my parents' house this afternoon for a reception. I would prefer to stay here with you all day."

He turned her around in his arms. "Don't you want the whole town to know we're married?"

"Grant, my hands are all wet."

He took her dripping hands and dried them on the front of his shirt. "Are you ashamed to have married me?"

"Of course not. What I don't want is for Marguerite to make any disparaging remarks to you or try to undo what we've done."

"I'm not afraid of your stepmother, and she can't undo this. You're my wife and will remain that way. 'What therefore God hath joined together, let not man'— or woman—'put asunder.'"

Isabelle took strength from his declaration, but Marguerite could be unstoppable when she set her mind on something. Though she'd likely not given up on having a lord in the family, she was no match for the Almighty.

Grant gave Isabelle a long, passionate kiss. One that reached deep into her heart, staking his claim in a way that no one could dispute. "What do you say we go back to bed?"

Before she could respond to his intriguing offer,

someone knocked on their front door.

Grant growled. "I'll see who it is and send them away."

"Who even knows we're here?" Certainly not her parents. They would expect her and Grant to be at the White Hotel.

He crossed the room. "No one." He opened the door to Oliver and Adelaide. "Except him."

Adelaide rushed in and gripped Isabelle's arm. "Mother has summoned us. What do you think she wants?"

Trouble, no doubt. *Oh, Marguerite, please leave us alone.* "I have no idea. The reception isn't until this afternoon."

Oliver shrugged. "Orders from on high. But she only wants an audience with the two of you ladies this morning."

Grant took Isabelle's hand. "Don't go. You'll see her this afternoon. She'll have to wait."

Isabelle touched his arm. "'What God hath joined together...'"

"Fine." Grant squared his shoulders. "If you're going now, then so am I."

Oliver gave a nod. "My thoughts exactly."

Isabelle liked the idea of reinforcements. "But I thought she wanted only Adelaide and me?"

Marguerite wouldn't be happy if they disobeyed her. But then her stepmother couldn't hold anything over her anymore.

Grant faced Isabelle. "None of us heeded their wishes on whom to marry, so why obey her call to appear before her?"

He had a point.

Isabelle glanced down at her work dress. "I need to change if I don't want to be scolded." She inclined her head toward her sister. "Help me with my hair."

Adelaide followed her upstairs to the bedroom.

Isabelle pointed to her two dresses hanging on pegs on the wall. "Neither of these will pass muster with Marguerite for a reception." She fingered the gray and pink dress she'd worn yesterday. "This one?" Then she touched the blue one she'd tossed in at the last minute. Impractical for life in this little homestead, but one of her favorites. "Or this one?"

"I don't know." A worry line formed between Adelaide's eyebrows. "I didn't pack an appropriate gown either. She'll be upset if we don't look our best at the reception."

"True." Isabelle shrugged. "Since neither one will make her happy, I think the blue one will make her less unhappy. And since we're going to the house now, we can choose more suitable ones there."

"Why do you think she's summoned only us?"

"I don't know." And why didn't she want the men to come as well?

Adelaide giggled. "I love being married. Oliver is so sweet and kind. Yesterday, when we arrived at his house, he put his hand on my stomach and said, 'This is *my* child in every way.'" She blinked tears from her eyes. "Isabelle, is it possible for me to be in love with my husband already?"

It did seem a bit soon, but she was happy everything worked out, and Adelaide would not only be taken care of but likely find love in the process. "I don't see why not. No one better to be in love with than your husband."

The foursome climbed into the provided carriage. Grant asked the driver to stop at the hotel.

Isabelle peered out the window. "Why are we stopping here?"

"I left word yesterday to have a telegram sent to my parents, informing them of the reception."

"I'm sorry they couldn't be here for the wedding. Do you think they'll make it?"

"I don't expect them to be able to leave on such short notice, but I wanted them to have a chance. I'll be right back." Grant exited the carriage and returned moments later, holding a piece of paper aloft. "They're coming and will arrive on the noon train."

"I'm so happy they can come. Now, I won't feel so bad that they didn't get to attend the wedding."

At the house, Isabelle and her sister, along with their husbands, walked up to their parents' front door. Should they knock? Or walk right in? "Is everybody ready?"

They all nodded.

Out of respect for no longer being under their parents' roof or control, she lifted the brass door knocker and clanged it twice. Unsure how her parents would greet her, she braced herself.

Sissy, the maid, opened the door and a wide smile bloomed on her face. "Why are you knocking? You don't have to knock on your own door."

"It's not my door anymore."

She inclined her head. "That's right. Come in. I'll let the missus know you've arrived." She slid open the parlor doors a couple of feet. "Your daughters have arrived." The maid pushed the doors all the way open in a hurry and stepped back in time for Marguerite to come barreling out.

Her stepmother stopped short and frowned at the men. "What are the two of you doing here? I specifically requested only my daughters. You may go." She gave them a dismissive nod.

Grant stepped forward. "We go where our wives go."

Marguerite narrowed her eyes. "The girls need to get dressed and ready for the reception. Do you have a formal evening suit?"

Grant shook his head. "Only my Sunday suit."

"That will never do." Marguerite turned to Oliver. "I presume you have one."

"I do."

"Good." She waved a hand toward the maid. "Sissy, take the girls up to their rooms to get ready."

Isabelle squared her shoulders. "Get ready for what?"

Her stepmother pinned her with a stare. "The *reception*. What else? You can't attend dressed like that. What would people think? Now go. Shoo. We'll find something appropriate for the young man to wear."

The young man? "*My husband* is fine the way he is."

"Not one more word. Your dresses are waiting for you in your rooms." Marguerite glided away. "Jackson?"

Sissy walked to the staircase. "Best do as she says. You know she'll get her way in the end."

Isabelle supposed so, and her stepmother hadn't

pretended neither of them had gotten married yesterday without permission. She seemed to have accepted it. Isabelle turned to the men to find out what they planned to do.

Grant nodded. "Go on. We'll be fine. We each need to pick up our parents anyway. We'll see you later."

She and Adelaide followed the maid up the stairs. As they reached the top, her father's voice drifted up from the bottom, likely speaking to the men.

Adelaide gripped Isabelle's arm. "What's Mother up to? You don't think she'll send Oliver and Grant away and not let them return, do you?"

Isabelle hoped her parents' dividing them from their husbands wasn't a ploy to separate them permanently. "I don't think Father would agree to that. Besides, if she tries something like that, our husbands wouldn't stop until they freed us and got us back."

Her sister smiled. "They would, wouldn't they?"

"They would." Isabelle parted from her sister and went to her room. The wedding gown she'd chosen last week hung on a dress form. Still as beautiful as she'd remembered. But Marguerite didn't expect her to wear that, did she? Isabelle was already married.

Adelaide came in and held the door open. "Put my wedding gown next to my sister's and my dressing table next to hers."

Sissy and Gwen carried the dress form with Adelaide's beaded gown. Two of the male servants carried the dressing table and chair. After a couple of minutes, everything Adelaide needed to get ready had been transplanted into Isabelle's room.

Her sister fingered Isabelle's gown. "This is so beautiful."

"So is yours."

"I know. I can't believe it."

By early afternoon, Gwen and Sissy had fussed, primped, and dressed Isabelle and Adelaide in the gowns they should have been married in.

Isabelle smiled at her reflection, pleased she got to wear it after all.

Marguerite swooped into the room, gave a nod of

approval, and handed each of the girls a string of pearls. Her eyes glistened. "I can't believe my girls are married."

Was her stepmother actually getting sentimental?

After a moment, Marguerite straightened, seeming to gain control of herself. "The guests have arrived. The men are in the study. Your father will escort you down together and hand you off to your respective grooms. Then you will cross to the parlor together and be announced." She exited as quickly as she'd entered.

Leave it to Marguerite to make too big of a production of this. But it wasn't much to ask to go along with it to have hers and Adelaide's marriages accepted.

Father, with a huge smile on his face, crossed the threshold of her room. He kissed each of them on the cheek. "Are my girls ready?"

"We are." Isabelle looped her hand around one of Father's arms, and Adelaide did the same with the other.

At the top of the stairs, Isabelle's breath caught at the sight of Grant in a formal suit, standing at the bottom looking up at her. As they descended the stairs, the voices of the guests hushed. Father transferred each of their hands to their husband's and joined his wife at the doorway of the parlor.

The foursome crossed to the room's entrance together.

Father cleared his throat. "I'm pleased to announce Mr. and Mrs. Grant Dawson, and Mr. and Mrs. Oliver Mallory."

The room erupted into applause. When it died down, Marguerite organized the receiving line, starting with Oliver's parents then Grant's.

Oliver's mother hugged Adelaide. "Welcome to the family."

Adelaide beamed a smile. "Thank you."

"I can tell my son is very happy with you."

"And I with him."

Both of Grant's parents hugged Isabelle. "We were afraid the two of you would never get together. We couldn't be more pleased to have you as a daughter."

"I'm honored to be part of your family."

Aunt Henny gave each of the girls a hug. "I'm so

delighted everything worked out for both of you."

After the receiving line had ended and while the guests mingled and ate, Marguerite spoke to Oliver's parents. "We refused to stand in the way of love. If a husband and wife don't have love, there isn't much point in getting married."

Isabelle almost choked on her punch. Marguerite didn't feel that way at all, but she apparently planned to weave this in her favor, as though everything had been her idea.

It didn't matter, as long as Isabelle could spend the rest of her life with the man *she* loved.

Grant, who hadn't left her side, whispered in her ear, "Do you think anyone would notice if we slipped away?"

Anyone being Marguerite. "She would notice." Isabelle didn't want to humiliate or hurt her father any more than she already had by marrying without his permission. "Can you last another hour?"

Grant heaved a sigh. "I suppose so."

Gazing at her husband, Isabelle didn't know if she could last a whole hour herself, sharing him with so many people. But she would have the rest of her life with Grant.

Who would have imagined when her parents had issued their ultimatum less than two weeks ago, she'd be married to her best friend. "Don't even entertain the thought of me giving up my bicycle."

"Oh, I entertain that thought, but know it will do no good. I've heard tell of a tandem bicycle for two. We'll get one of those."

"How fun. Don't those steer from the back? That's where I'll ride."

Grant chuckled. "We'll see about that."

Isabelle smiled to herself. He would see indeed.

Author Note

The Daughter's Predicament is set in a time when women had little control over the direction of their life. Their parents and especially the men in the family had the say in what they could do and whom they could marry. If a lady went against the wishes of their family, they could be cut off and on their own with no way to support themselves.

In this book, I enjoyed exploring Isabelle's dilemma. What if a young woman with dreams of romance had not one, not two, but three marriage proposals and a secret admirer? That could be interesting. But I couldn't make it as easy as choosing hero A, B, or C. What fun would that be?

I didn't want an obvious bad suitor. I wanted Isabelle's choice to be hard. I wanted to be able to see Isabelle end up with any one of her options and seeing that she could have been happy and have a good future.

Romance isn't always easy or straight forward. Some times other factors cloud the way and family interferes.

As a romantic at heart, I don't know what I would have done in Isabelle's situation. Do whatever was needed to help and protect a sister in need? Or let her suffer the consequences of her own mistakes, which would be far worse than helping her? It's not an easy decision. Depending on which way you look at the situation, both options have merit as well as their drawbacks.

I hope you enjoyed Isabelle's story, the second in the Quilting Circle series.

Happy Reading!

Mary

☺

If you enjoyed my book, I'd love it if you'd consider posting a review on Amazon, Christianbook.com, Goodreads.com, BarnesandNoble.com, BookBub.com or anywhere else books are sold or reviewed. Reviews are a tremendous help to authors! Thank you for anything you can do.

I'd love to connect with you. Readers can find me at:

FaceBook: Mary Davis READERS Group –
www.facebook.com/groups/132969074007619/

Blog: marydavis1.blogspot.com

Subscribe to my Newsletter:
marydavisbooks.us17.list-
manage.com/subscribe?u=cbe8a2ec4ef27cfcf51813f02&id=
82ad258f06

Amazon: www.amazon.com/Mary-Davis/e/B00JKRBJKE

GoodReads:
www.goodreads.com/author/show/8126829.Mary_Davis

BookBub:
www.bookbub.com/profile/mary-davis?list=author_books

DISCUSSION QUESTIONS

1. What was your favorite quote/passage? Why did this stand out and how could you use it in your own life?

2. How well does the book's cover convey what the book is about? Do you think the back-cover copy did a good job of indicating what this book is about? If the book were being adapted into a movie, who would you want to see play Isabelle? Adelaide? Aunt Henny? Oliver? Grant? Shane?

3. Which character did you relate to the most, and what was it about them that you connected with? Can you relate to Isabelle's predicament? To Adelaide's? To what extent do they remind you of yourself or someone you know? Do you empathize with the characters?

4. Describe the dynamics between Isabelle and her sister, Isabelle and her parents, Adelaide and her parents, Isabelle and Grant, Isabelle and Oliver, Isabelle and Shane. How do the characters change, grow, or evolve throughout the course of the story? Have you ever been caught in between two difficult decisions and felt like there was no right answer? How did you deal with that?

5. If you were in Isabelle's place and had to choose between marrying a good and kind man to protect your sister or another relative from disgrace and scandal, would you? Why or why not? Do you think it was fair of Isabelle's parents to demand this of her? Why or why not? Do you think living in the 1890s would make a difference and change your answer? How does the Bible verse to honor your father and mother play into this?

6. What are the major conflicts in the story? What events in the story stand out for you as memorable? What main ideas—themes—does the author explore? Are they relevant in your life?

7. Do you think the father of the baby got punished well enough by having to leave town suddenly? Would you have told his wife? If you would have, would that have made anything about the situation better? If it wouldn't, then why tell her? If you wouldn't tell the wife, why not? Would God want the sin brought out in the open? Or would he want people to turn the other cheek?

8. Did any parts of the book make you uncomfortable? If so, why did you feel that way? Did this lead to a new understanding or awareness of some aspect of your life you might not have thought about before? Has this novel changed you or broadened your perspective?

9. What do you think will be your lasting impression of the book and why? Did the issues that were raised touch or impact you in any way? Would you recommend it to a friend, and if so, why? Can you see yourself reading it again?

NOW—A SNEAK PEEK AT BOOK THREE

THE DAMSEL'S INTENT

RELEASING JULY 1, 2020

One

Washington State, Late Fall 1893

"Nick, there's something you should know. You ain't no boy like your cousins."

In buckskin pants and shirt, twenty-year-old Nick Waterby sat across the wobbly, pot-marked table from Sarah Combs, the only neighbor for miles around. "I know. Grandpa said I would be the *man* of the house and in charge when he passed over into heaven, which he did a few weeks back. You being our only neighbor, I came to you for advice. We buried him, but I'm not sure what to do now. We don't have enough provisions to last through the winter. Grandpa always got us what we needed. He'd leave for a day or two and come back with flour and coffee and the like. I don't know how to do that."

The grizzled old lady, tough enough to survive alone in the mountains, sucked in air through the gap between her two front teeth and shook her head. "You miss my meaning. Your grandpa meant well—was trying to protect you—but he's done you a disservice by keeping you hid away up in these mountains. You ain't no man—not in the true sense of the word. You're a woman like me."

"A woman? He'd've told me." Nick recalled the times she'd tried to talk to Grandpa about the differences between herself and her cousins, but he forbid her to speak about it. She leaned forward on the table. "Grandpa grabbed my arm real tight, and his last words were, 'Go to Kamola and find a husband. I should have told you sooner, but Nick, you're not a fell...' then he breathed his last. I don't know what he was trying to tell me. If he claimed I was a man, why would he tell me to get a husband? That isn't right. Did he mean I should get a wife? He would never talk about such things, so I could be getting them confused."

Sarah rubbed her lips, like she was trying to form the right words. "He was probably going to say you ain't no feller. You understand the word 'man' like being a person. A man and a woman are two different kinds of persons."

That made sense in light of Bible passages she'd read. "You mean like Adam and Eve. Male and female." Events in her life fell into an order she'd never been able to manage before.

"Exactly. You and I are female. Your grandpa and cousins are male. Your full name is Nicole. It's a right pretty girl's name. I told Ike he shouldn't be hiding you away up here in the mountains and dressin' you like them boys and telling you, you was just like them. You're not."

Nick had never been able to figure out the female thing when grandpa lumped her in with the boys as male. It made sense now. "I've known for a long time I'm different from my cousins. Pretty much ever since they arrived five years ago." Maybe that was why she'd felt a connection with Sarah, because they were both women. "Grandpa would never talk about it. He would get real upset if I asked, so I kept quiet. But I knew he wasn't telling me something. That something wasn't right."

The older woman patted Nick's hand. "He was powerfully afraid someone might hurt you iffin' they knew you were a girl. There be some pretty mean folks out there, and he did what he thought best for you."

"I could tell Grandpa wasn't like the trappers and

mountain men who wandered by our place now and then. He'd read them their letters, write their replies, and do sums for them. He had more learning than they did. He taught me a lot of things. Made sure I could read and write, but I suspect there's a lot he didn't teach me. Taught the boys reading, writing, and numbers too."

"You're right. There's a whole lot he didn't teach you. That's why you need to go to Aunt Henny in Kamola. Now, I'm not one to do much trusting of outside folks, but Aunt Henny is good people. You can trust her. It's time for you and your cousins to move into town."

"Move there? Leave the mountain? I've never lived anywhere else."

Sarah nodded. "It's time."

Nick's insides wiggled like she swallowed a snake. Grandpa never spoke well of town. "Grandpa wouldn't approve of us moving there, but I'll visit—just to see what it has—and come right back. Can you take me?"

"Sorry. I can't go to town. Follow the crick all the way down. You'll see the place. Aunt Henny can help you better than me. Take your cousins with you."

"I cain't take the young'uns. I'll leave them at the cabin. Will you check on them while I'm gone?"

"Rolfy's what—twelve now? Bucky's seven?"

Nick nodded.

"And you're seventeen or eighteen?"

"Turned twenty on my last birthday."

Sarah shook her head. "Has it really been that long? You're still too young to be up here on your own caring for those boys. It's best if all of you move into town. You're not gonna find a man to come back up here with you. There's a loose floorboard under your grandpa's bed where he stashed some money. You take that and find Aunt Henny. You tell her I sent ya. She'll help ya."

Nick knew about the hiding place and that Grandpa used what was in there to bring back provisions.

The next day, Nick trudged down the mountain. At the tree line, she stopped short and ducked behind a lodge pole pine. She saw a whole passel of cabins. Big ones. She'd never seen the like. There must be seven or eight of them, all bunched together.

Horses pulled carts with four wheels. What did a person need with four wheels? Was this that Kamola town Sarah told her about? She said there would be a lot of people. Nick'd never been around other folks besides her grandpa, cousins, Sarah Combs, and the occasional hunter.

She ventured out of the forest and scurried up a knoll and onto the heap of rocks there to get a better view of this Kamola and the cabins. She kept her shotgun in her hand. Grandpa said to never set down your gun lest a grizzly surprise you and your gun's too far away.

She gasped at the sight. There was more than eight cabins. A whole jumble of them every which way. Too many to count. What were so many doing together? The horses and carts moved along on the spaces between the cabins. Some of the bigger ones had two or four horses pulling them.

And people. Lots of people. How was she supposed to find one person in that mess? Like a colony of ants crawling all over an apple core.

Sarah had said for her to ask someone.

Nick came down off the knoll and strode toward the town of cabins and people and horses and carts. Too much to take in.

The first couple of cabins she came to had white, board fences all the way around them. When she reached a whole string of them attached together, she stepped up onto the long wooden walk along their front. These ones had large windows. She'd never seen glass so big. Grandpa's cabin had two, small, four-paned windows, and when the bitter winter wind blew, they let in all the cold. How did people stay warm with windows the size of walls?

She peered through the glass.

One man laid back in the oddest chair or was it a bed? He had shaving soap on his face. Another man held the razor blade, scraping off the white foam and whiskers.

She walked on down to the next window.

A man handed a brown-paper wrapped box to a lady.

The next had all manner of things stacked all around in rows and rows. Cans and lamps and blankets and fabric with pretty flowers, stripes, and plaids on them. Sacks with the words flour, coffee, and sugar spelled out on each. This must be where Grandpa got everything he brought back.

These were the strangest cabins. How did people sleep and eat with all those trappings?

She stepped off the porch as a man on horseback galloped down the dirt pathway.

"Hey, mister?"

He rode right on past without even stopping or saying good day. Grandpa always taught her to say a greeting to people when the occasional trapper or hunter had wandered by their cabin.

Two women, dressed in clothes like Sarah's but cleaner and without patches, headed toward her. Maybe one of them was Aunt Henny.

Nick tipped her hat. "Howdy. Do you—"

The women gasped and darted across the open stretch between the long cabins.

That wasn't very neighborly. Nick never would have done that to Sarah.

"Begging your pardon?" She said to the next person who sidestepped around her. Now she knew why Grandpa said towns were evil places. When a person wouldn't greet another, it wasn't worth the effort it took to speak. She should skedaddle back up to the mountains.

She spun around and faced a horse square in the chest. It startled and reared. She ducked and rolled out of harm's way and landed on her feet with her shotgun at the ready.

The horse settled, and the rider rode off down the long dirt patch.

A deep voice behind her said, "Nice move, kid."

Nick swung around.

The man laughed then put his fingers on the end of her barrel and pushed it away from pointing at him. He was a sight better looking than any of the trappers she'd met and had a warm smile that did something funny to her insides.

She lowered her gun. "Sorry about that."

"No problem. You moved pretty quickly out of the way of that rearing horse. A lot of people would have frozen like a pond in winter and gotten themselves injured under those hooves."

"Grandpa always said move fast or die."

"Words to live by." An amused twinkle flashed in his blue eyes. "If you're interested in work, I can always use someone like you who is fast on their feet and quick thinking."

"I'm not after work. I need to track down Aunt Henny. Do you know where I can find her?"

"Sure. Everyone knows Aunt Henny. But I've learned that she's not really anyone's aunt."

"Then why's she called aunt?"

"I've been wondering that same thing." He unwound his horse's reins from the hitching rail. "Come on. I'll take you to Aunt Henny. You planning to stay at her boarding house?"

"No, sir. She's gonna help me find a husband."

"A what?" The man stopped and snatched Nick's hat.

"Hey, give that back, thief."

"I declare, you're a girl under all that dirt and buckskins."

"Am not. Grandpa said I was to be the man of the house after he passed, but Sarah said I'm a woman."

He doubled over laughing. "Girly, you are no man."

"Stop calling me that." She swiped her hat from his hand and smashed it back on her head. "Are you going to take me to Aunt Henny or not? Point me in the right direction. I'm a good tracker. I'll find her."

"Oh, I'll take you there, all right. I can't wait to see her face."

Regardless of his beguiling smile, she determined not to like this man laughing at her the way he had. But he had been the only one kind enough to talk to her and offer her help, so he couldn't be too bad.

Henny turned the pie dough out onto her floured worktable in her kitchen and picked the sticky bits off her fingers.

Boots clomped on her porch.

She let out a frustrated groan. Why did a new boarder have to show up while her hands were sticky with dough?

The anticipated knock sounded.

"Just a minute. I'm coming." She grabbed a towel and wiped what dough she could off her hands. She covered the knob with the towel and turned it, opening the door.

That new rancher Shane Keegan and a buckskin-clad boy stood on her porch. "Good morning, fellows. What can I do for you?"

"This here... fella? is looking for you." Mr. Keegan swiped off the boy's hat. "But he's a she."

The boy-er girl grabbed her hat back. "You need to stop doing that." Her nearly black hair had been cropped, a little longer than a boy's. Hacked, really, to her shoulders. Between her hair and her clothes, no wonder Mr. Keegan thought she was a boy.

Henny pushed the screen open with her elbow. "Won't you both come in?"

Mr. Keegan tipped his hat. "I'd love to, if only to find out what this is all about, but I have a lady to see. Good day, Aunt Henny. Good day, kid." He tromped off the porch laughing.

The girl did look a bit unusual but nothing to laugh at. Henny would like to say she'd seen worse, but she hadn't.

The girl entered.

Henny closed the door and pointed to the entry to the parlor. "Stand right there. I'll be back in a moment." She washed the dough off her hands as quick as she could. Who knew what an uncivilized girl would get into? She drew two glasses of water and cut two slices of chocolate cake. Set the lot on a tray and grabbed two tea towels.

When Henny re-entered the parlor, the girl stood in the exact spot she'd left her in. Surprising. "You didn't move."

"No, ma'am. Grandpa said when he told me to do something, I was to do it without question."

Henny set the tray on a low table then draped one tea towel on the seat of a padded chair and the other on the backrest. "I hope you don't take offense, but your... clothes are a bit dusty." That was being kind. "Have a seat?"

"I don't mind. I can sit on the floor if you'd like."

"No. That won't be necessary." Henny didn't know what to make of this girl.

She sat. "You have a nice cabin. I never saw one so big. This town's full of large cabins like this. You must have a passel of people in your family."

"No. No family. This is a boardinghouse. I rent rooms to travelers and people who don't have or need a house of their own." Henny sat on the settee and handed her guest a glass and a plate. Did she know how to use a fork? "Water and cake. I thought you might be thirsty and hungry."

The girl's eyes widened. "I sure am. I haven't had cake in ever so long. Must be three years or more." She took the plate and glass. "Thank you, ma'am." She guzzled half the water then took a large chunk of cake on the fork and shoveled it into her mouth without dropping a crumb.

She knew what a fork was used for, said thank you and ma'am. Someone had taught her a few things.

"What's your name?"

"Nick. No, wait. Sarah told me to tell you my full name. Nicole Waterby."

"Sarah Combs?"

"Yes, ma'am. She's our neighbor."

"Our?"

"Me and my cousins."

Henny resisted the urge to correct her grammar. "I didn't realize Sarah had any neighbors. I thought she was up there all by herself."

"Have to go a bit farther up the mountain to get to our place."

"How old are you?"

"I turned twenty last month."

"How old are your cousins?"

"Rolfy's twelve. I left him in charge while I'm gone. Bucky's seven."

"Two boys, then?"

"Yes, ma'am."

"Mr. Keegan said you were looking for me?"

"Keegan? Is that his name? He was the only one who would talk to me. Everyone else gasped like they had seen a rabid coon and hightailed it away from me. But Mr. Keegan was right nice. He brought me all the way here. Nice, except for taking my hat and laughing."

"Did Sarah send you? Is she all right? I worry about her."

"Sarah's right as rain. She sent me here because my grandpa passed away."

"I'm sorry to hear that."

"He was pretty old. He told me to take care of my cousins—on account they are younger than me—and to go to Kamola to fetch me a husband."

Henny nearly choked on her cake. She coughed and patted her chest. "A husband? Did he tell you how to do that?"

"He was pretty bad off by then. He just made me promise to do it so I could take care of the young'uns." Nicole leaned forward. "Is there a special place I go to get a husband? Cuz I'm anxious to get back up the mountain."

Mercy. This girl needed help.

Shane rode down the main street of Kamola, fresh from the cattle drive. He'd sent his men on ahead to the ranch to check on things. He didn't want to waste any more time to find out Miss Isabelle Atwood's answer.

Before he'd left two months ago, he'd asked to court her when he returned with the intention to marry her. He knew it had been quick, but he liked her a lot, and he didn't want another man to steal her away while he was gone. He wanted to make her his wife and take her to his ranch outside of town. Though he hadn't thought about taking on a wife before Isabelle fell into his life, he decided he'd rather like to have a wife.

He'd gone to the bathhouse and washed off the trail dust and grime and bought a new shirt and blue denim pants so she wouldn't think him uncivilized. He shook his head and chuckled, thinking about that buckskin girl. She certainly was an unusual creature. But girl or not, he could use a fast thinking hand like her. Maybe he would talk to Aunt Henny and find out more about her.

He rode up to Isabelle's house, one of the larger ones in town, but by no means the wealthiest family. He knocked.

A maid answered the door. "May I help you?"

"Um. I'm here to see Miss Isabelle Atwood." Was that the correct way to make that kind of request for someone of her station?

She opened the door wider. "Come in."

He stepped inside the foyer.

"Wait right here." The maid slid open a pair of pocket doors, disappeared inside, and closed them behind her.

An expensive rug covered the marble floor. He skirted around it for fear of mucking it up with his boots that had picked up dust on the trek here. A dark-wood, curved staircase ascended to the upper level. This was one swanky place. Could Isabelle ever be happy stuck way out on his ranch? Muffled voices leaked through the doors, but he couldn't tell what anyone said.

The doors slid open, and Isabelle appeared. "Mr. Keegan, it's so good to see you." She crossed the entry and slid open doors on that side. "We can talk in here."

Mr. Keegan? That couldn't be a good sign. He followed her into a room that appeared to be a study with heavy furniture, dark paneling, and walls of books.

She sat on a little couch and pointed to a chair.

"Have a seat."

As he did, his stomach knotted. This meeting would give direction to his future. One way or another.

The maid entered with a tray and set it on the coffee table. "Anything else, ma'am?"

"No, thank you."

The maid curtsied and left.

Isabelle poured tea from a china teapot into two china cups and handed him one. "How did your cattle drive go?"

"Real well. I got a higher price per head than I anticipated." He took a swallow of the warm brew. "I think you know why I've come."

She gave him a sweet smile. "I do."

"I'm not gonna like your answer, am I?"

"Shane, I care about you a great deal."

"But you aren't going to let me court you, are you?"

"I'm sorry. I don't know if I could have been happy way out of town on your ranch. You deserve someone who wants all the same things as you. Someone who finds living on your ranch as exciting as you do."

"Did you marry the man your folks wanted you to?" He hoped not. She hadn't been enthusiastic about him.

"No."

"That hotel clerk? You're in love with him, aren't you?"

She nodded. "I am. How did you know?"

"You were always talking to him, always around him, and he gazed at you the way you deserve to have a man regard you. I don't think I ever looked at you quite that way. Maybe that's why I proposed. So he couldn't steal you away."

"But he did."

Shane shook his head. "He can't steal what wasn't mine to begin with. He obviously makes you happy. I can see it on your face. Is he going to marry you?"

She held up her left hand with a silver band on her ring finger. "He already has. I'm so sorry. I wanted to tell you, but I didn't know how to reach you on the cattle drive."

"No reaching a man on a drive." He stood. "I'll be

going."

She walked him to the door. "I hope you find the perfect woman. You deserve someone special."

The image of the buckskin girl popped into his head. She was special all right, but not necessarily in a good way.

He opened the door. "Isabelle, thank you for telling me yourself. You could have easily had your maid relay the information to me—or your father."

"I couldn't do that to you. You mean more to me than to treat you inconsiderately."

"Good day, Miss Isabelle." He walked down the steps and out to his horse.

Though in his heart, he'd known he was never good enough for someone like Isabelle, her refusal—even as kind and sweet as it was—still stung.

What should he do now? On the drive he had purpose—return to Kamola and court Isabelle. Now, he would simply head out to his ranch. That seemed lonely somehow. It never had before. Isabelle had changed his way of thinking. He would need to change it back to his solitary way of life. He could do that. Make ranching everything again. He'd been foolish to think otherwise.

Ask for this book at your local bookstore or any online retailer July 1, 2020